CROWN

ALSO BY MAY MCGOLDRICK

THE SCOTTISH RELIC TRILOGY

Much Ado About Highlanders
Taming the Highlander
Tempest in the Highlands
"A Midsummer Wedding" (novella)

THE PENNINGTON FAMILY SERIES

"Sweet Home Highlands Christmas" (novella)
Romancing the Scot
It Happened in the Highlands
Sleepless in Scotland

THE ROYAL HIGHLANDER SERIES

Highland Crown

HIGHLAND CROWN

MAY McGOLDRICK

St. Martin's Paperbacks

This is a work of fiction. All of the characters, organizations, and events portrayed in this novel are either products of the author's imagination or are used fictitiously.

HIGHLAND CROWN

Copyright © 2019 by May McGoldrick.

All rights reserved.

For information address St. Martin's Press, 175 Fifth Avenue, New York, NY 10010.

ISBN: 978-1-250-31497-0

Printed in the United States of America

St. Martin's Paperbacks edition / April 2019

St. Martin's Paperbacks are published by St. Martin's Press, 175 Fifth Avenue, New York, NY 10010.

10 9 8 7 6 5 4 3 2 1

To Ammara Mayya McGoldrick, with love

PROLOGUE

Abbotsford, the Scottish Borders
September 1832

Some say I'm a hero. Some call me a traitor.

My time grows short now. I feel nothing in my right side. My hand lies inert on the bedclothes. The apoplexy has robbed me of any useful employment. I've tried, but I cannot hold a pen. Not that it matters. Those exertions are behind me now.

Some will say that I, Sir Walter Scott—author of *Waverley* and *Rob Roy* and *Red Gauntlet*—invented the new Scotland. That I was the unfailing champion of the noble traditions of the past. That I revealed the Scottish identity all now wear with tartan-emblazoned pride.

What they say is a lie.

My family has brought down my bed and propped me up before the open window of my dining room. In the meadow outside, the yellow of the rockrose, the scarlet of the campion flower, the pure white of the ox-eyed daisies nearly blind me with their reckless brilliance. The water scratches over the pebbled shore of the Tweed at the end of the field, but instead, I hear the haunting voices of hungry, homeless Highlanders, dying by the thousands.

How many have died as the ancient hills continue to be cleared of their tenant farmers in the name of progress? Pushed from their homes, driven to the sea, to the cold, hard streets of our cities, to lands far away . . . if they survive the journey. All to make way for a few more sheep. All in the quest of a few more shillings.

I did what I believed at the time was right for Scotland. I convinced myself I could not let my country descend into the lawless chaos of bloody revolution, the throat of civility ripped out by the mob. It happened in France. The guillotine's dread machinery flew out of control, splashing far too much innocent blood into the streets in its ravaging thirst for the guilty. And the cobbled lanes of Paris were not yet dry when a new terror arose in the form of their arrogant tyrant Napoleon. I told myself I could not let that happen here. Not here. Not in my homeland.

But now I see the truth clearly, and the bitter gall of that knowledge rises into my throat. I spent a lifetime creating an image of Scotland I knew was not real. I closed my eyes to the suffering and the deaths of my own people, and instead told stories depicting the grandeur of an imagined Highland past. And as I worked, I held my tongue about the bloody decimation of the clans and their way of life. Men I dined with daily were profiting from the killing, and I said nothing. Worse, I, too, made money from it with my romantic tales.

Many are those who see me clearly. To them, I am Walter Scott—turncoat, bootlicking lackey of the British

Crown. They say I sold the independence of Scotland for a shabby box of tawdry and meaningless honors. They say that because of me, the Scottish people will never be free again. That I betrayed them for a wee bit of fleeting fame and the price of a few books.

Now, after all these years, I find myself forced to agree. And that is all the more difficult to bear because I lie here with Death stalking the shadows of Abbotsford.

He's been dogging my faltering steps for some time now.

This fever struck me as we returned from our travels. Rome and Naples, Florence and Venice. Those places had offered no relief. Death was coming for me. London was covered in yellow fog when we arrived, but the rest is a blur. They tell me I lay close to dying for weeks. I don't recall. Then the final journey home. The steady rumbling rhythm of a steamboat remains in my mind, but I remember very little of that. I only know that I am home now.

Two of my hunters have been turned out into the meadow. Fine mounts. The golden sun glistens on their powerful shoulders as they begin to graze. I wish I could be as content, but life has buffeted me about, and the choices I've made give me no respite. Nor should they.

My mind returns again and again to the upheaval of 1820, to the "Rising."

We called those men and women radicals, when all they wanted were the rights and freedoms of citizens. In the name of equality and fraternity, they cried out for representation. They demanded the vote. Some called for an end to what they saw as the iron fist of Crown rule. They wanted to sever our northern kingdom from

England and restore the ancient parliament of Scotland. In my lifetime, those men and women were the last chance for Scotland's independence, and I blinded myself to their cause. And when Westminster made it treason to assemble and protest, they willingly gave their lives. The heroic blood of the Bruce and the Wallace ran in their veins. I see that now. Too late.

That same year, that same month, as the blood flowed, I returned to Scotland from Westminster bearing my new title. Even now, I feel the weight of the king's sword on my shoulders. But as I reveled proudly in my accomplishments, the cities across the land were tinderboxes, threatening to explode in a wild conflagration of civil war. The weavers and the other tradesmen in Glasgow and Edinburgh had just brought the country's affairs to a halt with their strikes. Some of the reformers had courageously marched on the ironworks at Carron to seize weapons.

Scotland teetered on the brink of anarchy. I was afraid. So I took the well-worn path of weak men.

My single moment of courage came when I saved a woman who would help change the course of history.

Isabella Murray Drummond. A marvel of this modern age. A doctor, no less, who'd studied at the university in Wurzburg, where her eminent father held a professor's chair. When he passed away, she married an Edinburgh physician who'd gone to further his studies under the tutelage of her father. He was a widower with a growing daughter. She was a single woman left with a younger sister and a small inheritance. It was a marriage of convenience.

Isabella, who had the loveliness of Venus and the

bearing of a queen, saved me from losing my leg—lame since my childhood—after the carriage accident in Cowgate. I was carried to their infirmary. The husband was away, but I was fortunate that she was there, for Isabella was the very angel of mercy I needed at that moment, and her skill as a physician saved my life.

No matter my regrets, or what I do to right wrongs, or what I write to change the fate of Scotland, some will always think me a traitor. I know now that I have helped in giving away my country's chance for independence . . . perhaps forever . . . in return for a peace that was profitable for a few. But one thing in my life that I'll never regret was my action on that woman's behalf when the time came.

The news spread across the city. Isabella Drummond's husband was dead, and she was in hiding with her sister and her stepdaughter. The government had declared her an enemy of the Crown, placed a bounty upon her head. Her husband's rebellious allies wanted her, as well, believing she'd inform on them.

I succeeded in helping the women escape from the city, far to the north where they would board a ship bound for Canada. She was to join all those Highlanders who were journeying to a new life. But she would never board any ship. She would never reach the shores of that far-off place.

For on the rugged coast of the Highlands, she disappeared . . . and lived a truer adventure than ever flowed from my pen.

CHAPTER 1

Sleep the sleep that knows not breaking,
Morn of toil, nor night of waking.
—Sir Walter Scott, "Lady of the Lake,"
Canto I, stanza 31

Duff Head, Northeast Highland Coast
June 1820

"Hard times been choking folks around here for a long while, and most of them would sell their own kin if they thought there's a ha'penny to be made from it." Jean paused and fixed her eye on her guest. "And one look at ye, and they'll know yer good for more than that."

A loud pop from the driftwood fire in the old woman's hearth drew Isabella's gaze. Sparks rose from the blue and lavender flames, struggling to find their way up the chimney. Wind and rain from the storm hammered fiercely at the shutters and the cottage door.

From what she'd learned on the journey here from John Gordon, Jean's nephew, the village that huddled around the cove in the shadow of Duff Head consisted of no more than a few dozen families of fishing folk trying to scratch a meager living out of the sea. Desperate. Hungry. Poor. Though she'd always lived her life in the city—Wurzburg, Edinburgh—she'd known many people like them. They didn't frighten her.

The soldiers pursuing her posed the real danger.

A ha'penny, Isabella mused. She was worth a fortune. These Highlanders knew nothing about the thousand pounds sterling on her head—the bounty offered by the government to anyone who could bring her back to Edinburgh alive to face interrogation, trial, and a public execution. Certainly, Jean had no knowledge of this. Nor did she know of the lesser amount bandied about by the radicals for her corpse to guarantee her silence. Both sides wanted her dead.

"I've lived here my whole life. The sea makes ye hard, and these folks are hard as stone," the woman continued, perhaps reading a hint of skepticism in Isabella's face. "They give their loyalty to no one. In the Rising of '45, they wouldn't fight for any side. If ye weren't born here, yer an outsider. To them, even the Bonnie Prince was a stranger. And they don't trust strangers."

If only her husband, Archibald, had been a little more like them, Isabella thought. Perhaps he'd still be alive. But it was his nature to take a side. And now, she and her sister and his daughter were running for their lives from the same butchers who cut him down in his own surgery as he tried to care for injured men. Men who'd simply stood up as citizens against a line of British Hussars in the streets of Edinburgh.

"Yer a stranger and an unprotected woman traveling in the Highlands. An easy mark, to be sure," Jean warned. "They'll figure ye to be carrying at least a shilling or two, and they'll cut yer throat for it. And then yer carcass'll go into the sea. Them waters have swallowed up more than a few strangers."

The older woman's dire prediction was surely an

exaggeration, but the fate that Isabella faced if she fell into the hands of the British was not. Her late husband's friends, newly released after being held by the authorities, had often been brought to the surgery bearing horrible wounds. Their bodies had been broken. Unspeakable tortures had been inflicted on them. And it mattered naught if they were man or woman.

"Ye keep to the cottage," Jean ordered, her tone as sharp as the needle she stabbed into the mending on her lap. "And if by chance anyone sees ye here, ye say nothing, ye hear? Ye look no one in the face, and ye answer no questions. If there's anything to be said, I'll do it."

Outside, the storm continued unabated, and the wind whistled and rattled loose shutters. The stone cottage, poor as it was, provided safety and a thatched roof to keep most of the weather out. The rustic meal they'd shared of stewed fish and bannock cakes warmed and filled her. She was grateful to have it. The journey north through the Highlands had been wet and rough.

"I appreciate you taking me in like this."

"I took ye in because my nephew asked me to . . . and gave me enough for yer room and board. But I don't know what John is up to. Other than yer name, he didn't say much about who ye are or where ye came from or where yer headed. But he's a good lad, and he's all the kin I have left. I trust him." The hard glare softened with affection. "He says to me, all I need to know is that yer a good woman and some vile Lowlanders'll pay to get their hands on ye. Says I'm to keep ye hidden for maybe three days. He'll come back for ye."

Jean's nephew had gone back to Inverness to book passage for Isabella, her sister, and her stepdaughter on a ship that would carry them across the Atlantic to Halifax. But that meant three days of worrying and waiting before she was reunited with Maisie and Morrigan. Still, she hadn't let the lawyer tell her where he'd placed the young women in the port town. Isabella was afraid she'd be forced to divulge their whereabouts if she fell into the hands of her British pursuers. She had to keep faith that John would do right by the girls. He'd been charged by Sir Walter to look after them all until they left Scotland.

Isabella's gaze fixed on Jean's trembling right hand. She'd noticed it before while the woman was eating, though her hostess tried to hide the infirmity. Now Jean's needle could not find the target, and she sat back in her chair in frustration as the piece slipped off her lap to the stone floor. Isabella bent over and fetched it, along with the woman's darning mushroom.

"Let me finish this for you." Sitting across from her, she studied the threadbare stocking. There was hardly anything left of the heel to work with, but she put the needle to the task. From the corner of her eye, Isabella saw Jean using one hand to try and quiet the other.

The Shaking Palsy. Jean's shuffling gait, the forward stooping, the occasional wiping of drool from the corner of the lips, and the trembling hand that wouldn't be controlled confirmed it. A disease with no cure that would become increasingly difficult to manage for a woman of advancing years who lived alone. Especially living in a place as desolate as this lonely outpost. Duff Head was a rocky bluff pushing out into the cold green-grey swells of the sea to the east of Inverness. And Jean's cottage sat like a hunchbacked sow between two stone-studded hills below the coast road, away from the village. She had no neighbors close by. Isolated as it was, Isabella understood why John suggested this would be a safe hiding place for her.

Her own difficulties aside, it was troubling to think Jean lived alone, out of reach of immediate help if she needed it.

Isabella made another covert survey of the cottage. The iron cooking pot was too heavy, and earlier, when Jean had struggled to swing it out from over the fire, Isabella had jumped to help her. The threadbare rug on the stone floor certainly presented a hazard as the ailing woman dragged her foot. If she fell and broke an arm or a hip, she could lie there helpless forever. "Does anyone visit you?"

Jean bristled. "If someone comes to the door, I'll do the explaining. I'll say yer Mrs. Murray, a friend of a cousin, on yer way down from the Orkneys. Heading to the Borders, ye are. Resting here for a few days. That's all they need to know."

Murray was her family name, and she'd lived as Isabella Murray for twenty-eight years until she'd married Archibald Drummond six years ago and returned to Scotland, to a homeland she hardly knew.

"I only asked out of concern for you." Isabella looked at the gaps in the shutters where rain-drenched wind was coming through. And the thatched roof was hardly watertight. A stream was running down one wall and pooling in a dark corner. "I'm sure a cottage like this requires a great deal of upkeep and—"

"I manage. Always have and always will. And I'm not about to hearken to John's talk of forcing me to live with him." The cap sitting atop the grey hair bobbed in agreement. "Feet-first is how I'll go. That's how my sainted husband left our house, and they can take me out the same way."

Isabella had known very little about John Gordon's aunt before they got here. Their entire trip north, she'd been more worried about getting Maisie and Morrigan beyond the reach of the men who would surely be chasing them.

"The curate does his duty and looks in on me once a fortnight when he comes through. And the women in the village stop by with a basket now and again."

The door shook from the force of a gust of wind. Jean followed Isabella's gaze and frowned.

"If one of them comes calling, remember what I said. No talking. Even a whisper of that Lowland accent'll give ye away."

"I'm quite good at following directions. I'll cause you no trouble."

The roof of the cottage shook as if in disagreement and showered them with broken bits of thatch.

Trouble. Isabella plied the needle to the stocking. Trouble had been a constant companion to her from the moment Archibald brought them all back to Scotland, to their house on Infirmary Street near the surgical hospital. In Wurzburg—thanks to her father's tutelage and influence—she was living a quiet and productive life as an accomplished physician and surgeon, well-versed in the science of medicine, privileged among her sex for being allowed to practice in a profession dominated by men.

Archibald had promised all would be the same in Edinburgh. Neither of them pretended that theirs was a love match. It was a marriage based on respect. It would meet their mutual needs, for her sister and his daughter would be provided for. She could practice medicine in his clinic and lead the same kind of life in Scotland. But he'd only spoken half the truth; he said nothing of the other part of himself.

He was a political idealist, a reformer, and his nationalist consciousness had reawakened the moment he stepped foot on the soil of his homeland. From then on, her husband led two lives. One, as a respected and learned doctor who was sought after by Edinburgh's elite. And the other, as an activist whose evenings were constantly filled with secret meetings and radical efforts to change the repressive direction of the government in London. But that covert life of his, Isabella wanted no part in. She was Scottish by birth, but she'd lived nearly her entire life away from this land. Scottish nationalism and reform were lost on her, for she'd dedicated herself to one passion: medicine.

The collapse of embers in the fireplace tore away a barrier in her mind, and suddenly she was back in her house in Edinburgh. Back in the midst of the mayhem of that fateful day in April.

It had been a day of strikes. Weavers had ordered a shutdown of the city. Shopkeepers shuttered their windows and doors. Protests has been organized in Glasgow and in smaller towns as well.

The government's response was direct and brutal. Troops on foot and horse attacked without warning, riding down and beating protesters in the street. After the clashes, eighteen were carried back to the clinic in their house with severe injuries. They hadn't enough room for all the patients. Bleeding men lay moaning on the floor, in the hall, on the table in the kitchen. Some were not conscious.

Archibald saw to those wounded lying in the front rooms. Morrigan worked at her father's elbow. Isabella set the broken leg of a six-year-old boy, an innocent by-stander knocked down by the mob trying to disperse and trampled on by the ironshod hoof of a cavalry steed.

She'd just put the boy upstairs on her own bed when the sound of shouts and pounding outside drew her to the window. Red-coated militia crowded the street in front of the house.

"Soldiers!" Maisie cried, rushing into the room. "Here. Demanding to be let in!"

Sharp, clawing fingers of fear took her throat in a viselike grip. Isabella was no fool. She knew what was happening on the streets of the city. She was well aware of the identity of some of the wounded they were tending to downstairs at this very moment. She knew the roles these men were playing in the unrest.

"Grab your cloak," Isabella ordered. "Go down the back steps and wait by the kitchen door while I fetch Morrigan. You two must leave the house."

As she raced toward the stairs, the sound of the front door splintering from being battered open was followed by shouts. Her feet barely touched the boards as she flew down the steps.

The front rooms—always a place of order and healing—were a battlefield. Tradesmen and women fought fiercely against the invading soldiers in blue and red jackets. She'd never seen such brawling. More shout-ing. A gunshot.

Pushing through the chaos, she found her husband sprawled against a wall, blood spreading across his white shirt and waistcoat. He'd been shot in the chest.

"Why?" she screamed at the men who continued to pour into the house. She crouched beside Archibald, pressing both hands to the wound, trying to staunch the flow of blood.

"You can't help me," he breathed, pushing her hand away. He looked behind Isabella. "Take her from here. Go. Please."

Fighting continued all around her, but she worked relentlessly to save her husband's life. Time stood still, and the air took on a nightmarish hue. Though Morrigan was right beside her, the young woman's keening cries had a distant, muffled sound. Still, Isabella struggled. But it was too late. Archibald knew. He shuddered, faded, and was gone.

How she was able to get to the back of the house, pulling Morrigan behind her through the bedlam, Isabella could not later recall. But Maisie was waiting for them in the kitchen, standing before the barred garden door. Before Isabella could pull it open, someone outside began knocking. There was no escape. They were surrounded.

"Don't forget what I told ye," Jean's barked order cut into the memories and jerked Isabella back into the present.

She took a deep breath. The knocking was real. The haunting chaos of Edinburgh dissolved in an instant. Isabella peered through dim firelight at the door.

Jean crooked a finger at her again before pushing to her feet and shuffling toward the entrance.

Isabella's stomach clenched. Had they found her? The farther they'd traveled away from Edinburgh, the more days that passed, her worry of getting caught only increased. The accusations of her involvement, the news of the bounty on her head, overtook the travelers and raced ahead of them. Eyes of strangers followed her. She feared being taken at every roadside stop. And the suspicion of her husband's friends that she'd be a liability to them if she were captured only magnified the fear. Long before they'd reached Inverness, word had spread that both sides wanted her.

The door creaked, and the old woman put her shoulder against it to stop the tempest from shoving it open wide. Jean nodded to whoever was outside and stepped out into the storm, pulling the door shut behind her.

Isabella left the sewing on the chair and moved away from the fire. Near the foot of the cot sat her bag. Her faithful and courageous Edinburgh housekeeper had hidden the three women in her son's dank, airless dwelling in Cooper's Close in Canongate and delivered her medical instruments a few days after the attack on their house.

The door was the only entrance into the cottage, and Isabella was trapped. Two windows cut through the thick walls. A stiff leather hide hung low on the wall near the fire, and she wondered if it might provide access to a woodshed or an animal pen. She picked up her cloak and bag but stopped.

It was foolish to think about running. Even if she were able to get out that way, where would she go? She didn't know the country around her. Her sister and stepdaughter were somewhere in Inverness. Their next meeting was to be aboard a sailing ship bound for Halifax. But even that part of their plan was vague. The only thing Isabella had any confidence in was that John was coming back for her.

All of their futures lay in the hands of John's colleague Walter Scott. *Sir* Walter Scott now. A generous man, he claimed he needed to repay a debt to Isabella, using his own funds and risking his own liberty.

The door pushed open again and Isabella stood still, holding her breath and letting it out only when she saw Jean come back inside alone. The old woman latched the door behind her.

"Someone knows I'm here?"

"They don't," Jean said, going back to her place by the fire. "And that's all the better for ye."

"What did they want?"

"Nothing that concerns ye."

The answer didn't make her feel less anxious. She was caught in a blind alley and recalling what she'd gone through only reinforced the helplessness of her position.

"Is there anything I need to know? Or be worried about?"

"Aye. Plenty." Jean looked sharply at her. "But no matter what happens, ye gave me yer word ye won't be leaving this cottage."

"I shan't. I have nowhere to go. But what do you mean 'no matter what happens'? Do you expect trouble?"

"Ye ask too many questions," she snapped.

"With good reason," Isabella replied, softening her tone. "I've been through a great deal of trouble, and none of it I asked for."

The old woman paused, keen grey eyes studying

Isabella's face. "This storm is blowing hard from the north. When that happens, we got to be prepared for what the sea gives up. That's why someone was at my door."

A shipwreck, she thought. How the villagers lived was none of her business. She put down her bag.

"The sea is a harsh mistress," Jean continued. "And seafaring folk must ply their trade, no matter the weather. The sea takes, and the sea provides; that's the way of things. Now, ye go to bed."

CHAPTER 2

Come as the winds come, when
Forests are rended;
Come as the waves come, when
Navies are stranded . . .
—Sir Walter Scott, "Pibroch of Donald Dhu"

The *Highland Crown*. His home. His pride and joy. His dearest possession after twenty years at sea. But there was no saving her. His beloved ship was lost.

Stinging, wind-whipped water—chill and sharp as ice—lashed at Cinaed Mackintosh's face as he squinted through the rain at the mortally wounded brig he'd sailed through a dozen storms as fierce as this one. He lived a good life aboard her. She had the speed to outrun many a ship with far more canvas. She could maneuver in the tightest spots and in the highest winds. She needed it, for they'd operated on both sides of the law. He'd been fortunate indeed in his years as master of this vessel. But his good luck had run out the moment *Highland Crown* was driven up onto the godforsaken rocks of this Scottish coast.

Cinaed's eyes burned from the brine. His ship was lying nearly on its side. The masts had been reduced to splinters, and the wind and crashing surf continued to drag the hull over the jagged reef, tearing huge holes in the timbers and threatening to tumble her into the wild green maelstrom of the sea. He peered toward the patches of black shoreline that appeared like momentary rends, opening and quickly closing in the shroud of dark mist enveloping his vessel.

Two longboats bearing his crew had already disappeared into the storm. The booming sounds of rollers crashing in the distance told him reaching shore was no certain feat.

The ship shuddered and groaned as a wall of water struck and washed over everything, briefly submerging Cinaed and his second mate, a former gunner, who clung to a torn ratline. A handful of men, the last of his crew, struggled nearby to keep the third longboat from swamping.

Not even a day ago, they'd been sailing up from Aberdeen to Inverness. When the storm struck, it hit fast and hard.

It pained him to do what needed to be done now. In a secluded inlet east of Inverness, Cinaed was to deliver his cargo, but that plan would never be played out. On the other hand, he couldn't allow those goods to fall into the hands of just anyone. The political sympathies of the folk living along this coast and across the Highlands were never a certainty, and he didn't want any of the consequences of discovery to fall on his crew.

"Burn it," he ordered. "You know what to do."

His second mate nodded grimly and climbed through the hatch leading into the bowels of the ship.

Not long after he disappeared, another watery surge hammered at the boat. The *Highland Crown* lifted and then dropped, breaking the keel like a wrestler's back. Cinaed held tight to the tattered lines. Worry for his man pushed him toward the hatch. The entire vessel moved again as a section of the bow of the brig heaved, broke off, and began to slide into the sea. Around him, lines snapped and planking exploded like dry kindling. Then, the bow was gone, and only a few casks and crates and splintered timbers remained to mark her passing.

He knew it was only a matter of time before the rest of the ship would follow, spilling its cargo into the churning, grey waves. He didn't want to lose another man. Reaching the hatch, he called down into the dark recesses of the hold. The fury of the storm obliterated any chance of an answer.

He dove through the hatch, moving swiftly through the lower decks in search of his gunner. Cinaed found him, his leg trapped against a bulkhead by one of the very casks he'd set out to destroy. The mate's eyes flashed white with terror. He was holding a lantern at arm's length.

Hanging the light from a beam, Cinaed found a pole and managed to lever him free. Half carrying, half dragging the man, he made his way back to the deck.

"Help him," he shouted at the sailors when they'd reached the submerged gunwale. Another wave crashed over them, but the ship held steady, for the moment at least. Standing in the froth, he handed the gunner into the longboat. "Cast off and get clear. If she rolls, you won't have time."

"Come with us, Captain," the helmsman shouted through the wind.

The ship moved with the grinding shriek of wood on stone.

"Do as I say."

He waited until the longboat cast off the lines. What was left of the *Highland Crown* now joined the tumult of the storm in trying to stop him from reaching his destination. A railing collapsed and tumbled over him, nearly taking him with it into the sea. He climbed over rigging and ducked a spar that swung at his head like a club before he plunged through the hatch.

The lantern swung where they'd left it. With one last look at his cargo, he lit the fuse. With a hiss, the sparks shot toward the kegs, undulating like a fiery serpent. He had no time to consider the loss of all that he'd scratched and fought and bled to build in his life.

The longboat was battling the waves on the leeward side when he reached the open deck. Cinaed leaped into the churning sea. The chill of the water knocked the breath from his lungs. A wave drove him under.

As the sea enfolded him in her arms, the pain of his loss was a dirk driven into his heart. He was not a rich man. He was not born to wealth with a university education or a bought commission or a loving patron ready to cushion his fall. He'd been rejected by the only family he knew. And now the winds of ill-fortune had dashed Cinaed upon a stony shore, ripping from him his home, his life, his future. Beaten back from all he'd gained, his path had been decimated. Was he strong enough to start again?

He turned his gaze up toward the heaving froth of the sea and clawed his way upward. Bursting through, he swam toward the longboat.

Eager hands reached out to help him clamber on board.

"Row, lads," he ordered, climbing into the stern. "All you've got now."

Behind him, the *Highland Crown* exploded in a rapid-fire series of blasts, and pieces of the vessel rained down on the longboat. Cinaed stood beside the helmsman and looked back at his precious ship. What was left of the hull on the reef was on fire, and black smoke billowed above her.

A knot formed in his throat as he watched her burn. Then, lifted by the storm surge, the ship washed off the reef and sank from sight. Planks and rigging were all that remained, burning as they tossed on the tumultuous waves.

Cinaed tore his eyes away and turned to the task at hand, getting his men safely to shore. Through the murk and heavy mist, a rocky point appeared, jutting out from some unseen mainland.

"What's behind us is gone," he shouted above the wind. "Row hard, men. The shore is near."

CHAPTER 3

With head upraised, and look intent,
And eye and ear attentive bent,
And locks flung back, and lips apart,
Like monument of Grecian art,
In listening mood, she seemed to stand,
The guardian Naiad of the strand.
—Sir Walter Scott, "Lady of the Lake,"
Canto I, stanza 17

The loud bang shocked her awake, and Isabella sat bolt upright.

Looking about her, she remained where she was for a few moments and tried to clear away the filmy webs of confusion. She couldn't quite grasp her surroundings. The place was unfamiliar, and she couldn't remember how she'd gotten here or why she was here. It was like a dream she could not escape.

But was the bang part of her dream?

She blinked and tried to clear her head.

Jean, John Gordon's aunt. Isabella was in the Highlands, in the old woman's cottage. The driftwood fire on the hearth had burned down to embers, casting a flickering glow over the floor and the walls and the humble furnishings.

The door swung hard, driven by a gust of wind, and banged once more against the scarred table by a shuttered window. A briny gust swept in through the open door, spattering the stone floor with rain that glistened like drops of amber.

Fanned by the sweep of salt air, the meager flames leapt up momentarily, and she glanced around the small cottage.

The woman was nowhere to be seen.

A quick series of explosions propelled Isabella to her feet. The blast was close, and she hurriedly yanked on her boots. Throwing on her cloak, she crossed to the door and peered out into the rain. Here on the Highland coast, the night sky retained the dismal grey hue of twilight throughout the summer, never yielding completely to the blackness of more southern climes. Even the storm clouds failed to blot out the dim light. But a second sun was burning brightly on the water. She stepped out onto the hard-packed sand and stared through the windswept rain at the wild scene before her.

Not a half mile from the stony beach, nearly cut off from view by heavy mists, the remains of a burning ship lay on a reef. Flames and smoke rose high in the sky.

Smatterings of villagers lined the black stretch of strand, pointing toward the wreck. A few men stood on a jagged ridge of rock projecting out into the raging surf. The attention of Jean's neighbors was riveted on the events offshore, but Isabella moved cautiously to a vantage point on the shadowy side of a line of large boulders leading down into the sea. From here, she could see and not be discovered.

A thick swirling cloud obscured the reef for a few moments, lifting just as a wave carried the burning vessel off the rocks. Shouts and curses peppered the air as the ship went under. Isabella had no experience with shipwrecks, but she guessed the sinking was a hard blow to the scavengers waiting on shore.

Before long, villagers began to wade out to gather the few casks and parts of the ship being carried in ahead of the crashing rollers. Working together, they dragged their meager treasure up onto the beach.

Isabella recalled that a visitor had come to Jean's door earlier. They must have seen the ship hit the reef. They knew this was coming. *The sea takes, and the sea provides; that's the way of things.*

Through the mist, she espied a single longboat foundering near the rocky point. It disappeared into a trough, and when it rose again, the boat was riding lower in the water. Wind and waves were buffeting it about.

A shot rang out from the rugged point.

Isabella gasped and took a couple of steps forward as a man in the longboat fell backward, tumbling out and disappearing into the surf. From where she stood, she could not see who fired the musket, but it was clear to her that the villagers were determined to scavenge what they could. They wanted no survivors to muddy their claim. And they would not brook the existence of any interfering witnesses either.

Pressing a fist to her stomach, Isabella watched the longboat fight to turn away from the rocks. A moment later, it disappeared into the mists.

Villagers continued to pull wreckage from the water, but she looked on with unseeing eyes. Lost in thought as the rain beat down on her, she considered the absurd naïveté of the life she led. Isabella had devoted her entire existence to healing people. But in the real world, men regularly ended each other's lives without hesitation or regret. She'd seen it. In Edinburgh, her own husband had died from a bullet fired by some soulless man in uniform. Even as they ran from the house, she'd seen the bodies on the streets, ridden down by the very men who were supposed to protect them. And she'd seen it here. Now.

How long she stood there, she didn't know. But suddenly she became aware of Jean hurrying toward her from the cottage. The old woman reached her and plucked at Isabella's cloak.

"I told ye to stay inside," Jean said fiercely, motioning toward the door. "This is village business. It's no business of yers. Get back inside afore someone sees ye."

"Who set the ship on fire?"

"They did, the blasted curs." She spat in the direction of the water. "They wanted to deny us whatever they were carrying."

"A villager shot a man in the boat," Isabella said, unwilling to forget what she'd seen. "In cold blood."

"I saw nothing of that. And neither did ye."

No law. No principle. No compassion. The only thing that mattered was one's own survival. This is how they lived. And, she guessed, how they'd always lived. This was why John brought her here. Still, it was difficult to witness. But she had to remain silent. Three days, she reminded herself. Three more days and she'd sail away from the Highlands. And the events of this night would fill only one thin chapter in the tragic memoir of her life in Scotland.

"Go in, I say." Jean peered through a gap in the boulders at the villagers. "Now. And don't be talking of shooting. We've got no guns in the Highlands."

Isabella planted her feet when the old woman tried to push her back toward the cottage. A movement at the sea's edge drew her eye. At the base of one of the boulders that cut off this narrow stretch of stony beach from the long strand leading to the village and Duff Head, a man was dragging himself through the wind-whipped foam. Just above the waterline, he sank onto the beach.

"Someone from the ship!"

Jean gripped Isabella's arm tightly. "I see no one."

She shook herself loose of the older woman. "I care nothing about salvaged goods. Your villagers can keep it all. But that man needs help."

"Wait. Ye can't."

For many, being a physician meant following a dignified profession, one that generally garnered respect and modest financial benefits. But to Isabella, it was an obligation and an honor. She always treated her chosen path as a responsibility. It didn't matter who or what the patient's circumstances were. Friend or foe, poor or rich, she did the same for all. She'd been given a gift that she was determined to use.

She moved quickly down the stony slope to the water's edge, and Jean stayed close behind her, grumbling the entire way.

The man's longish dark hair was matted with seaweed and grit. His face was half-buried in the stones and sand. He was clearly a large man, tall and broad across the shoulders. From the well-made wool jacket and from the quality leather of the boots, she decided he was no ordinary tar. He was either a passenger or an officer from the ship.

Isabella put her back to the gusts of rain and crouched

beside him. Putting her fingers on his throat, she felt for a pulse. His skin was clammy and cold.

"God willing, the dog's dead," Jean mumbled, hovering over her.

"Your wish might come true. He's more dead than alive."

If this was the man who was shot, she imagined there'd be no mercy shown if the villagers found him alive. And his body would never be found. The rising tide was washing up around his boots.

"Help me turn him over."

"I'll not help ye with any such thing. And if ye have any sense, ye'll leave him be and let the sea take him."

Isabella wiped the salty rain from her face and pulled his arm, managing on her own to turn him onto his side. A growth of beard covered his face, but his skin was pale as ash, his breathing shallow. Taking hold of his jacket, she rolled him onto his back. Her hand came away red. She pushed his coat open and saw a hole in his black waistcoat an inch or so above the heart. Blood was seeping from the wound.

"I knew it." She pressed her hand against the wound to stop the bleeding.

"Let him go."

She pressed harder. The storm and the rage of the sea blended with Jean's warnings before fading away. Her mind was transported back to their house in Edinburgh. The stranger's face was Archibald's. Warm blood oozed through her fingers. All her years of training and she hadn't been able to save him. His life had just slipped away.

Isabella would not let this man die.

Archibald was her friend, her mentor, and her teacher. Just as when her father died, losing him had slapped her down with the cruelty of life's uncertainties. The responsibility for the well-being of her sister and her stepdaughter was overwhelming. In a moment, she'd been stripped of the ideal existence she'd been living. At four and thirty years of age, she had to learn how to survive. She had to run for her life.

"Not much is washing ashore." Jean's voice came to her from the gap in the boulders, where she was watching the villagers down the beach. "Folk'll be coming this way to see if anything drifted this far."

Blood continued to pulse from the wound.

The old woman shuffled back to Isabella's side. "Ye have to go in, mistress. Now. They won't be any too happy with this one."

"I can't let him die. Not again. I can't," she said, her voice belonging to a stranger.

Isabella reached for a clump of seaweed that washed up beside them. She pressed it into the wound. The bullet was still in him. If she could extract it, sew the wound shut, she could stop the bleeding. It was the only way to save him. Ten years ago, she'd helped her father operate on the bloodied men carted back to Wurzburg from the battle at Leipzig. After a week, they'd still carried Russian musket balls and shrapnel in their festering wounds. The death rate had been dreadful.

The bag containing her surgical instruments was beside the cot. "Help me take him up the hill."

"This one will never see the inside of my cottage. Just leave him."

"I'll drag him up there by myself, then."

Jean tugged at Isabella's cloak again. "Yer daft, woman. Ye remember nothing of what I said last night, do ye?"

The patch of seaweed was helping staunch the flow of the blood. Isabella looked up at the sandy stretch, trying to decide on how she could get him up the hill.

"Ye listen to me now, mistress—"

"I am *not* leaving him," she cut in sternly. "Do you hear? I am not letting him die out here on the beach. Now, you do what you see fit. But if you want to deliver this man up to your friends, then you can just hand me over with him."

The older woman let go of the cloak and straightened up, staring at her as if she were a creature with two heads.

They both started at the sound of someone calling from the beach beyond the boulders. A man's voice.

Too soon, Isabella thought. Her bravado was being tested. "I stand by my words."

"Stay down and don't move," Jean hissed. "Mind me now."

The urgency in the old woman's voice sank in. Isabella crouched beside the injured man. She kept firm pressure on the seaweed over the wound.

Concealed by the boulder at the edge of the water, she watched Jean climb with surprising agility onto the rocks to head off the villager.

"Oy, Auld Jean. Anything come in along this stretch?"

From where Isabella waited, she could see the man was carrying a stout cudgel.

"Nay, Habbie. Not a thing, curse 'em," she wailed. "The dogs blew it up rather than giving us our deserving share. And what purpose does that serve, I'd like to know."

"If any of them boats land nearby, I'm thinking the lads'll be taking it out of their hides."

"Well, that blast was a fine show, to be sure," she remarked. "What do ye think they had in there to go to such trouble?"

"French gold and Old Boney's crown, no doubt. Wouldn't want that lot to fall into the wrong hands." Habbie laughed. "Though maybe they was carrying a weapon or two."

Illegal in the Highlands, Isabella thought.

"And maybe a keg of powder or two?"

"Ye could be on to something, woman. Wouldn't be the first smuggler to run too close to the Head."

Isabella frowned at the man lying motionless in the sand beside her. A smuggler.

The sound of others calling from the beach drew the villager's attention. "Come for us if anything washes ashore. Don't be dragging any crates out of the sea by yerself."

"Of course, ye fool. I'm too auld to be doing anything like that."

Isabella didn't know if it was safe yet to let out a breath of relief. The sailor or the smuggler or the passenger or whoever this man was, remained unconscious. But beneath her palms, she could feel his beating heart. He was not giving up.

She watched Jean make her way back down.

"Thank you," Isabella said. "Now can you please help me drag him up to the cottage?"

"Best look at him again. The blasted cur looks dead enough to me."

"He's not dead. He—"

The words caught in her throat as a hand shot up and long, viselike fingers clutched her windpipe, squeezing hard.

Isabella gasped for air, stunned by the attack. She tried desperately to yank herself free of the deadly grip. She tried to claw at his face but couldn't reach. Her nails dug into his wrist, but he wouldn't let go. His eyes were open but unfocused. He was intent on murder, and there was nothing she could do to stop him.

Her lungs threatened to burst. This was the end, she thought. Her destiny was not to die beside Archibald and his rebel comrades in Edinburgh, but here, alone, her life choked out of her in a storm on a Highland shore. Jean would surely push her body into the sea, and her killer's body would soon follow. Maisie and Morrigan's faces flashed across her mind's eye. The two would need to survive without her, Isabella decided, feeling herself losing consciousness. They had each other, and they were no longer children but strong women. They would need to be.

But her end didn't come so quickly. Unexpectedly, the man released his grip with the same suddenness that he attacked her. Isabella fell backward onto the stony beach, coughing and trying to force air back into her chest.

One breath. Her lungs protested. Another breath. She was breathing. Breathing. She held her bruised throat.

Jean was crouched beside the man's head, proudly waving a good-sized rock in her hand.

"This time I'd say the sea dog really *is* dead."

CHAPTER 4

O, Woman! In our hours of ease,
Uncertain, coy, and hard to please,
And variable as the shade
By the light quivering aspen made;
When pain and anguish wring the brow,
A ministering angel thou!
—Sir Walter Scott, "Marmion,"
Canto VI, stanza 30

Cinaed looked up into a woman's face. Fine black eyebrows arched over brown eyes that were focused on his chest. Thick dark hair was pulled back in a braid and pinned up at the back of her head. Intent on what she was doing, she was unaware that he was awake.

Her brow was furrowed, and lines of concentration framed the corners of her mouth. The grey travel dress she wore was plain and practical. She was not old, but not young either. Not fat, not thin. From where he lay, he guessed she was neither tall nor short. She was beautiful, but not in the flashy way of the women who generally greeted sailors in the port towns. Nor was she like the eyelash-fluttering lasses in Halifax who never stopped trying to get his attention after a Sunday service. He didn't bother to assess the pleasant symmetry of her face, however. The "brook no nonsense" expression warned that she wasn't one to care what others thought of her looks, anyway.

But who was she?

The last clear memory he had was seeing a flash from the shore. The next moment his chest had been punched with what felt like a fiery poker. Everything after that floated in a jumbled haze. He recalled being in the water, trying to swim toward some distant shore. Or was he struggling to reach the longboat again?

Cinaed didn't know what part of his body hurt more, the fearsome pounding in his head or the burning piece of that poker still lodged in his chest.

"Where am I?" he demanded. "Who the deuce are you?"

Startled, she sat up straight, pulling away and scowling down at him. In one blood-covered hand, she held a needle and thread. In the other, a surgeon's knife that she now pointed directly at his throat.

"Try to choke me again and I'll kill you."

"Choke you? For the love of God, woman!"

His ship. The reef. The explosion. He closed his eyes for a moment and tried to clear away the fog. Everything he'd been through struck him like a broadside.

The *Highland Crown* was gone. He'd detonated the powder himself. Where were his men? He'd climbed into the last longboat. They'd been fired at from the beach. He'd been shot.

Cinaed grabbed the knife-wielding wrist before she could pull it away. "Where are my men?"

An ancient woman in Highland garb slid into his line

of sight behind the younger one. She was making sure he saw the cudgel she had over one shoulder.

"This one is worth less than auld fish bait, mistress," she taunted. The crone was ready and obviously eager to use that club. "And thankless, too, I'm bound. I was right when I said ye should never have saved him."

Should never have saved him. He released the wrist, and the hand retreated. But the dark-haired woman didn't move away. As if nothing had happened, she dropped the knife on the cot, out of his reach. The brown eyes again focused on his chest, and she put her needle back to work.

He winced but kept his hands off the woman.

By all rights, he should be dead. A musket ball had cut him down and knocked him into the water. He should indeed be finished. Someone on shore had tried to kill him.

But he was alive, and apparently he owed his life to this one. Gratitude flowed through him.

"Want me to give him another knock in the head?" the old witch asked.

"Last stitch. Let me finish," she said in a voice lacking the heavier burr of the northern accent. "You can kill him when I'm done."

A sense of humor, Cinaed thought. At least, he hoped she was joking. She tied off the knot, cut the thread, and straightened her back, inspecting her handiwork. He lifted his head to see what kind of quilt pattern she'd made of him. A puckered line of flesh, topped by a row of neat stitches, now adorned the area just below his collarbone. He'd been sewn up by surgeons before, and they'd never done such a fine job of it. He started to sit up to thank her.

That was a grave mistake. For an instant, he thought the old woman had used her cudgel, after all. When he pushed himself up, his brain exploded, and he had no doubt it was now oozing out of his ears and eye sockets. The taste of bilge water bubbled up in his throat.

"A bucket," he groaned desperately.

The woman was surprisingly strong. She rolled him and held a bucket as his stomach emptied. She'd been expecting this, it appeared. However horrible he was feeling before, it was worse now as the room twisted and rocked and spun. Long stretches of dry heaves wracked his body.

"Blood I can deal with," the old woman grouched from somewhere in the grey haze filling the room. He heaved again. "By all the saints!"

"I'll clean up later. Don't worry about any of this. Go sit by the fire, Jean. You've had a long night."

Cinaed felt a wet cloth swab the back of his neck and his face.

Jean mumbled something unintelligible about "weak-bellied" and "not to be trusted" and "a misery." When he hazarded a glance at her, she was glaring at him like some demon guarding the gates of hell.

"Does my nephew know that yer a doctor?" she asked, not taking her eyes off of him as she snatched up the knife and handed it to the younger woman.

A doctor! He lifted his head to look at her again. She was definitely a woman. And a fine-looking one, at that. He was still breathing, and she'd done an excellent job on whatever damage had been done to his chest by the bullet. But the possibility of any trained physician, or even a surgeon, being here in this remote corner of the Highlands was so implausible. Male *or* female.

"John knows."

"But ye say yer not a midwife," Jean persisted, a note of disbelief evident in her tone. "And not just a surgeon, in spite of all them fine, shiny instruments in that bag of yers."

"I trained as a physician at a university. But I'm finding that my abilities as a surgeon have more practical uses wherever I go."

University trained. Cinaed stole another look at her. She had an air of confidence in the way she spoke and acted that convinced him that she was telling the truth. And for the first time since the *Highland Crown* struck that reef, he wondered if his good fortune was still holding, if only by thread. Lady Luck, apparently, had sent him Airmid, his own goddess of healing.

Long-forgotten words, chanted over some injury, came back to him from childhood. *Bone to bone. Vein to vein. Skin to skin. Blood to blood. Sinew to sinew. Marrow to marrow. Flesh to flesh . . .*

From the floor, she retrieved a bowl containing bloody cloths. A musket ball lay nestled like a robin's egg on the soaked rags. By the devil, he thought, his admiration nearly overflowing. She'd not only stitched him together, she'd dug the bullet out of him.

The deuce! He'd never seen anyone like her. Frankly, he didn't care if she came from the moon to practice medicine here. He owed his life to her.

"And a woman doctor, to boot," Jean said. "Imagine that. I never knew there were any."

Cinaed lifted his head to catch a glimpse of the heart-shaped face next to his. The eyes were dark and beautiful, but she wasn't seeing him. Her attention was on wiping the sweat from his face.

"I never knew there were any either," he managed to say before bending over the bucket and vomiting again.

In this remote and godforsaken Highland shore, where people shot at the survivors of a sinking ship, he'd been saved by a doctor.

"After digging that ball out of him, did ye sew him up wrong?" Jean asked. "Is that why his guts are spilling out into my bucket?"

"He's throwing up because you hit him with a rock."

"What choice did I have? Yer a stranger here, but the dog was throttling ye. Had murder in his eyes, he did."

Cinaed did vaguely recall fighting. He was on a beach. The pain in his chest was intense. He thought someone was cutting out his heart. He felt a twinge of guilt.

"I didn't. I wasn't. No mur . . ." he managed to rasp out, trying to keep down the next gallon of boiling seawater rising into his gorge.

"I was trying to save your life, but you decided to choke the life out of me," the doctor said calmly. "You deserved the knock on the head."

Yet she'd still extracted that ball from his chest and put him back together. Steps shuffled off across the floor. Old Cerberus was returning to her lair. At least the woman doctor didn't belong to this tribe of brutes who tried to kill him. He should apologize—thank her, at any rate—but he couldn't. The bile was in his throat again. Every limb felt dead to him. His body ached, and his face was suddenly burning with fever. He only wanted to close his eyes and shut everything out.

She gently rolled him onto his back and lowered his head onto a soft mound.

The hellish upheaval in his stomach was easing now that it was empty. The doctor stood and crossed to the fire, and Cinaed studied the inside of the cottage for the first time. The smell of fish and a wood fire permeated the air. One door, two windows, a thin beam of daylight cutting across the smoky interior. The old woman sat at a wooden table, mumbling what sounded like complaints at no one in particular. The storm seemed to be lessening outside. His clothes were wet, so he couldn't have been unconscious for too long.

Carrying strips of cloth, the doctor came back and crouched beside him. Her hands were cool, and he welcomed them on his fevered skin. Her touch moved with competent assurance as she cleaned and covered the wound on his chest.

In his entire life, no woman had ever treated him so tenderly. Certainly, he'd known the soft touches of plenty of harbor lasses, but their interest in him was more closely connected to the coins in his pocket. He'd been at sea for most of his days and never had a real home to call his own. He'd never had a woman who cared for his needs without wanting something in return.

He studied her face again.

Her nose was straight. She had a wide, lush mouth. The hollow curve beneath her high cheekbones fascinated him. He didn't know why, but he found himself fighting the impulse to reach up and erase the furrowed crease in the middle of her brow.

Cinaed's eyes drifted shut. It was too painful to move,

to think, to decide how he could repay his debt to her. To this doctor.

Then suddenly, he was back on board the *Highland Crown*. The storm was again raging, and huge waves were battering his brig. Men were trapped in the stern, and he had to save them before the ship was driven down into the bottomless abyss.

Isabella laid a blanket over the man, leaving the dressed wound exposed. She wanted to know if it began to bleed again.

She hadn't removed his boots from the long legs that hung over the end of the cot. His size alone made him quite imposing. And his reflexes were quick, despite his injuries. She touched the tender skin of her throat and rubbed her wrist where his grip had bruised her. He was a rough man, but considering all he'd gone through and the strangeness of waking up in this cottage, she understood his reaction.

He was extremely lucky to be alive. The ball had missed his heart and lodged itself in the flesh close to the collarbone. Half an inch in any direction and he would have been killed, to be sure. Isabella was glad he'd been unconscious while she'd operated. She didn't want to think how he would have responded if he'd woken up while she was digging about in his chest.

"Well, is yer sea dog going to live?" Jean called from the table.

"He's young and strong. So long as he doesn't come down with a fever, he should recover."

"How soon can we turn him out?"

"If you think he'll wake up and walk out of here in the next hour, I'd say you're expecting too much."

Jean shoved a bowl to the side and grumbled under her breath. The fire hissed back at her. Having two outsiders here clearly wasn't what the old woman had bargained for when she'd agreed to help her nephew.

If the man were found under her roof, Jean would be facing a great deal of trouble with her people. Helping Isabella hide in the cottage paled in comparison with concealing and nursing someone from the wreck.

Whatever John gave his aunt from Sir Walter, she thought, it wouldnt be enough.

Isabella picked up her instruments and dropped them into a pot of water boiling over the fire. Her attention stayed on the old woman's hands. The excitement of last night and this morning had made the shaking worse. She wracked her brain for something she could do to help Jean. Somehow, she'd have to repay her for the risks she was taking.

She started to clean her equipment. For a moment, her thoughts turned to her father, a student of ancient Roman medicine. In his teaching, he'd always been a strong though lone advocate of cleanliness. But what mattered most to him would not have been the conditions under which she'd operated. She'd saved a man that many others would have allowed to die. Isabella had no doubt what she did last night and today would have made Thomas Murray proud.

"I don't understand ye." Jean's hand was shaking hard enough to cause a soft, steady drumming on the table.

Isabella left her medical instruments in the pot and dried her hands on her skirt.

"I don't understand going through all this trouble," Jean complained. "To be sure, he'll kill us both when he's strong enough."

Isabella hadn't had enough time to think everything through. Last night, she'd run up to the cottage and fetched a blanket. Rolling the man onto it, the two women struggled but somehow managed to drag him inside where she'd immediately operated.

He was wounded, and she needed to help him. It had been the same in Edinburgh. Sick and injured men and women had arrived at their door, and she'd reacted. She had very little interest in whether they could compensate her and her husband for their care. And what was to become of her patients in the future was the worry for another day.

Jean's short temper boiled over. "I can't have it. Ye, I might be able to explain. But him?" She snorted.

"Perhaps he'll *want* to go when he wakes up," Isabella suggested. Of course, it was impossible. She'd seen enough gun wounds to know her patient was in no condition to walk out of this place alone.

"What if he doesn't?"

She didn't have all the answers. And right now, the thought of making a decision for someone else was overwhelming.

The trials of these past weeks never left her. She'd lost Archibald. Maisie and Morrigan's future depended on her making good, clear choices. She had little faith that all would turn out well for any of them. But one thing Isabella was certain of was that she'd done right. And saving this man had restored a vestige of the confidence she had in herself and her abilities. She still had a purpose to serve.

As powerless as she'd been feeling while her life collapsed around her, she still had something valuable to offer.

"I can't handle him when he wakes up," Jean kept on doggedly. "And neither can ye. I say we drag him back to the beach now and let—"

"Take this," Isabella cut in, slipping the gold ring from her finger. Archibald had given it to her on their wedding day. A token she was ready to part with.

She'd spent her youth studying and working beside her father while many other young women dreamt of love and courtship. She'd had no interest in such things in married life. And as for Archibald, his true love had been Morrigan's mother, the woman he'd lost a year before he offered marriage to Isabella.

None of the past mattered anymore. He was gone, and a different life lay ahead of her. She laid the ring on the table in front of Jean. "It's yours."

"Why give me this?"

"To pay for his keep," Isabella said, motioning toward the sleeping patient. "He's lost a great deal of blood. To let him stay and mend."

Jean picked up the gold ring and turned it over, staring at the engravings.

"Let him stay until your nephew comes back. John will know what to do with him."

Her hostess had confirmed this morning that, because of the fiery explosion, not much of value had washed ashore with the wreckage from the ship, and the villagers would certainly be blaming the crew.

Isabella had witnessed how ruthless they could be. She had no doubt this man's fate would be sealed the moment they put him back on the beach. They'd kill him if for no other reason than to satisfy their anger over what had been destroyed.

Jean pushed the ring back toward Isabella. "I've seen wedding rings afore, and I'll not take yers. But while we're at it, where is yer husband?"

Isabella shook her head, too tired to explain. It was safer this way. "Can he stay or not?"

The old woman started to say something, but then she stopped short. Her head cocked toward the door. Immediately, she was up and moving. Pushing open a shutter a crack, she peered through and motioned to Isabella to stay quiet.

"Habbie the Ranter's got his cart down on the strand," she hissed.

Isabella took an involuntary step back. The fire in the hearth blocked her retreat. "Who is this Habbie?"

"A low, troublemaking cur. The same one that came looking for salvage afore."

"Will he come this way?"

"He might."

Anger unexpectedly sparked up within Isabella. She'd been through this before. Trapped in their house. Soldiers breaking in at every door. Archibald had died in her arms. And while they were in hiding, word had come that the protesters they'd been ministering to had either died or been dragged off to the horrors of Bridewell Prison. She couldn't save them, and she couldn't protect them. Isabella had never seen herself as a fighter—in the physical sense—but right now, she was ready to pick up Jean's cudgel and swing it at the head of the first person who tried to force his way into this cottage.

"He's coming. Hide."

"Where?" Isabella asked as the woman started to un-
latch the door.

"Through there," she said, pointing to the leather hide
hanging low on the wall. "It's just a wee space for keeping my wood dry. Take him with ye. I'll try to keep this
one outside, but I might not have a say in the matter."

Jean went out and pulled the door closed behind her.

Isabella's hands shook as she darted toward the wall.
Pulling the stiff skin aside, she stuck her head into a
dark space that she'd barely be able to stand in. She
quickly shoved driftwood aside to make room, but in the
end, the space was barely large enough for one person
to hide. It would have to do. She hurried back to the
wounded man's side.

"Help me," she whispered, prodding him. "I need you
to wake up."

She received only a low moan in response. She had no
time. Casting aside the blanket, she lifted one booted leg
off the cot and then the other. Going behind him, she
raised his head and slipped her arms around his chest.
He was too heavy.

"I'm sorry." She gathered her strength. "This won't do
your injuries much good, I'm afraid."

Pulling with all her might, she managed to tip him off
the cot.

Isabella froze at the sound of a gruff voice.

"Oy, Auld Jean. Fine day after such a wild blow,
wouldn't ye say?"

"So yer out for a stroll in the weather, Habbie?" Jean
replied in a scoffing tone. "Are we going to make these
daily visits, then?"

They had to be standing right outside the door. Taking hold of her patient's boots, Isabella dragged him toward the hiding place.

"Don't care for my company, auld woman?"

"When did I ever?"

Isabella paused to catch her breath. Jean asked about the events of the night, and Habbie told her that none of the longboats landed nearby. He was out looking for anything else that might have washed in with the tide.

She pulled the wounded man again, and he groaned softly as his head bumped along the stone floor. As she backed through the low opening, she banged her own head hard on the lintel.

Crawling through, she managed to haul most of his body into the space. Why did he have to be so tall and broad? When she had no more room to pull, she climbed back over him, heaved his shoulders up, and forced him through the opening. He was moaning low, and Isabella held him in a sitting position, breathing hard. She hoped she hadn't torn his stitches loose in moving him.

"All right, Habbie. Out with it," Jean said to her visitor in a scolding tone. "What're ye doing down here?"

"I told ye, I'm out looking for anything from the wreck. What little there is, the lads are sorting it up at the kirk."

Isabella's patient wouldn't stay upright. There was nothing she could prop his back against. Bracing herself, she shoved him in another inch or two. If anyone stepped inside the cottage now, she'd be in plain view.

"Nothing washed ashore on the beach here, as ye can see. So ye can just be on yer way."

"Now that ye mention it, there's marks in the sand leading right to yer door. Something was dragged up here since the storm."

Isabella broke out into a cold sweat. How careless of her not to go back and sweep away the track. The thought had never entered her mind. But it wouldn't have mattered. She'd had no time to do it. Her patient had needed immediate care.

Jean's voice was rising in pitch. "Yer a bold piece of work. Out with it. Ye think I come on some treasure and decided not to share it with the folks in the village."

Isabella recalled what Jean said before about being able to explain her presence, but that didn't seem like a good way to go now. She pushed at the pieces of wood on either side of the opening, desperately trying to make room for herself to crawl in behind the man. Driftwood shifted, clattering in the darkness of the storage space. She'd gained very little.

"I made no such accusation. But since ye got nothing to hide, ye won't mind me taking a look."

Panic washed through her. Half of her body was still protruding into the cottage.

"Come in and see for yerself, if ye must, ye nosy cur."

Giving the man one more shove, she crowded in after him.

The door of the cottage opened at the same moment Isabella dropped the leather hide in place. She was on her knees behind the wounded man, using her body to hold him in a sitting position.

Her patient murmured something, and she quickly covered his mouth with a hand.

"Please, for the love of God," she whispered softly in his ear. He smelled of sea and night. "If you make a noise, neither of us gets out of here alive."

Isabella felt the man's back and shoulders grow tense,

taking some of his weight off her. His head rolled slightly but remained drooped forward, and she prayed he was awake enough to understand what she'd just told him.

She heard their voices inside the cottage.

"Do ye see? Nothing. No treasure. Only blood I been cleaning off my floor from the fish that went into my stew last night."

Blood on the floor. Her bag lay open by the cot. A few of her medical instruments still sat in the pot by the fire. Her travel cloak hung from a peg on the wall. Isabella felt her stomach tighten and grow queasy. She wondered how observant this Habbie was. Indications of her presence lay in the open all over the cottage.

Footsteps came close. Isabella pressed her face against the wounded man's back as she started to shiver. Fear washed through her, paralyzing her. If he pulled back the leather covering, there would be no escape.

She was like a trapped animal watching a hunter approach.

"Satisfied?" Jean barked. "I told ye I've nothing here."

Habbie gave no reply, and Isabella tried to imagine what the villager was staring at now. The silence was the most chilling. She had no idea if the man had ever been inside Jean's cottage before. She didn't know if he could identify those things that did not belong. He had to be armed. Her back was to the makeshift door, and prickles of fear ran down her spine. If he lifted the hide, he'd see her. And how was she going to defend herself?

Cold sweat covered her brow. She worried that the drumming of her heart was loud enough to be heard outside. A large hand slipped around hers in the darkness, and she was relieved to know she was not alone. Her fingers entwined with his. She welcomed their strength. Her body molded to him. His wide shoulders were a wall, offering shelter. Her cheek brushed against his coat, and she breathed in the warm scent of the man and tried to calm the fears.

"That'll do, Habbie," Jean snapped. "If yer planning on staying around here any longer, ye can just get down on yer knees and clean that floor for me."

"If ye think I'll be doing yer chores, ye really are a daft auld cow," the villager answered with a scoffing snort. A chair scraped on the stone floor. "What's that?"

"What?"

All of Isabella's fears surged through her again.

"This ring. Where did ye find it?"

Her wedding ring. On the table. Isabella bumped her forehead again and again on her patient's back. Of course, Archibald could not give her a plain ring. She'd told him she needed no ring at all. Not to be put off, he'd bought her an ornate gold band of obvious value.

"Found it. On the beach a fortnight ago. It's mine."

"Don't look like it sat in the sand even a minute. Looks brand-new. I'm thinking it came from that wreck."

Jean cursed him roundly. "Damn me, if ye think I'll let ye take it."

Please, Isabella pleaded silently, let him have it and be gone. The thought became a reiterating chant in her head. She wanted him to be gone.

"How ye going to stop me, eh?" The sneer was evident in his tone.

"Give it to me, I say."

"Save yer wind, auld woman. I'm keeping it."

"Ye'll not be going out of here wi . . ."

The sound of the old woman's cry was followed by a crash and splintering wood. Immediately, Isabella felt the wounded sailor struggle to move. She couldn't sit still and let Jean be injured by this thieving bully. He was one person against the two of them. Safety be damned. As she began to untangle herself, Jean called out.

"It'll take more of a man than *ye* to hurt the likes of me," she said in a voice that Isabella realized was intended for her. "But yer still a foul and nasty dog. True when ye was a wee chack, and truer now. Ye'll burn in hell, to be sure."

"Try to take this from me again, and I'll send ye straight to hell ahead of me. Make no mistake," Habbie taunted. "Come on, if ye want it. I'd as soon tie a rock around yer neck and throw ye off the Head as look at ye."

"This is what we've come to in this village now, is it? Ye wait until the curate hears that ye struck me down."

Thoughts of violence crossed Isabella's mind, and she wasn't alone. Her patient was straining against her hold on him. She pressed her cheek against his back, trying to instill patience.

"Ye go right ahead. Tell 'em all." Habbie paused. "Go ahead, auld hag. Pick up that stick of yers. It'll be the last thing ye do in this world."

"If my auld man was still alive, he'd—"

"Yer auld man's been gone many a year, so come on and raise a hand to me. Yer just another mouth to feed in this village. I tell ye, no one here'd miss ye."

Let him go, Isabella pleaded silently. Please, Jean. Let him go.

The leather hide behind Isabella shivered as the cottage door opened. He was leaving. Thank God. She listened to the fading footsteps as Jean continued to shout her complaints after him about a "vile world where folk rob their own and auld women are struck down by brutes."

A moment later, the door closed, and Isabella heard the warning whisper.

"Stay where ye are."

"Are you hurt?" Isabella asked.

"I'm fine. Don't ye worry about that. If ye'd come out, it would have gone worse for all of us."

Fear was slow to make room for any feeling of relief. Her heart continued to pound. In her mind's eye, she saw him bursting back into the cottage, tearing away the hide, and dragging them out of their hiding place.

"Let me out of here." The voice was deep and grim. He let go of her hand.

She inched backward, trying to make more room for him. But there was nowhere to go. His size filled the space, heated the air. Her body shaped itself against him. Isabella didn't think she'd ever been this close to a man, other than her husband.

"Not yet. Jean will tell us when it's safe."

He didn't like her answer. She could feel the muscles flex in his back.

"Where are we?"

"We're in a cottage not far from Duff Head."

"He's still not gone back to the cart," Jean's whisper cut in. "Don't ye move. Hear me?"

"Why are you hiding?"

He sounded abrupt, impatient, but his tone calmed her. Regardless of his injury, he exuded courage. She imagined it was a matter of time before he pushed her back and climbed out.

"Because I don't belong in these parts," she answered. "I'm only staying here for a few days."

"That doesn't explain why you're hiding."

His voice carried a trace of the Highland burr. She wondered if he was from anywhere nearby.

"Who says I'm hiding?"

"You're here in a hole too small for a pair of rabbits, curled around me like a worn wool blanket."

Jean's blow to the head obviously hadn't done much damage to his astuteness. He was absolutely right. Her knees had moved, and were straddling his hips. Her skirts were pushed up.

"Who are you?" she asked, trying to distract him from questioning her or noticing her encroaching position.

"Cinaed Mackintosh, owner and ship's master of the *Highland Crown*, the brig that's now strewn all over that reef."

Isabella had known from his clothing that he wasn't an ordinary seaman.

"Move," he ordered. "I won't lie here like a . . ."

Suddenly, a hide covering a narrow gap on the outside wall flew open and light flooded in. Stunned that there was another opening, Isabella stared at the silhouette of a man filling the doorway.

"Well, what do ye know? Two castaways."

Habbie. He was carrying a stout cudgel. Everything she'd feared was coming true.

"Auld Jean," he shouted. "That wee knock ye took was but the first . . ."

Isabella felt Cinaed lean forward, and an instant later she gasped. A knife pulled from his boot flashed in the dim light as it flew across the enclosure.

CHAPTER 5

Soldier, rest! thy warfare o'er,
Sleep the sleep that knows not breaking;
Dream of battled fields no more,
Days of danger, nights of waking.
—Sir Walter Scott, "Lady of the Lake,"
Canto I, stanza 31

Cinaed Mackintosh was not a murderer by trade or profession. He felt no obligation to fight for God or king or
country. Long ago, he'd decided the Almighty had to be
tired of all the killing, and no king had ever deserved his
loyalty. When it came to fighting for Scotland, the place
of his birth, he believed enough blood had already been
spilled in a land that would never be free. Still, that didn't
stop him from causing trouble for the enemy when the
need presented itself. He acted because he was fighting
for the people. They were the only thing that mattered.

Cinaed had never served in any army. He'd narrowly
avoided being impressed into the Royal Navy years ago.
But he knew that many Highlanders had taken up the
sword for the English who defeated them at Culloden.
They'd fought and bled and died in a dozen wars for
the glory of the Empire. They were fools, killing and lay-
ing down their lives for the aristocrats and the moneyed
elite who scorned their very existence. These Highland

warriors were lost men who allowed themselves to become nothing more than killers for hire.

Cinaed could kill if he needed to. He would kill to survive, and burying that knife in the heart of the blackguard had been an act of self-preservation. If he hadn't acted, if he'd missed his mark, the two of them hiding in their wee rat hole would be dead, and he was certain it wouldn't have gone too well for the old woman.

The doctor was quick to get around to the back of the cottage, and Jean was right on her heels. He heard their voices outside. The villager was dead. He knew that already.

As Cinaed tried to listen, his head still pounded, and the burning pain in his chest was not improving. He felt as weak as a newborn, but thankfully his mind was clear.

He could not imagine being in a worse situation. This brutish dolt had found them with very little difficulty. It was only a matter of time before others came looking as well.

Cinaed dragged himself out of the cramped space and slowly pulled himself to his feet. The table near the window had been smashed into kindling. He looked around the cottage for any weapon he could use. The doctor's surgical knife was the sharpest and the most lethal thing he could find.

Moving from one window to the other was painful, but he had to ignore that. Outside, no other people were visible on the beach. Cinaed's gaze immediately moved to the rocks out on the sea. A different kind of pain pierced his chest. Charred driftwood and torn pieces of the sail were all that was left of his brig. No longboats in sight and no bodies along the shore.

Raised voices drew him outside. Around back, the two women were arguing. The dead man lay on the ground between them. Their quarreling stopped as soon as they saw him. Feeling a bit light-headed, he leaned back against a stone wall of the cottage.

"Ye can just take this stubborn chit and go," Jean ordered him. "And I mean *now*."

"This man should not even be out of bed, never mind go anywhere," the doctor asserted, eyeing him with concern before turning her frown back on the older woman. "But when we *do* go, you need to come with us."

"Yer sea dog is well enough to throw a knife and kill a man," Jean grouched. She turned her back on the doctor and shuffled toward Cinaed. "At the top of the strand, down past these rocks, ye'll find Habbie's cart where he left it. Ye take it. And take *her*. Follow this path up to the coast road. Less than half a day's ride and ye'll be in Inverness."

The younger woman refused to be ignored. "And just how are you going to explain this dead villager?" She pulled at Jean's sleeve. "How can we explain to John that we left you in this predicament?"

"Don't ye be worrying about telling my nephew anything."

"I don't care what you say. You're coming with us."

Jean pulled her sleeve free and spoke to Cinaed. "My nephew, John Gordon, always stays at the Stoneyfield House on this side of the port. It's right on the coast road, so ye should have no trouble finding it. Deliver this one to him. Ye might as well keep the cart and the horse, for Habbie won't be doing any more hauling in the future." She waved off the other woman like some annoying insect. "And don't forget ye owe her yer life. Taking her to Inverness is the least ye can do to repay her for all she's done."

Inverness. Perhaps some of his crew had made it safely to shore and found their way to the port town. After delivering his cargo, he was supposed to continue on to Citadel Quay at Inverness. He was to be paid on delivery by his kinsman Searc Mackintosh.

Worse, those who'd been expecting him would be seriously disappointed. Months of planning and waiting and secrecy had all come to naught. And Cinaed doubted they would be very agreeable about helping him get a position on another ship or find his crew.

He had to get back to Canada somehow if he were ever to begin rebuilding. But whatever he had to do, it needed to start in Inverness. This blasted hamlet was nothing but a death trap for him. If the villagers found him, they'd hang him for sure. He had the blood of one of their own on his hands.

"We're going," he said abruptly, motioning to the doctor. "Now."

"Not without her." Her eyes flashed. She pointed at the corpse, ignoring him. "This brute threw you about for a paltry ring. I don't want to think of how they'll treat you after this."

"Ye'll be the death of me, woman," Jean huffed, digging in. "Go. Leave me be. I know how to lie, and they'll believe what I say."

"The way this one believed you?" the doctor scoffed.

Soft footfalls. From the direction of the beach, someone was creeping up on them. Cinaed edged over to the corner of the cottage. The women continued to argue, paying no attention to him. He'd been only nine years old when his clan had rejected him and sent him away to become a ship's boy. Good instincts and quick reflexes had saved him from harm many a time. More often than not, he sensed danger before it struck.

"You say the ship's captain owes me his life," the younger woman snapped before softening her tone. "Well, I feel that I owe you mine. When the village discovers this man's body, you'll not be safe here. Come with us now. Your nephew can bring you back if you wish it. But I'm not leaving you here alone."

The sound of breathing told him someone was listening around the corner of the cottage. Cinaed moved fast. Reaching around, he grabbed a collar of a greasy jerkin and yanked the stalker off his feet, slamming him to the ground. Putting a knee on the scrawny back, he pressed his knife to the throat of the wide-eyed intruder.

"Don't," Isabella shouted, rushing toward them. "Don't kill him. He's only a boy."

"I'm no boy," the lad protested, squirming like a speared fish and craning his neck to glare up at Cinaed. "I'm a grown man and worth ten pox-eared sea rats. Ye let me go, and I'll show ye in a fair fight."

The boy was tall and thin, and his eyes flashed fire at the indignity of his position. He couldn't be more than eleven or twelve years old. Shaggy hair stuck out from a woolen cap and a filthy jerkin covered equally filthy pants. He was doing his best to act tough, Isabella thought, but his bravado looked more like stupidity at the moment.

"The lad's just a wee fool," Jean told them. "Habbie

uses him to run and fetch. Teaching him to be a lowdown dog, same as him."

The ship's master appeared to have no intention of letting the boy up or fighting. His gaze was focused on what they could see of the beach. Isabella continued to be shocked by his speed and his strength, despite the newly stitched hole in his chest. Trapped with him earlier, she'd never seen him reach for his knife. And when she got to Habbie's body behind the cottage, she'd been amazed by the precision of his aim.

He was now using her scalpel as a weapon. He had to be in tremendous pain, and yet he showed no suffering. His stern face was pale but the picture of concentration. He was as relentless and vigilant as a scout scanning the area for any potential dangers. Despite the unbuttoned coat and vest, and the torn and bloody shirt beneath, he was clearly ready to do battle. She couldn't help but be impressed. More than impressed.

Isabella was certain she'd never in her life met anyone like him. She didn't even think men like him existed outside of stories. Wounded warriors who rose above physical pain and debilitating injury, who never gave up even in the face of certain annihilation. Like the mythic heroes of ancient times. Prometheus, Hector, Odysseus, Achilles's Myrmidons. She recalled the Athenian warrior who carried the news of victory from the plains of Marathon.

"How many more are with you?" Cinaed asked, sparing the boy only a glance as he withdrew the blade.

The young one didn't answer fast enough and got a knee jammed harder into his back for his trouble.

"No one," he yelped. "I was down by the cart waiting. When he didn't come back, I thought to see what happened to him."

The boy turned his head and his eyes fixed on Habbie. His mouth hung open for a moment. Suddenly, he didn't look like the young tough he was trying to be. In Isabella's eyes, he was no more than a child unable to fathom the sight before him.

"What have ye done to him?" he croaked, staring wildly at his captors before looking back at Habbie. The high-pitched wail made it clear he'd seen the handle of the knife protruding from the man's chest.

Isabella was tired of the bloodshed, but she wasn't about to blame the ship's master for the dead man lying at their feet. She doubted that any explanation or any plea would have convinced Habbie to let them walk away unharmed. She was a physician. In the past, she'd found it impossible to condone the taking of another's life. But this case was an exception, and she couldn't bring herself to assign guilt. If Cinaed hadn't acted, more violence would have occurred.

"He knew ye was up to no good, ye auld hag," the boy cried out. "He was right, and ye had to kill him for it, didn't ye?"

Only moments ago, Jean had been arguing that she wouldn't go to Inverness with them, despite the dead body on her doorstep and evidence that she'd been harboring two strangers in her cottage. Isabella hoped the older woman would now see things differently. This boy's words would go a long way with Habbie's friends in the village, and he wouldn't be alone in accusing her.

Suddenly, the boy began shrieking for help.

"Quiet," Cinaed barked.

But the lad only cried out louder. With a determined sigh, Cinaed pushed the lad's face into the sand for a moment. That was enough to frighten him into silence.

"What will it be, Jean?" Isabella asked softly. "We can't stay here all day. Others are sure to come."

The old woman nudged the dead man with the tip of her shoe, a look of sadness and resignation on her face. Crouching beside the body, she took Isabella's wedding ring out of Habbie's pocket. Then, without ceremony, she pulled the knife from his chest and wiped it clean on his jacket.

"No point in wasting anything of value on this one," she murmured. "I'll just tidy up my home afore we go."

Relief washed through Isabella. No one could have foreseen the series of events they were dealing with. As it was, trouble and death had found their way to Jean's cottage door. Staying here was not a viable option.

John Gordon would surely see that when they all reached Inverness. The man was capable enough to handle the details for spiriting three fugitive women out of the country; he'd know what to do for his aunt. And he could find a place for this one to recover. Perhaps the captain had his own people in the port.

As Jean started for the front of the cottage, she gave the knife to the ship's master and placed the ring in Isabella's palm.

"Ye better be killing me too, ye auld witch," the boy cried, talking tough to Jean, since she was the only one of the three that he might be able to handle. "I'll tell everyone what ye done to Habbie. Ye won't be getting away with this, hear me?"

Isabella had raised a sister and a stepdaughter from the time they were slightly older than this boy's age. Putting aside their education and the life of privilege they'd grown up with, neither of the girls were reckless. They both were thoughtful and shrewd when it came to danger. She'd witnessed Maisie and Morrigan's behavior since they'd fled their home. And they were anything but stupid.

"Have at it. Kill me too. I'd fancy seeing ye hang for it."

This one, Isabella thought, was stupid.

As the captain shook his head, she saw the tug of a smile that quickly disappeared, replaced by a frown. He seemed as amused as he was unimpressed with the foolish whelp squirming beneath his knee. She imagined he'd commanded many boys as young as this one aboard his ship. And she was glad that he was in control of his temper and not about to give the lad his wish.

Cinaed called to the older woman before she rounded the corner. "What should I do with him?"

She paused and then shrugged, looking from Isabella to the captain. "The lad's right. Two killings amount to the same thing. Ye'd best cut his throat. They can only hang ye but the once."

CHAPTER 6

So shall he strive, in changeful hue,
Field, feast, and combat, to renew,
And loves, and arms, and pipers' glee,
And all the pomp of chivalry.
—Sir Walter Scott, "Marmion,"
Canto V, Introduction

"You *told* him to kill the lad."

"Go on. Say it again. Just keep on accusing an auld woman unjustly," Jean argued. "Ye two are the ones running from the law. I've got no say in what ye do or don't do."

Listening from behind them in the cart, Cinaed had already learned the doctor's name was Isabella Murray. He knew she was married, for the two women had argued fiercely about a wedding ring that Jean would not accept from her as some sort of payment. There was no discussion of any husband, however.

He shifted his body slightly to look over his shoulder at her. She was a bonnie thing, and he couldn't let go of their time in the woodshed. She must have dragged him there by herself. And there was the moment when he'd known she was frightened. He'd so much wanted to hold her, to tell her he wouldn't let the blackguard in the cottage hurt her.

"It was ruthless of you even to say the words," Isabella retorted.

Jean flicked the reins just to keep the broken-down cart horse from wandering off the coast road. The journey had been slow, but since the old woman's cottage was on the Inverness side of Duff Head, at least they didn't need to go through the village in the stolen cart. Still, Cinaed was watchful of anyone following them. So far, he'd seen no one.

"Ruthless? Bah!" Jean scoffed. "Do ye truly have no idea how to put the fear of God into bold lads? That scrawny cur was showing no respect for his elders at all."

"And you don't think ordering the boy killed was a bit much?"

"Killed? Killed by who?" Jean asked in a mocking tone. "Ye wouldn't kill anyone if they were ready to cut yer throat. And there's no way that man sleeping back there would have killed the boy either."

Isabella turned to look back at him, but he pretended to be unconscious.

"His name is Cinaed Mackintosh, and he was the master of the ship that went aground," she said, returning her attention to Jean. "That alone tells me he must be pitiless, or he would never be in a position of command."

Cinaed lifted one eyebrow. Interesting that she'd have that opinion of ship captains. Knowledge of navigation and general seamanship, expertise in the unique idiosyncrasies of the ship, confidence in one's ability to lead hard men through difficult situations—these were qualities of a successful ship's master. But in his experience, lack of pity was not a requirement for the job.

"Habbie deserved what he got," the older woman asserted. "What yer sea dog . . . yer ship's master . . . did was right. He defended us from harm, sure as I'm sitting here. So don't go casting dirt on the captain's good character."

"His *good character*?"

"Yer too young to be repeating me."

"This makes *no* sense," Isabella declared, stealing another glance back at Cinaed. "Fewer than a dozen civil words have been exchanged between you two. And yet you're ready to defend his character?"

The cart wheel hit a deep hole, splashing rainwater left by the storm and jarring the three of them. Jean grabbed the doctor's elbow to keep her from bouncing out while a lightning bolt of pain shot through Cinaed's chest.

"I've a canny sense about folks, and I know how to get along in the world. Ye don't."

"I know how to *get along*, as you call it," Isabella said hotly.

"By St. Andrew's beard, I swear if I left ye on yer own in these parts, ye'd be dead in half a day. Me, on the other hand, I could survive on a rock in the ocean with bit of broken glass and an auld boot. And I wouldn't even need the boot."

The snort from the doctor was unexpected, and the old woman sent her a sideways look.

Cinaed found their argument entertaining. He liked them. Both of them. Isabella more, and not—he told himself—because he fancied her looks or the tone of her voice. She'd saved his life.

"I know how folks think," Jean continued. "I can tell when they're worth a lick, and when they're not. When my nephew left ye with me, ye didn't hear me complaining, did ye?"

Beyond the fact that he knew Isabella was a university-trained doctor and that she was married, where she came from and what she was doing in the Highlands were still a mystery. And now, for the first time, Cinaed was hearing talk of some nephew and his involvement.

"He gave you money to house me."

"I knew ye was worth saving the moment I saw ye. And the same goes with this one back there. I trust him."

"And when did you decide that?" Isabella was quick to ask. "Did you trust him last night on the beach when you were insisting that I roll him back into sea? Or was it this morning while I was still stitching him up and you were telling me he'd probably murder us both?"

Neither Jean nor Isabella was ready to yield in this argument, and Cinaed felt his eyelids becoming heavy. Trust him or not, no harm had come to the lad. He was trussed up and lying on the floor of the cottage. The older woman said that no one from the village would come looking for the two until sometime late in the day. By then, she figured, they'd already be in Inverness.

With a dead body outside and a bound lad inside, Cinaed didn't care to be caught by a mob looking for justice. He hoped Jean was right, for he was in no condition to be fighting anyone right now. He stole a look back in the direction they'd come. They were probably still closer to Duff Head than Inverness.

The cart hit another hole and jolted the passengers again. Grimacing, Cinaed waited for the pain to subside. The bullet hole in his chest was throbbing, and he could see fresh blood on the bandages. Helping him into the back of the cart, Isabella had told him how important it was to let her know if he started bleeding again.

He decided it was more likely he'd die at the hands of pursuing villagers than he would from losing too much blood. Pulling the doctor's travel cloak over himself, he closed his eyes.

The few things that the women had packed into the cart offered very little cushion, but he knew he needed to rest. Soon, despite the discomfort, sleep overtook him, and dreams rolled over him like cresting waves in a stormy sea, stealing the breath from his lungs and driving Cinaed ever deeper into the briny darkness.

Gorse-covered hills loomed up on either side of the black, fast-flowing river that tumbled along beside him. He was on foot, running hard. Shadows like wisps of haunted mist sprang up, and formless terrors pierced him with chill shards of fear.

Behind Cinaed, angry voices spread out in a threatening line of pursuit.

As he ran, familiar mountain summits came into view, huddled beneath thick Highland clouds. The path rose and fell, and the sounds of men grew louder, closer. A thickly forested glen appeared, and he made a dash for it. As darkness closed around him, the path gave way to a thick floor of pine needles that he could smell with every step he took. His chest was burning, but he knew he couldn't stop. The sounds of his pursuers, crashing through underbrush, continued to grow louder, hemming him in, pushing him forward.

Cinaed's legs were no longer flesh and bone. They felt more like bags of sand and rock. A light appeared through the trees.

Someone caught hold of his hand. He glanced over,

trying to shake himself free of the grip, but he could see no one. Still, he could feel the weight dragging at him. Then a voice inside spoke; he needed to carry it to safety. He gripped the hand tightly and pulled the unseen companion along.

Suddenly, he was nearing the edge of the forest. The light was blinding, but the angry voices were right behind him. As he burst out of the darkness, a new spurt of strength flowed into his chest. Cinaed knew where they were. His destination lay directly ahead. But he couldn't see it through the thick blanket of fog rolling in from the mountains. Still, he *knew* it was there, ahead of him, perched on a hill. Safety lay just ahead, if he could only make it.

He flew over the path and the wet grass. The acrid tang of smoke hung in the air. He could feel the pursuers' panting breaths and the pounding of their footsteps. The curtain wall of an ancient fortress emerged on the hill, its black, iron-studded door open.

Sharp objects poked him in the back. They were right behind him. A gun fired and a bullet whizzed past his ear. The hill was steep, but the gate was there. Cinaed clutched the invisible hand. He couldn't let go. His home, his people were just beyond the door, waiting for him. They'd be safe.

His feet barely touched the wooden bridge crossing the wide ditch outside the wall. The massive portal began to swing shut. He wasn't going to make it. He cried out, but his plea was drowned by the shouts and curses behind him. The entrance was moving away.

Then, at the last moment, with a burst of speed, Cinaed clutched the hand of his unseen companion and slipped through. The great door slammed shut.

Standing with the high wall and the door at his back,

he stared uncomprehendingly at the sight before him. No family awaited to greet him or enfold him in their arms. No castle yard surrounded him.

Cinaed was standing at the edge of a jagged cliff. Mountain peaks spread out in the distance, their tops covered with snow that sparkled in the blinding sunlight. And a thousand feet below, a river raged, white-capped and deadly, through a rock-strewn valley.

The cliff edge began to crumble beneath his feet, and as he scrambled backward, he banged up against the wall.

Cinaed struck his head hard, but it wasn't against any stone wall. Cautiously, he lifted his head off the planks of the cart as it lurched forward. He opened his eyes. The cart had turned onto the coach road from the rutted coastal track.

He raised an arm to block the golden afternoon sun. No one was holding his hand. But his breathing was ragged, and his body was soaked with sweat. He threw the cloak off him. The fiery pain in his chest was a sharp indicator that he was no longer asleep, but the dream wouldn't leave him right away.

The thick curtain wall, the wide ditch, the gorse-covered hills lining the river valley. He knew them. The Highland fortress in his dream was Dalmigavie Castle.

Cinaed thought of the letter he'd received from Lachlan Mackintosh before sailing for Scotland. The laird of Dalmigavie had invited him to visit.

The Mackintosh clan had cast him out as a child, however, and he wouldn't be going back to them now. The dream had simply been a reflection of his thoughts. He'd destroyed the letter after reading it, but it still angered him. Cinaed needed no one.

He ran a weary hand over his face, forcing himself to focus on the business at hand.

Inverness. His men. It would be a massive relief to find they were alive. They had wives and children who were waiting for them. Able-bodied sailors were always in demand. They would get back to Halifax. As for himself, he had kin here. Searc Mackintosh would help him find a way of getting back.

Jean's voice broke into his thoughts. "We're almost there. It's time ye told me the rest of it."

He raised his head to look around. The grassy land on either side of the road stretched out flat as a table, glistening from the rain. Not a stone's throw away, Moray Firth sparkled in the sunlight. They must have passed the road to Fort George a while back, for up ahead he could see a large merchant brig and two schooners busily taking in sail. The ships had to be getting close to the mouth of the River Ness and the port.

Jean was keeping after Isabella. "Ye might as well tell me. I'm already an accomplice in whatever heinous crime ye've committed."

Cinaed's attention was drawn to the doctor. He wanted to know this as well.

"You must trust me when I say, the less you know about me, the better."

He stared at Isabella Murray's dark green travel dress and her ramrod straight back. She'd loosened her bonnet strings, and the hat now hung back between her shoulder blades. She was rubbing her long, slender neck. Wisps of hair were loose and danced in the wind. The woman had to be dog-tired. The *Highland Crown* had run up on the reef early last night. He expected the villagers probably witnessed every stage of his ship's demise. Later, when he'd washed ashore, she'd been on the beach and had cared for him straight on until morning.

He recalled the hand he was holding in the dream. He owed Isabella his life, and he wondered if she was the companion he'd pulled along at his side.

"Ye must've committed a terrible, terrible crime, I'm thinking," Jean pressed, unwilling to give up. "Or ye wouldn't be running away and hiding, as ye are."

"I've committed no crime."

"Ye must've. Out with it, lass. Passing counterfeit coins? Selling bad oysters to innkeepers? Did ye murder the Lord Mayor's cat?"

"I've done nothing wrong."

"Then what? Ye admit they're after ye. So ye must have done something. Ye must, at least, have a long, sad tale of how yer being wrongfully accused."

The younger woman's shoulders lifted in a shrug.

"Ye wouldn't be the first or the last, I expect. Especially ye being a woman and all. And my John wouldn't have come all the way from Edinburgh with ye unless there's a story to it. He's told me many a time he works on the trials of some tough folk, but I know him. The lad also has a soft heart for those the world has tramped on."

The doctor's lips remained sealed. Isabella simply stared straight ahead, offering nothing.

Cinaed couldn't imagine what kind of trouble Isabella Murray would be in. She was a rarity as a woman doctor. Of course, her chosen profession alone could draw the law down on her, depending on where she decided to practice medicine. But why would she need to travel all the way to the Highlands?

"At least tell me *who* it is that's after ye, so I don't say the wrong bloody thing to the wrong bloody folk."

"You say we're almost there?" Isabella asked, obviously trying to curtail the interrogation. A young woman with secrets. Cinaed had plenty of them himself.

The old woman fell silent for moment, and her tone was pained when she spoke again.

"If that's the way ye want it, all well and good. But know this: I was fine living my life afore ye arrived at Duff Head. And even after, I could've managed if I'd just left yer sea captain in the surf. But I listened to ye. Trusted yer judgment. And now, I've lost everything I could call my own. I've let ye drag me from the place I've lived all my days. But ye still don't trust me a lick. But go on and hold yer tongue, if that's the way ye want it."

Isabella shifted uneasily. For a moment, Cinaed thought she'd jump off the cart rather than give in to Jean's questioning. He was relieved when she didn't. Finally, she fixed her gaze on the older woman.

"*Everyone* is after me."

"Everyone?"

Isabella nodded sharply, clutching the edge of the cart with a white-knuckled grip. "But those I fear most are the British soldiers. Right now, your nephew is trying to secure passage for me, so I can escape this country."

Cinaed lifted himself on one elbow. He was as surprised as Jean looked.

Before she mentioned the soldiers, Cinaed was beginning to wonder if Isabella was being sought for the murder of her husband. She *had* been trying to give away her wedding ring. Not that he believed she was capable of it, but he'd already been thinking of reasons that would justify her actions. If that were the case, however, she'd be fearful of magistrates, and not specifically British soldiers.

"What have ye done, mistress?" Jean asked gravely.

"I told you before. The less you know, the better." Isabella looked away.

"I grant ye, ye've made me believe the matter is serious. But how serious is it? Are we talking a hanging offense?"

Another long pause hung in the air, and Cinaed watched the woman's profile. The tense flicking of her jaw muscles, the bite of her bottom lip, the tremor that she quickly tried to mask, all told him she was fighting a battle inside. The same protectiveness he'd felt when they'd been holed up in that wall, rushed through him again. She hadn't asked for it, but he wanted to help her.

"Talk to me," Jean persisted gently, putting her wrinkled hand on top of her companion's. "Tell me, lass."

"I'm quite certain I'll face torture at their hands until they get the answers they want. And after they're finished, I'll hang until they cut me down and behead me."

Cinaed sat up in the cart, feeling his insides clamp tight. If her face and words weren't so grim and serious, he'd think the whole thing preposterous. How could this woman be facing such dire consequences? It had to be a mistake. He glanced ahead of them, his hand feeling involuntarily for the knife in his boot. If they were out looking for her now, he'd need more than sgian dubh if they came upon any soldiers. He wished he had a pistol. Or at least a sword.

But hanging and beheading? Treason was the only crime he knew of that the British punished in such a way, and the authorities had been throwing the word around quite a bit lately.

People had been angry since the end of the war, and it was getting worse. In every port and city, he saw evidence of social unrest. In London and Liverpool and Glasgow and Edinburgh. And he'd heard it was true in the rest of the country as well. Whether it was the weavers of Manchester or the farmers of Ayrshire, people were on the edge of revolt.

"You're connected to the radicals in Edinburgh?" he asked.

Isabella twisted around so fast that Jean had to take hold of her arm so she wouldn't fall out. The alarm in her eyes quickly gave way to a guarded wariness.

"I am connected to no one," she said too quickly. "I carry the banner for no political movement. I take no side."

"And still, you're wanted for treason."

"I said nothing of treason."

"You mentioned the punishment for it."

Her hand moved involuntarily to her throat. Cinaed wondered if it was a reaction to the thought of the punishment for her crimes, or if she was recalling the bruise he'd caused.

He wasn't willing to let go of his questions. She was clearly in trouble. And he knew better than anyone that being this far north didn't put her outside the reach of British law. Every ocean crossing, he'd been taking men and women that the government called rebels to Canada or America. He knew firsthand about their fight and the tenuous nature of their existence here.

"Thistlewood, Davidson, Tidd, Ings, Brunt." He watched the blood drain from her face.

"I don't know them."

The Cato Street conspirators. Last month in London, all these men had been hanged and beheaded.

"Lord Kinloch."

She shook her head, her gaze refusing to meet his.

Cinaed guessed she already knew the man's other name. The Radical Laird. Since December, Kinloch had been in hiding for speaking out in favor of reform. The government was calling for his arrest.

"Hardie and Baird and others from Glasgow are rotting in prison, waiting to be tried. They'll surely hang. Why are they chasing *you*, Isabella?"

"Please. Stop."

He heard the desperation in her tone. She was frightened. And from the bits and pieces of information he'd heard, she didn't want to involve anyone else in her troubles.

Cinaed saw her turn to the road. He couldn't fault her hesitation, for she knew nothing about him. Nothing but the little he'd told her.

"This here is Stoneyfield House," Jean told them, gesturing ahead.

Her announcement put an end to the conversation, and Isabella's relief was palpable. She turned her gaze toward the inn.

Cinaed knew this place. Or rather, knew *of* it. Not so much the inn, but the area. Looking toward the firth, he saw the stone cottages of fishing families clustered along the edge of a protected inlet, surrounded by boats and

nets and drying racks for their catch. To the south, beyond the rambling stone inn, with its enclosed yard and
stables, farm cottages studded the flat fields, cooking
smoke rising above their thatched roofs.

Not far beyond the bordering swath of forests, the moors
of Culloden and Drummossie lay, the wooded hills rising
above. The blood of the Highlands stained those fields.

Just around a bend ahead, a small kirk sat with its
squat steeple. Like so many village kirks, its bell had
rung out for the Bonnie Prince, calling his Jacobite
forces to gather. The sounds of pipes and war drums and
cannon had grown silent—for now—but many would
never forget the sacrifice of those who had died and the
brutality of those who had carried the day.

The cart rolled past the entrance to the inn yard and
stopped.

Cinaed inched off the cart and forced his fevered
brain to focus on their destination. The inn sat on the
coach road between Inverness and Nairn, and from the
activity in the stable yard, it appeared to be doing good
business. The door of the tavern was open, and a trio of
farmers was going in.

"Ye'll not be coming in with us," Jean told him. She
climbed down and came around to where he was leaning against the cart. "Ye can just climb back up and go
on yer way."

Isabella was slow to get down. She kept her face
averted from the inn as she pulled up her bonnet.

"Perhaps I should wait," he said, unable to tear his attention away from the doctor. He was worried about her.
"What if your nephew decided not to stay here?"

"He told me he'd be here." The old woman started to

reach for their bags, but Isabella was already pulling them to the end of the cart. "Ye don't need to worry. I've known the innkeeper for twenty-five years. He'll look out for us."

As Cinaed raised his hand to help with the bags, pain flashed through his body, shooting from his chest up his neck and setting his head ablaze with blinding heat.

"You're injured," Isabella said. Her face was still pale. "I can manage this."

Cinaed was satisfied that an understanding had passed between them. At least she knew he was aware of her predicament. She'd have his friendship if she chose to accept it, although in his current condition, he was more of a liability than a help.

He was reluctant, but he let go of the bags. "I don't feel comfortable leaving you two alone here."

Jean waved off his concern. "The innkeeper'll give us a place where we're out of the way until John returns."

"Let me at least bring your bags in for you," he offered, wondering how the devil he'd accomplish it if she agreed. "I'd like to see you settled."

One grey eyebrow lifted. "Yer daft, man. Look at ye. Yer a bloody mess. Ye'll draw more attention than if we hung a placard about our necks. Nay, ye can help us best by getting as far from here as that auld nag'll take ye."

Isabella moved around the cart and, without asking his permission, pulled open Cinaed's coat and waistcoat. She didn't spare a single glance up into his face, focusing her attention on the bloody bandages covering the wound on his chest. She ran cool fingers over his burning skin. He wanted to reach up and take her hand. Cinaed was relieved to see a soft blush had crept back into her cheeks.

"You're bleeding again." She frowned.

"A few other things needed tending since you sewed me up."

As she pulled the bandage away from the wound and leaned closer to get a better look, Cinaed admired the dark lashes against her pale skin. She pressed the flesh beneath his collarbone and a shaft of red-hot iron ran him through. It was all he could do to remain still.

"You're feverish and bleeding," she said, shaking her head. "You'll need a physician wherever you're going."

He needed *her* care. But he wouldn't ask. Inverness was his destination. Searc Mackintosh was no doctor, but he could find him one.

More important, he had unfinished business with Isabella. He tried to tell himself he'd already done enough in return for her saving his life, but he knew it was a lie. She put her own life in jeopardy for him. And after what he'd learned, she was in greater danger than he was right now.

"Do *you* want me to come inside with you?" he asked, his voice low. The words were only intended for Isabella. "I can wait until you've met up with her nephew."

Her eyes met his, and for the length of a heartbeat he lost himself in their rich golden-brown color. He knew so little about her, but beneath that serious exterior, there was a courageous woman he wanted to spend more time with. He had things he wanted to say to win her trust. Her hand suddenly snapped back from his chest, and she stepped away. Unexpectedly, a blush bloomed on her cheeks.

"Thank you. As Jean said, it's best if you go. Some of the stitches have pulled. It's critical you find help and a place where you can rest for a fortnight, at least. Your wound needs time to heal."

He took her hand before she could step away. "Thank you." His voice sounded oddly husky, even to himself. "I mean it."

She waved him off and reached for her travel bag. "I hope you have good luck in your travels, Captain."

As Isabella slung her bag over her shoulder and crossed the road alongside the old woman, Cinaed drew a painful breath.

"You're a fool," he murmured to himself, watching her walk away. "She's a married woman. And she's wanted by the British authorities. Both of those things mean trouble you don't need."

Still, he was struck by a strange sense of loss. But how could he lose something that he could never have?

CHAPTER 7

And said I that my limbs were old,
And said I that my blood was cold,
And that my kindly fire was fled,
And my poor withered heart was dead,
And that I might not sing of love?—
How could I, to the dearest theme
That ever warmed a minstrel's dream . . .
—Sir Walter Scott, "Lay of the Last Minstrel,"
Canto III

Isabella was no stranger to offers of protection. Her father, her husband, Sir Walter Scott, John Gordon.

And now Cinaed Mackintosh.

So many men—friends and associates of her father— had felt the need to be protective of her. It had been the same in Edinburgh. All due to the uniqueness of her position as a female physician, she supposed. But no offer from a man had ever effected her like Cinaed's words.

Her involuntary response took Isabella completely by surprise. The flush in her face, the sudden tumultuous fluttering eruption of warmth inside. *That* was new to her.

Before her marriage, she'd always found herself to be immune to men who made the conscious effort to attract her. She was fully aware of it when they tried to be charming, flirtatious, forward. The captain was attempting no such thing. He'd spoken the truth, as frightening as it was. And at the same time, he respected her need for privacy. Still, Cinaed Mackintosh had breached the wall that shielded her heart.

She'd married Archibald for protection. For herself and her sister. And for a chance to pursue her medical career. But now he was gone. She'd always appreciate everything he'd done for her. Her response to Cinaed was a surprise, but she felt no guilt about it.

"It's not too late," Jean said, breaking into her thoughts as they approached the inn's tavern door. "I heard what he said. If ye want, we can put a blanket over his shoulder. Ye both can wait right by this door until I find out where my John is boarding."

"I can't." Her objection was too fast and sharp, and she drew a curious look from the older woman. Isabella fumbled to explain. "More than likely, half the village are coming after us from Duff Head. If he comes in with us, the cart will be out there on the coach road. They'll know we're here."

"We can move it into the stable yard."

"The captain is badly wounded. He'll not be able to fight anyone."

"Well, mistress, I wouldn't say the man's good for naught, even with that wee hole in his chest."

Isabella entered the tavern room ahead of Jean. She didn't want to discuss this any further. Of course she didn't want to leave him alone in his condition. She *wanted* to take him by the hand and have him come in, for him and for her. And though she would not say it to Jean— she could barely admit it to herself—it bothered her to think he was about to disappear from her life forever.

All these mad thoughts had to be the result of exhaustion. Isabella couldn't remember the last time she'd slept. Jean, on the other hand, appeared to be holding up fairly well.

The older woman stationed Isabella just inside the door with their travel bags, giving her curt directions. She was not to ask or answer any questions, under any circumstances. She was simply to wait until they found out the whereabouts of her nephew.

Jean crossed the wide room to the innkeeper, who sat closeted behind a wide serving plank, puffing away at a pipe and reading a newspaper. Behind him, a half-dozen casks lined a wall, and above him, empty tankards for beer hung from hooks.

Standing in the shadows, Isabella held her cloak over her arm and cast furtive glances about the room. Of the dozen or so tables, only two were occupied. The trio of farmers who'd entered before them had joined a fourth farmer. Cards sat on the table, but no game had yet commenced. By a window, two more men who appeared to be traveling merchants sat engaged in a serious conversation over an open ledger book. A waiter in a worn black vest and apron, with greying hair that stuck up like that of an angry hedgehog, leaned against a wall near a wide fireplace. He was critically eyeing a young potboy who was carrying a pitcher of beer over to the farmers. A small, smoky fire burned in the fireplace with a kettle hanging above the flames. The smell of roasting mutton and potatoes wafted in from some distant kitchen.

The waiter reluctantly pushed away from the wall and slouched over to Isabella. In a somewhat peevish tone, he asked if she'd care for a table, but upon receiving a shake of her head for his trouble, the man stumped back to his original place.

As they traveled up through the Highlands, John Gordon had taken care to choose which inns or houses they stopped at, which door they used to enter or exit, and where they ate. Always securing a private dining room for their use, he'd made sure the three women had been constantly shielded from public attention. Standing in the tavern now, Isabella felt exposed and vulnerable.

One of the farmers was watching her, and she could catch occasional snatches of talk between the men. She understood Jean's insistence on her remaining silent. The native Gaelic language of the Highlands had been outlawed seventy-five years earlier—after the Jacobites' defeat by the British—but more than a few native words still peppered the conversation. In addition, the accents were rich, and the way they pronounced words was very different from the way she spoke. She'd be singled out as an outsider the moment she opened her mouth. And she could already tell that Duff Head wasn't alone in its dislike of strangers. The longer she stood waiting by the door, the more hostile the looks.

Isabella was relieved when Jean shuffled back to her. The look of disgust she fired over her shoulder signaled her dissatisfaction with whatever answer she'd received.

"Arrive without welcome. Leave without farewell," Jean spat disdainfully. "That's the way of it with this owner."

Leave without farewell. Isabella tried to comprehend the meaning of the words. If John Gordon was gone, where could he be? She never should have sent the captain away. She should have waited to know for sure that

Jean's nephew was definitely at the inn. The complication of where they would go from here and how she could reach the girls pricked her with needles of alarm.

Jean sat herself on a bench at a nearby table.

"Is John here?" she asked, joining her.

A half-dozen fishermen poured through the door, boisterously calling for beer and filling the space in front them.

"Aye. That he is. Or this poor excuse for an innkeeper thinks so, but he says he can't be too sure until he speaks with his wife."

"I thought you said you knew the man."

"I did. The last owner." Jean spat on the floor. "This vile toad and his wife run the place now. Says the auld fellow passed away over a year ago. I don't think John knew this inn was being run by the likes of this one. When I asked him if he remembers my nephew, the fool brazenly said he only remembers guests by the size of the tips they leave."

Isabella hoped John was generous with servers.

"How long ago were you here?"

Jean shrugged. "Maybe two years since."

Or maybe three or four years, Isabella thought, already recognizing Jean's tendency to forget things.

"So where is the innkeeper's wife?"

"He doesn't know where she's gone off to. Says she'll be back soon enough. Though how he knows that is beyond me."

Isabella reached into her cloak for a money purse she kept there. "Why don't you go back and offer him something? Perhaps a shilling will help him remember if John Gordon is staying here or not."

"We're not giving him anything," Jean said firmly, putting her trembling hand on top of Isabella's and stopping her from producing any coins. "That greedy toad'll take the money and still be of no help. I could see the way he was looking at me. Just an auld fishwife beneath his notice. I offer him yer money, he'll take it and immediately forget the reason I gave it to him."

"Perhaps I should speak to him."

The old woman's stern shake of the head spoke of the pointlessness of such suggestion.

"Don't make things worse, mistress. We'll just wait here. Be patient."

An impossible feat. Isabella wished she could summon some of Cinaed's cool confidence. In that wild moment when they'd been discovered back at the cottage, he'd known exactly what he had to do. And he'd done it. While she could function perfectly in a medical emergency, this violent new life she'd been thrown into required different skills. Perhaps while she'd been learning surgery, Isabella thought, she should have learned other uses for a knife.

A headache gnawed at her, and she rubbed her temples. She tried not to think of his recitation of the names of all those men who'd already been swept up unjustly.

The feel of his broad back against her cheek, she'd not forgotten. Nor the reassuring hold of her hand. The image of Cinaed standing by the cart was back. The man's blue eyes matched the early-morning sky. Or that rare blue of the ocean in summer. They enthralled her with the promise of finding treasures in their depths. The long curls of his dark hair framed the strong angles of his jaw and the effect, combined with the growth of beard, was alluring.

Isabella expelled a frustrated breath, trying to shake off thoughts of Cinaed Mackintosh. She had to. She didn't need him. She only needed a whisper of faith that all would be fine.

"I believe the Queen of Sheba's arrived."

Jean nodded in the direction of a stout woman wiping her hands on her apron as she came across the taproom toward them. From the way the waiter and potboy jumped when they saw her, Isabella knew she had to be the innkeeper's wife. As she drew near, she and Jean both stood, but the woman looked only at her, at the bags, and at Isabella's forest-green carriage dress before addressing her.

Before they'd left Duff Head, Isabella had changed out of the bloodstained travel dress she'd been wearing into this one, which was of higher quality material and required no cloak in good weather. She'd intended to change into it once they'd boarded the ship for Halifax or after they arrived. But the blood from surgery had given her no choice. And she was limited to the two pieces that her housekeeper had hurriedly tucked in around her medical instruments while they were hiding from the authorities in Edinburgh.

"Are ye a lady?"

The question took her by surprise, and she was relieved when Jean—suddenly behaving like a mother bear—put herself between them.

"Ye'd be only talking to me, if ye please," the older woman snapped. "So what is it now? Do ye have an answer about my nephew?"

"Who is she?" the woman asked, trying to look around Jean for a better view of Isabella.

"Not that it's any business of yers, but she's a friend of my cousin, traveling from the Orkneys. Now is John Gordon staying with ye here or not?"

The innkeeper's wife stepped around Jean and addressed Isabella. "What are ye doing in Inverness?"

"What's it to ye?" Jean barked, trying to put a stop to the questions. "My companion can wait outside if that'd help ye to answer me."

"What's yer name?" the woman asked, persistent.

"To be sure, yer the most impudent—"

The innkeeper's wife raised her hand so quickly, Isabella thought she was about to slap Jean. "Can't she speak for herself?"

The customers in the tavern grew silent, and every eye turned in their direction. Isabella knew there would be no end to the woman's questions until she spoke herself.

"Mrs. Murray," she said, trying to imitate Jean's accent.

"Ye don't sound like folk from the islands." The woman cocked her head and looked at Isabella with open suspicion. "Are ye from Stromness? I know folk from there."

"Nay, she's not from there, ye bold piece," Jean snapped. "She's down from Kirkwall, if ye must know."

"I'm a governess," Isabella broke in before the two came to blows. "For a family in the Borders. I was only visiting Mrs. Gordon's cousin in Kirkwall. I'll be returning south in a few more days. We heard her nephew was staying here, and I hoped to pay a call while I'm in the area. That is, if you'd be kind enough to tell us if he's staying at Stoneyfield House."

The woman considered the reasonableness of the answer as she ran her eyes over the travel bags again before letting them linger on the purse still in Isabella's hand.

"We have a room for the two of ye, if ye care to stay."

"That would depend on your answer." Isabella waited, pasting a pleasant smile on her face.

The burly woman thought for a moment and then made up her mind. "Aye, yer Mr. Gordon is staying with us. But he's not here at present."

Tremendous relief washed through her. Arriving in the Highlands, Isabella's primary concern was the safety of Maisie and Morrigan. John had assured her that he had trustworthy connections in the Inverness area. They'd be protected and well cared for. But right now, he was the one person who knew where they were. It would have been horrible if she'd lost the means of communicating with him.

"We'll wait for him," Jean said waspishly. "Ye can just show us his room."

The innkeeper's wife shook her head, waving for the potboy. "Nay. Don't ye be thinking I'd trust ye to wait in anyone's room. But I'll have the lad here show ye to a private dining room, and I'll send someone to fetch ye when Mr. Gordon returns."

Waiting in a private room, Isabella thought, sounded far preferable to sitting here under the baleful stares of the farmers and other customers. She picked up their bags before Jean could do it.

Upon receiving his directions from his employer, the potboy glanced at the bags in Isabella's hands and sent a worried look at the innkeeper's wife.

"Off with ye, scamp," the woman said, cuffing him lightly. "Ye know which dining room."

As they crossed the taproom toward the back of the inn, hostile stares followed their every step. Following the lad through a narrow door, they made their way down an unlit corridor past a flight of stairs ascending into darkness. Presently, the boy stopped at a closed door and turned to say something to Isabella but decided against it. After opening the door for them, he stepped back and they entered.

The dining room, airy and well-lit from open windows, wasn't empty. At the end of the table, a British officer laid his fork down. He stood and donned a dark blue regimental jacket ornamented with rows of gold braid down the front. At the sound of the door closing behind them, Isabella turned to find a second blue-coated soldier blocking their retreat.

CHAPTER 8

Norman saw on English oak.
On English neck a Norman yoke;
Norman spoon to English dish,
And England ruled as Normans wish . . .
—Sir Walter Scott, *Ivanhoe*

The fire in his chest flared up with every labored breath he took. Some unseen hand was twisting a hot poker around in him, igniting every organ from his throat to his entrails, and the ache in his neck, collarbone, and shoulder seemed to be getting worse.

Cinaed wiped away the sweat standing out on his face. His shirt, soaked with perspiration, stuck to his body. At the same time, a chill lay like an icy blanket around him. He couldn't remember the last time he'd experienced such physical agony. Perhaps he never had.

The downward turn started when he'd tried to climb back into the cart. He might as well have been trying to scale a castle wall or climb the mainmast of his ship using one hand. And with each passing second, his body betrayed him more. He needed to find a place, a room, a hole, where he could crawl in and sleep. Somehow, he needed to fight off this fever.

Searc Mackintosh. He was slippery and untrustworthy

as a greased snake—he'd grown even more so over the years—but Cinaed knew he was kin and his only hope. Twenty years ago, he'd taken in and cared for a distraught and friendless boy sent down from Dalmigavie Castle. Even now, when he thought back to the time spent in that labyrinthine house near the mouth of the Ness, the smell of malt houses and the river filled his senses. It was all so different from the clean mountain air he knew. But Searc had kept him safe until a ship was found that would carry him to Halifax. To a new life.

Sitting in the cart with the reins in his hand, however, Cinaed couldn't bring himself to leave. Common sense told him the women were settled inside the inn and he should go, but his instincts ordered him to stay.

Vague arguments rolled back and forth in his mind. Perhaps it wasn't his instincts he was hearing. Perhaps it was simply that he didn't want to leave her right now. After all, the place looked like any other roadside inn. More customers were making their way to the door. Farm lads and fishermen, looking to enjoy a pint or two before going home to their supper. In the stable yard, a lanky lad with a shock of red hair was rubbing down a horse by the gate.

Cinaed needed water. He needed rest. And sitting in front of the inn for too long would draw unwanted attention. He should continue on to Inverness. A few more minutes.

He wasn't sure what he was looking for. In fact, he wasn't sure of anything, but still he couldn't bring himself to go.

Hours went by, or perhaps only minutes. There was no telling the difference. His throat was rough and parched as old shark skin. Finally deciding that sitting on a stolen cart on the coach road was stupidity of great magnitude, he flicked the reins. The quiet kirkyard around the bend seemed to offer a better choice than pulling in to the stable yard.

Driving around the back of the kirk, Cinaed reined the cart in under a tree beside a well near an empty curate's cottage. He was growing weaker, but he managed to climb down from the cart. Drawing up a bucket from a well, he drank deeply and watered the old cart horse.

Where he sat, he had no view of the door of the Stoneyfield House. A plan formed in his mind. It wasn't a particularly good one, but it was better than staying here. Cinaed ran his fingers through his hair and assessed the state of his clothing. Total disarray. Gingerly, he pulled the edges of the shirt together over the wound and buttoned up his waistcoat and coat all the way. He was disheveled, and his clothes indicated he'd been through a rough time of it. But unless he began bleeding profusely on the tavern floor, he didn't think anyone around here would pay any attention to it.

Heading back down the road toward the inn, Cinaed felt each jarring step like a bolt of lightning coursing through his body. The shivering only seemed to be getting worse. His body was failing him, but his mind was becoming clearer. He would simply walk inside and pretend not to know the two women. If they were in the tavern with Jean's nephew, all well and good. If they weren't, then over food and a drink, he'd ask a few questions of the server and find out what he could.

As he stepped up to the door, the lanky stable lad with the red hair came running out and barreled into him. The young man went sprawling in the dirt, and a missive flew out of his hand and dropped at Cinaed's feet. He picked up the letter as the lad bounded up and held his hand out for it.

"A delivery?" he asked. "Didn't I see you in the stable yard just now?"

"Aye, but the master told me to run with it."

"Where to?" He started to hand the letter back to him.

"Fort George," the young man answered.

Cinaed jerked a thumb toward the open door. "Is the innkeeper friendly with the soldiers at the barracks?"

"Nay. This ain't from the master. It's from them two officers who been lounging about the back dining room all day."

Perhaps it was due to her training as a physician and the work she'd done as a surgeon. Perhaps it was an innate quality she'd always possessed. Whatever it was, Isabella had the singular ability to focus in the midst of chaotic situations. When the moment called for it, nothing could distract her from her purpose.

With all the coolness she could muster, she gazed at the British officer and this room in which they'd trapped her. The dining table contained a variety of food and drink. Outside the open windows, a few livestock sheds and coops for fowl stood between the inn and the open fields.

She'd felt it in the taproom. The vague responses Jean had received from the innkeeper. The delay before they had an answer about John Gordon's whereabouts. A trap had been set, and she'd walked right into it. And now, she would keep up the pretense of ignorance until they exposed their hand. Regardless of being caught, Isabella forced herself to stay calm. She could see no path for escaping this predicament, so she simply focused on what she could control—her confidence and her conduct.

"Humble apologies, sirs," Jean told them. "We've been sent to the wrong room. To be sure, we wouldn't care to be bothering ye at yer dinner."

"You're mistaken," the soldier by the door replied, one hand resting on the pistol he'd stuck into his belt, the other on the handle of his saber. He was making it clear they wouldn't be leaving. "We directed the innkeeper to have you brought here."

"What for?" Jean asked sharply.

"We'll ask the questions," he barked in reply. "And you, old woman, will keep a civil tongue in your head."

Suddenly, Jean's legs began to give way, and Isabella took her arm as she leaned on the table to steady herself.

"You will state your names." The soldier by the door continued to speak. The officer at the far end of the room had yet to say anything.

Isabella was no expert on military uniforms, but she'd lived through the French wars and she could distinguish the difference in rank between the men. The shorter of the two, standing by the door, wore the stripes of a sergeant on one sleeve. The silent one, taller and powerfully built, was an officer, distinguished by gold braided epaulets on his shoulders.

The sergeant, with thinning, long blond hair, wore a moustache that partially hid a scar running from the edge of his mouth to his jawbone. The officer had no visible marks, and his lustrous brown hair was fashion-ably curled with sideburns that extended well below his ears. His pale blue eyes were fixed intently on her face.

"I'm Mrs. Gordon. Of Duff Head. This is Mrs. Mur-ray. She's visiting friends and kin in Inverness. We're looking for no trouble. We only came here to visit my nephew. He's in the law trade in Edinburgh. Perhaps ye know him. John Gordon."

A muscle in the officer's face twitched. The next mo-tion of the head was insignificant, but it was understood by his subordinate.

"Your bags," the sergeant ordered. "Put them on the table."

If they were looking for confirmation of who she was, her medical instruments would be proof enough. Isa-bella noticed Jean trying to hide her hands in the folds of her skirt. They were trembling badly.

Neither woman moved to pick up the bags. With a growl of disgust, the sergeant deposited them on the table and started to open one.

"Stop," Isabella said sharply enough to make the soldier hesitate. She would never allow herself to be some sheep led to slaughter. She'd fight every step of the way. She turned to the officer. "I have given you no permission to paw through our belongings."

"You think we need permission to—" the sergeant began.

"You will *not* speak when you are not being ad-dressed," Isabella asserted powerfully, cutting him off. "You have a superior officer here. Have you forgotten your place?"

She waved a hand as if he were an annoying insect,

softening the edge in her voice as she directed her words again to the other man.

"If you would be so kind, sir, as to tell us exactly who you are and what business you have with us?"

The sergeant, reddening from his collar to the roots of his hair, opened his mouth to interject again but was waved to silence again, this time by his commander.

"Finally, she speaks." The smirk pulling at the corner of his mouth told her he was impressed.

"And you, too, have finally decided to join the conversation," Isabella retorted. "If that's what we're to call it."

To study medicine as a woman and to convince a patient that she was as capable of treating them as any male physician, she had to appear confident, sometimes even arrogant.

Isabella's shoulders and neck ached from holding up the imaginary crown she was wearing for this occasion. Her father always told her that she was more of a queen than any woman sitting on a throne in Europe. That she was able—when it was called for—to wrap herself in regal aloofness. Frailty empowered an opponent, while a show of strength always diminished their advantage. At this moment, she needed to utilize all her strength.

"Your name, sir?"

"Lieutenant Ellis Hudson of the 10th Royal Hussars, at your service." He bowed rigidly. "This is Troop Sergeant Davidson."

Isabella refused to curtsy and could only manage a slight nod. She kept her chin high. She held the officer's gaze without a flinch.

"You will tell us why you're detaining us, sir."

He motioned to the dishes of food on the table. "Would you care to sit and join me, Mrs. Murray?"

"Thank you, but we have other plans. Now, you will kindly answer my question. Why have you brought us in here?"

"Mrs. Murray, you say." He let the name roll off his tongue as if he were savoring the taste. "I have an excellent memory for faces."

The man paused, letting the comment hang like a threat between them. Isabella raised an eyebrow and waited.

"And how is your memory, ma'am? Do you recall the last time we met?"

Isabella kept her face composed and impassive even as beads of sweat began to run down her spine. She'd lived for six years in Edinburgh. During that time, she'd come in contact with a number of English officers at social events and at the university. She didn't remember Lieutenant Hudson.

"We've never met. I would certainly recall."

The officer tsked his disappointment. It was clear he knew who she was. He trailed his hand along the chairs as he sauntered toward her, but Isabella knew there was nothing casual about this man. She knew what lay ahead. She also knew these men would show no mercy. She braced herself for the worst, for she would not be telling him what he wanted to hear.

"Never is so definite." He paused at the corner of the table. "I can even tell you when we met."

He began counting slowly on his fingers. Isabella understood his deliberateness. Each tick was intended to intensify her nervousness. He was about to place her neck on the execution block, but first he wanted her to see the glint of the sun on the blade and feel the sharpness of the edge.

"Twelve weeks," he said finally, dropping his hands to his side.

The day of the attack on their house. Tending to Archibald, she had been blind to the faces of the soldiers charging in. And later, she'd thought of nothing but getting Maisie and Morrigan safely away. Anger now formed like a fist in her chest. He had been there.

"Your home on Infirmary Street had a fine clinic, did it not?" he taunted.

She bit her tongue and looked into the man's coldly assessing eyes. He could have been the officer in charge of the raid. He could have been the soldier who had pulled the trigger that killed Archibald. The blood of all those who'd been murdered that day and in the days that followed were on this man's hands.

"I was hoping for an introduction," he said with false affability. "You were quite inspiring, leading your distraught stepdaughter calmly through the violence while we restored order to that gang of riotous traitors."

Those were the most difficult steps she'd taken in her entire life. Dragging the nearly hysterical Morrigan away while she knew her duty was to stay and fight to keep her patients alive.

"But then you disappeared. Were you in a hurry to hide that rather volatile stepdaughter or your quiet, sensible younger sister?"

Isabella wanted to scream. Did he have them? How could he know how different the two girls were unless he'd already arrested them?

"I can understand your impulse. Such beautiful young women. But what a foolish notion, to think that any of you could put yourselves beyond the reach of His Majesty's justice."

No, she reasoned. The information about the girls could have come from servants and neighbors, as well as from Archibald's colleagues at the university.

But why, then, this game of cat and mouse? If he was certain of her identity, then why not simply arrest her and drag her off to Fort George and from there to Edinburgh?

Unless he wasn't sure.

Another thought occurred to her. Perhaps he didn't think he and his sergeant were sufficient to escort the notorious traitor to prison. He had to know the radical dissenters would be loath to see her in the hands of the British authorities.

She'd seen no other soldiers in the tavern. Perhaps he was waiting for help to arrive. The sergeant still stood by their bags. She wondered if they thought she could be carrying weapons. Another punishable crime.

"I have no recollection of you. We came here to see John Gordon. So unless you know his whereabouts, our business is finished."

She turned to Jean and motioned toward the door. But before either of them could grab their bags, the sergeant stepped forward and took hold of Jean's arm in a bruising grip.

"Let *go* of her! This *instant*!"

Isabella's bark was commanding enough to cause Davidson to release the old woman's arm and take an involuntary step back.

"But I do know of John Gordon's whereabouts," Lieutenant Hudson said icily, unaffected by Isabella's wrath. "He was arrested this morning and is on his way to Fort George at this very moment."

"Arrested?" Jean gasped, having found her voice. "On what charge?"

"Assisting in the flight of an individual wanted for high treason."

All of Isabella's fears ignited within her like some molten fireball. To protect the girls, she'd wished to be kept ignorant of their hiding place. But now, John Gordon's arrest exposed everyone. She thought of Sir Walter and wondered if he ever imagined that by assisting her, he was putting himself at odds with the same king who'd just knighted him.

"Treason?" Jean wailed. "We're simple, honest folk. What do we know of treason? Who could my nephew know that would be involved in such nonsense?"

Isabella's mind was on the two people who mattered most to her, the ones she'd sworn to protect. And now she was helpless to do anything for them. Neither Maisie nor Morrigan had any charges against them. But she knew that wouldn't stop these brutes from using them to force damning information out of her.

The lieutenant walked to a side table. He moved with lithe, catlike grace. Retrieving his sword, he strapped it on and picked up a pistol.

"We'll be going soon. But before we do, would you care to explain to this woman who you are?" he asked, tucking the firearm into his belt. "Or does she already know? Which of course makes her an accomplice, as well."

The avalanche of so-called British justice was already cascading down on them. For Isabella, there was no protection. Her courage was depleted. But she couldn't allow Jean to become a casualty in this tragedy. She sent her companion a look of silent gratitude.

"This woman knows nothing of any of this," she said, facing her captors. "She has nothing to do with any of it. I only paid her to bring me here. Let her go."

Before another word could be uttered, a loud knock sounded, and the door swung open. The innkeeper stood awkwardly on the threshold.

"Beg yer pardon, sir, but—"

"Out!" the sergeant roared, beginning to close the door.

"But I've a gentleman here. Says he's a ship's master. Making a ruckus, he was, in the taproom. Says he has a complaint about two women." He paused and stared at Isabella and Jean. "About these two, or I'll be hanged."

"I warned you that we were *not* to be interrupted," Davidson barked.

"Wait," Lieutenant Hudson ordered. "What complaint?"

"The gentleman says these two shot him with a pistol. Then they trussed him up and threw him in the back of their cart, he says. Left him there to die."

Suddenly, the innkeeper was pulled back from the doorway, and Cinaed walked into the room, causing the sergeant to step back.

"I can speak for myself." His voice was hoarse and weak.

Isabella was never happier to see anyone in her life, but he was not in very good shape. His coat and vest were gone, and there was fresh blood on his ruined shirt.

He closed the door, but as he turned and took a step into the room, he staggered. Isabella caught him by the waist before he fell. The man was burning with fever, and he leaned heavily on her.

"You are bleeding again," she murmured. This wasn't good. After all he'd gone through, the stitches had to have ripped free. He tried to take another step, but he was too heavy. She couldn't support his weight, and he began sinking to the floor.

"What is this?" Hudson demanded, coming closer. "What do you have to say, man?"

Cinaed sat, holding her as she eased him down. "These two women kidnapped me."

He had to be delirious with fever. Last night he'd tried to choke her, so she knew Cinaed was capable of anything in this state.

Isabella started to open his shirt, but he caught her wrist.

"Let me see what's happened to your wound," she said.

Their faces were close, and their gazes locked. No word was spoken, but she saw clarity in his blue eyes.

"Who is this?" Hudson leaned over to see for himself. "How do you know him?"

Isabella didn't see Cinaed's hand move, but suddenly he was holding the officer's pistol with the muzzle pressed up under the lieutenant's chin.

CHAPTER 9

So daring in love, and so dauntless in war,
Have ye e'er heard of gallant like young Lochinvar?
—Sir Walter Scott, "Lochinvar," Canto V

The man's ice-blue eyes reflected the barely restrained fury of a killer. Not just any killer, he was an officer in one of the British empire's elite mounted regiments, trained in the craft of death.

Isabella had good reason to be afraid.

"Your weapons," Cinaed ordered. "Place them on the table and step away."

Luckily for all of them, he was smart enough to realize Cinaed wouldn't hesitate to pull the trigger.

"Do it, Davidson," the lieutenant growled, never losing eye contact.

Whether he killed this man or not, Cinaed's life was changed forever. His decision was made in the taproom. He could have walked away and gone to Inverness and gotten a berth on the next ship to Halifax. But he didn't. When he stepped into this room, he was giving the British authorities a face. A face that he'd kept hidden from them for all the years of his illegal activities. The face they'd been searching for since he'd stolen a revenue cutter and ran it aground eight years ago. He was now a target.

And the man on the other end of this pistol was capable of destroying him.

Davidson put his pistol and saber where he was told, but his eyes were darting across the room, looking for some advantage.

"And that knife in your boot." Cinaed waited until the sergeant complied, then spoke to the officer. "Now you. Slowly."

The lieutenant unfastened his sword and slid it onto the table. He, too, was carrying a knife, which he tossed up with the other weapons. Cinaed released his grip on the man's coat, and the officer stood up, straightening his clothing.

"I am Lieutenant Ellis Hudson of the 10th Royal Hussars. You'll hang for this."

"Too bad you won't be around to enjoy it." For years now, his hangable offenses against the crown had been piling up. He could die only once. He gestured toward Davidson. "The penalty is the same if I kill you both right now."

Behind him, Jean quickly latched the door. He had no worry about the innkeeper. The man and his wife were too frightened to cross him now. They'd taken his money and would do his bidding, but he'd made it clear they'd be dead if they failed him.

"Back up." Getting on his feet was painful, but Isabella looped his arm around her neck, helping him up.

He stole a look at her. A touch of color was slowly creeping back into her fair complexion. It must have been terrifying, finding these two waiting for her. He surveyed the dining room. Not the best of situations. There was only the one door. The space around the table was narrow, and if one of them upended the table, or grabbed Isabella or Jean, the field of battle would change drastically. And, by the devil, the stakes were high. They could all quite easily die here at the hands of these soldiers.

The sergeant was edging toward the table.

"Don't." Cinaed pointed the muzzle directly at the commander's heart. The man stopped. If they decided to charge him, he couldn't take out both men, not in his present condition, but he'd make sure the officer was dead.

A wave of light-headedness washed over him. He was unsure how long he'd be able to remain standing.

"Jean, slide the weapons down to the end of the table." A moment later she had them out of reach and was holding the pistol with both hands.

"You," he barked at the sergeant. "Join the lieutenant. Both of you stand by the window."

"You've made a grave mistake." Hudson's voice was as low and dangerous as the growl of a mad dog. "A fatal mistake."

"One of us has," he replied. "But I'm holding the pistol."

Cinaed needed to buy some time. In spite of his tough words, his body was failing him. For a moment, he thought his knees were about to give beneath his weight, but Isabella caught him around the waist. He focused on his adversary's face. Nothing went unnoticed by the lieutenant. He was an adder ready to strike.

"Who are you?" Hudson demanded, ignoring the taunt. "And who sent you?"

"No one sent me. I work for no one but myself."

The officer looked at Isabella. "If no one sent you, then that makes you a vile opportunist and a mercenary."

He could call him whatever he wanted, Cinaed thought, so long as he followed instructions.

"Then you must know," the lieutenant continued, "that the Crown is willing to pay far more for her than any sum the rabble is offering."

Hudson's superior tone was becoming irksome, but Cinaed waited. He had questions about exactly who the "rabble" might be, but this was not the time to ask. He noticed when the man's attention turned to Jean. Still holding the pistol, her hand shook excessively but she stayed true with her aim.

"The old woman is with you?"

"The old woman is with me."

"If she didn't shoot you, then you must have enemies nearby. They'll surely be after you to finish what they'd started."

Hudson was stalling. He was waiting for the message to Fort George to come back with results. He was also biding his time, looking for an opening. Cinaed noticed the man focus on his bloody shirt. Most likely, he'd already decided where he'd punch or kick to make him drop the weapon.

Cinaed leaned against the table, forcing himself to stay alert.

"You recognized Mrs. Drummond and thought you'd make a quick profit from some treasonous radicals. We can protect you if you're willing to make a deal. A far better deal."

Mrs. Drummond. Cinaed shot a glance at Isabella

and tried to decide why the reformers would have placed a bounty on her. Her stoic expression gave nothing away. Drummond must be her husband's name.

"Whatever they've offered you, the Crown can do better," Hudson repeated, inclining his head slightly toward his subordinate. "Tell him, Davidson. Tell him how much this woman is really worth."

"A thousand pounds sterling, sir."

As the words floated in the air, Cinaed felt Isabella's body go tense. No wonder she was worried that everyone was chasing after her. It was true.

"But you'll never collect it," Davidson continued.

"Shut up," the lieutenant snapped.

"He won't, sir. Not after drawing on a king's officer."

"Or after shooting one?" Cinaed suggested, his voice icy as the grave. "Along with a worthless sergeant?"

Isabella walked away from him and stood by Jean. He hoped she wouldn't fall for the game he was playing.

"Why does the Crown want her so badly?" he asked.

"She's the wife of Archibald Drummond, a ringleader of some radicals causing trouble in Edinburgh."

Cinaed had been right in assuming she was connected to the reformers in the city.

"Do you want her in order to get to her husband?"

"The scoundrel Drummond is dead, his body dumped into a paupers' grave with the rest of that scum." The officer directed his reply toward Isabella, and Cinaed realized he was deliberately gauging how much pain he could inflict. "He was killed resisting arrest the day my men rooted out his den of spies and troublemakers."

The room began to spin, and he squeezed the handle of the pistol harder, trying to bear down. He needed to hold on for just a while longer. "You killed the husband. What do you want with the wife?"

"She was a collaborator in her husband's seditious activities. She knows the names of all the traitors. She's the key to crushing this subversion of the king's laws in the city."

Now he understood why the radicals would also place a bounty on her head. She knew too much.

Hudson took a step away from the window, and Cinaed raised the pistol until it was pointed directly between the man's eyes.

"If you attempt anything so foolish, Lieutenant, I'll shoot you dead where you stand."

"You're the fool," Hudson replied, his voice low and threatening. "This woman is nothing to you, and we'll never allow you to take her."

Cinaed glanced down at Isabella, impressed by her show of courage. She didn't cringe at all but met the man's gaze with matched hostility.

"This is my final offer," the lieutenant said, turning his attention back to him. "You will leave behind my sword and pistol and walk out that door. In return, I shall pretend the past few minutes have only constituted a slight misunderstanding. In addition, I shall have Davidson make arrangements for you to collect the reward."

"The thousand pounds?" Cinaed raised a brow to make sure they confirmed the amount. "All of it?"

"All of it."

"You *do* take me for a fool, Hudson," Cinaed scoffed. "You'll have me arrested the moment I appear to collect the money."

"Nay, sir. I swear to you, on my honor."

"Allow me to be the first to tell you, Lieutenant, that your word of honor is meaningless in the Highlands."

The first gong of the kirk bell seemed to come from a long distance. He hoped he hadn't imagined it. But another one followed soon after, and then the next. Cinaed allowed his relief to show with a smile as the tolling of the bell filled the sudden silence in the room.

"Bloody hell," the sergeant cursed, looking out the window. "Why's that bell ringing?"

Hudson held up a hand to silence his subordinate. "This is your final chance," he threatened. "Take the pistols and go. And we'll let you take the old woman with you, too. But you must leave Mrs. Drummond."

"You clearly know nothing of the Highlands, Lieutenant," Cinaed taunted, before pausing and listening. "And the bells."

With the pistol still leveled on the two men, Jean moved to the windows at the end of the room and threw open the shutters.

"Oh, they'll be coming soon now," Jean predicted triumphantly.

"Who'll be coming?" Hudson snapped. "What is this nonsense?"

Davidson shifted uncomfortably. "The locals here use the bloody church bells to call for help, among other things."

"To help whom?" the lieutenant asked, not comprehending.

"To help us." The old woman cackled.

Hudson smiled and motioned triumphantly to the

window. "Let them come. The more Highlander blood we draw in one day, the more cause for celebration. For you'll soon know I've sent for troops, as well. They should be here any time now."

In any brawl, in any battle, the sweetest moment was when a man knows he's bested his opponent. Taken him by surprise. Beaten him at his own game. This was that moment.

"The lad with your message was waylaid," he replied, tossing the letter he'd taken from the boy onto the table. "I believe your request for help somehow fell into the wrong hands."

Angry patches of red appeared on the lieutenant's cheeks. His hand went for the place where his saber should have hung. Coming up empty, he sent a murderous glare at his subordinate. The bell continued to ring out.

"The Highlanders in this area will be coming, Lieutenant," Cinaed assured them. "And they'll be armed too, even though the British authorities are foolish enough to think there are no firearms to be found around here."

For the first time since he'd walked into the room, Isabella addressed them directly and disdain dripped from her words. "When they catch you and I tell them who and what you are, you'll be treated with as little mercy as the scores of innocent people you've murdered. You will disappear without a trace, and true justice will be served."

As she finished, Hudson took a step toward her, hate flashing in his eyes. But the sergeant pulled him back.

"So now let me tell you *my* final offer," Cinaed said, pausing until he had the man's attention. "You will go out that window behind you, and you will run as fast and as far as your legs will carry you before the men I've summoned get here."

Isabella started to protest but stopped as a furious pounding commenced at the door.

Cinaed waved his pistol toward the window. "And I wouldn't recommend using the coach road, for out here on your own, unarmed, you'll be quite vulnerable. And every Highlander knows the only enemy of the common folk is you."

The hammering on the door grew louder, and the sound of shouting in the hallway was the last straw for the sergeant. "Please, sir. We need to go now."

Dragging Hudson to the window, he scrambled through, pulling the furious officer after him.

"How could you let them escape?" Waves of anger for these soldiers washed over Isabella as she watched them disappear beyond a rise in the fields. She whirled on Cinaed, speaking over the continued banging on the door. "Hudson was at my house in Edinburgh. He's a murderer and . . ."

She forgot the rest of what she was going to say, for Cinaed was about to fall over. She rushed to his side, and he handed her the pistol.

"When they get back, don't hesitate to shoot him right between the eyes." He draped an arm around her shoulders to steady himself.

She'd never fired a pistol, but by heaven, she'd use it now. She'd happily give them a reason to hang her if she could stop that killer. She was a condemned woman anyway. Jean pushed a chair up behind him, and Isabella handed her the firearm before helping Cinaed sit.

She was so grateful to him, and she had so much she wanted to say. He'd done the impossible. Only minutes ago, she'd nearly given herself up for lost, and now she was ready to exact retribution on behalf of decent folk who now lay dead.

Isabella had no idea how he'd managed it, or what he'd said to convince the farmers and fishermen in the tavern to come to their assistance. The church bell continued to ring, and she expected an army of people descending on them at any moment.

"Should we open the door?" she asked.

He was struggling to keep his eyes open. She placed her hand on his forehead and was alarmed by the heat.

His fever was a result of the gunshot in his chest. Considering everything he'd gone through since she'd operated this morning, it was a miracle he was still alive. She had to move him to a bed and clean the wound and possibly stitch him again. Then they would need to wait. Wait and hope that he was strong enough to last until the fever broke.

The persistent knocking continued. She turned to Jean. "Open the door and tell them the soldiers have escaped. They need to go after them."

"I'll talk to him," Cinaed interjected, his voice weak.

Jean unlatched the door and yanked it open. The surprised innkeeper stood on the threshold, his meaty fists up in the midst of his banging. His eyes went wide when he saw the pistol in Jean's hand. He took an immediate step back.

"Inside," the old woman ordered.

Wringing his hands, he surveyed the room before

taking a few cautious steps past Jean. He emitted an anguished moan when he saw Cinaed slumped in the chair. "Don't say he's dead?"

"It's your lucky day. I'm still alive."

Barely, she thought. The whites of his eyes were bloodshot. His eyelids drooped as if the exertion were too much to keep them open. The muscles in his jaw clenched as he tried to control the shivering.

"And they're gone?"

"They're gone."

The man ran his fat fingers through his hair. "I done just as ye said."

Cinaed reached into the purse at his belt and took out some coins. He held them out. "It was all well done."

"And the lad?" the innkeeper asked as he took the money.

"Go tell him to stop ringing the bell."

Isabella stood for a moment, unsure of what had just happened. Was it possible this had all been a bluff? No mob was standing at the door, trying to get at the officers. There was no one in the hallway at all. No one but the innkeeper.

"And when the lad brings the cart, change that horse for a fresh one and bring it to the back door. I don't want to go out through the taproom."

The innkeeper started to back toward the door, keeping an eye on the pistol in Jean's hand.

"And not a word to anyone out there. Understand?"

With a nervous nod and a hurried bow, the man scurried out, closing the door behind him.

"No one is coming?" Isabella flicked a hand toward

the window. She didn't know if she should panic or laugh. "The bell wasn't calling anyone? You paid a boy to ring it?"

He leaned forward, his forearms on his knees. She knew his head had to be exploding with pain.

When Cinaed burst into the room, bloodied and heroic, she'd never been more impressed with a man. Now she was practically speechless at his brilliance. It was all a ruse, except for his blood and heroism. "You made Hudson believe . . . you made me think . . ."

"Didn't I tell ye I know a fine man when I see one?" Jean's low chuckle confirmed it. She slapped Cinaed on the back, and Isabella had to dive forward to catch him before he fell off the chair.

"We don't have much time." His voice was hoarse, and he struggled to get the words out. "They'll be coming back and bringing every soldier they can spare from Fort George. We need to leave now."

She didn't know how far it was to the fort or how long before Hudson and his men returned. Still, she couldn't leave here without finding out what she could about John Gordon. So much had gone wrong. He was the only link she had to the location of the girls. Feelings of desperation filled her chest, squeezing the air from her lungs. She couldn't go. Perhaps *someone* at the inn knew who John's friends were. He'd only been here a day, but if he sent a message, someone would have taken it to them. She had to find a clue to their whereabouts.

"I can't just run and leave my nephew to these dogs," Jean announced.

They knew everything else about her. Isabella decided to explain the rest of it.

"My sister, Maisie, and my stepdaughter, Morrigan, are somewhere near Inverness. John hid them with people he trusted. There's a chance someone here knows where they are. I can't leave until I know."

"We can't stay here," he repeated.

Even as she talked, she understood the futility of staying. She'd doubted they'd have any support here once Hudson and his Hussars returned.

Isabella tried to stay calm, but a frantic fear was edging into her. "They've taken him to Fort George. What happens if he breaks down and tells these monsters where my family is?"

"He is a Scot. And a Highlander." He addressed Jean. "Is he not?"

The old woman's face lit with a glimmer of hope.

"I've sailed past Fort George a dozen times. With a few good men, we can rescue him. But the three of us can do nothing right now."

She crouched before Cinaed. The fever chills had taken full hold of him. It took great effort for him to talk. His face was covered with sweat. She wiped the perspiration from his brow.

"I need only a few minutes to ask questions. I have some money. The innkeeper helped you. If I pay him, he might do the same for me."

He took hold of her arm and brought her face close to his. She could see nothing but the blue of his eyes.

"Listen to me. They'll kill you. There isn't a man in this inn who doesn't know by now that the British want you. And there's a cloth manufactory not five miles from here. The weavers are the reform leaders here as well as in the south. Any one of them in that taproom could have heard that you're wanted. They'll turn you over to one side or the other to collect the bounty. Do you understand?"

She did. The innkeeper and his wife had already betrayed them to the British. But they'd cooperated with Cinaed. Of course, from the way the man acted just now, she guessed he'd given them no choice.

She mustered all her courage. What would it matter if she lived and her family was taken? She would never forgive herself if someone like Hudson got his hands on them. "I cannot just run away."

His hold loosened. His fingers trailed along the line of her jaw before his hand dropped away. She sat back on her heels.

"Take me to Searc Mackintosh. In Maggot Green in Inverness. Near the Black Bridge. He's kin. He'll shelter us. It's near enough."

Isabella looked over her shoulder at Jean, wondering if she could make any sense of this direction.

"We'll find it." The old woman stuffed a pistol in each of the bags. "He's right, mistress. We can do no good here for my John nor for yer lasses. And there's no point staying and letting these lowlife curs at ye."

Here, two strangers were coming to her rescue. Continuing to risk their lives to help her.

"I owe you so much," she whispered, mopping the beads of sweat from his face. "You could have gone, and you'd have been better off for it. But you stayed. You saved my life. I can never repay you for what you did today."

He opened his mouth to answer, but she recognized how quickly he was sinking. She put her fingers to his lips.

"You are a fighter."

Of all the people she'd cared for over the years, of all the sickbeds she'd been called to, no situation matched this moment. She was desperate to get him through this, but her education and her years of training were meaningless. Everything told her he needed to lie quiet in a clean bed. He needed fluids and medicine. But she could give him none of that. He was right; the soldiers would be back, and they had no time.

"You're going to live." The assurance was as much for herself as for him.

Resigned to their plan, Isabella was trying to decide how she'd get him into the cart when the innkeeper arrived. The stable boy was on his heels.

"He's not strong enough to make it out of here on his own. You'll need to help us. We'll use the chair as a litter."

A moment later, they were making their way out into the corridor and through a back door. It took all four of them to lift Cinaed from the chair into the waiting cart. His eyes opened as she climbed in beside him, while Jean took the reins.

"They'll be back here looking for ye." The innkeeper's eyes were scanning the fields to the north. "What should I be telling them? I don't care to hang for helping ye."

"You didn't help," Cinaed murmured hoarsely. "Say a handful of men you didn't know came in with me. One of them went to the kirkyard and started ringing the bell. They held a knife to your wife's throat. We forced you."

"But where should I say ye all came from?"

"Duff Head," Cinaed muttered, looking up at Jean.

The old woman shrugged.

"Duff Head," the innkeeper said, stepping back.

Jean flicked the reins, and a moment later, they were on the road to Inverness.

Isabella raised his head and pushed a travel bag beneath it. As the cart rolled past the kirk, she covered him with her cloak.

"So you do believe in revenge, Captain Mackintosh."

His face was grim. "I'm missing three longboats filled with my men. I have no idea if they're dead or alive. But if any of them came ashore at Duff Head, I know their fate. Those villagers almost killed me. They deserve what's coming to them."

"They'd have killed us all, to be sure," Jean said sadly. "The sea provides, and the sea takes her due."

Isabella was about to say something more, but the words withered in her throat as the sound of hooves drew her eyes back along the road. In the distance, a detail of mounted British soldiers was thundering toward them.

At the head of the line was a rider taller than the rest. Lieutenant Hudson.

CHAPTER 10

Come fill up my cup, come fill up my can,
Come saddle your horses, and call up your men;
Come open the West Port, and let me gang free,
And it's room for the bonnets of Bonny Dundee!
—Sir Walter Scott, "Bonny Dundee"

A half-dozen men were bearing down on them along the coach road, and Cinaed knew there was no point in trying to outrun them with a single horse pulling an old cart. Their pursuers were coming hard on fresh horses.

He forced himself into a sitting position. Escape was impossible. A stone's throw from the road, long stone walls and ditches enclosed large flat tracts of land that had once been farms. Now flocks of sheep grazed unperturbed around the ruined walls of ancient cottages. Across the fields, a grove of tall trees stood like an island of deep green, but they'd never reach it in time, and it offered little protection. They had nowhere to hide and nowhere to run to.

Behind him, Jean was muttering curses under her breath, and Isabella was sitting with her back straight as a mainmast, cool disdain on her face. She was a goddess of composure in the face of grave danger.

No matter how sick or injured one might be, he thought,

nothing was more jarring than knowing one could die at any minute. Forcing himself to ignore his pain and exhaustion, he focused on the soldiers.

"Hudson and his bloody skip jacks made good time." He drew a deep breath as he flexed his shooting hand. "Where are the pistols?"

"Jean has one in that bag beside her. The other is here," Isabella answered, taking it from her travel bag and quickly sliding it under the edge of the cloak.

His fingers closed around the handle, and he left the pistol where he could reach it when the time came. He pulled his knife from his boot and placed it beside the firearm.

Unless Hudson had ordered them killed on sight, which was unlikely, they had two choices. They could fight—and that would be a brief skirmish, at best—or they could allow themselves to be taken. The end result would be the same. They'd be dead.

Isabella was drawing a scalpel from her bag and secreting it in her dress.

She shrugged. "I plan to fight them. I'll die before they arrest me. If they take me, my death will be far more dreadful."

Their thoughts were sailing on the same tack.

As the Hussars rode up and came to a halt, they formed a half-circle around the cart. Cinaed placed his hands where they'd be seen.

"I'd like to thank you for ringing the bell. It certainly worked in my favor," Hudson said as he nudged his horse forward. His pistol was pointed directly at Isabella. Davidson lagged a few judicious steps behind him.

Cinaed would put his bullet into Hudson's brain and,

before being cut down by the others, make sure his knife found Davidson's heart. What happened after was out of his hands. His fingers inched toward the edge of the cloak.

Hudson was still crowing like the cock of the roost. "Unlike your cowardly Highlanders, who no longer have the heart to show up to do battle, my men responded to the sound of the bell. Davidson and I were met before we'd traveled far."

"Terribly embarrassing, was it not," Cinaed taunted, "to have your own men find you running back to the barracks with your tail between your legs?"

Hudson reined his horse to a halt not fifteen feet from the cart. Davidson moved to the side where he'd have a clear shot at Cinaed.

"A very impressive performance on your part," Hudson said, ignoring the insult. "As fine as any actor in London. I'm quite curious to know just who you are."

In a moment, he'd be their worst nightmare. The angel of destiny. The reaper of souls.

He scoffed, not deigning to answer. From running a revenuer ship aground to conveying rebels to safety to what he did today, he'd been a scourge to them. The Highlanders called him the *son of Scotland*.

Of late, while folk all over the Highland were being subjected to every imaginable savagery as a way of "encouraging" them to emigrate to some new land, Cinaed had been using the *Highland Crown* to bring powder and guns to those who chose to resist. He was giving them the means of fighting for their land. And for a better price than they could get from other weapons smugglers.

This blue-jacketed fool and his seagoing cronies had

never come close to catching him. They'd never learned the name of the captain who'd slipped by their naval patrols and beneath their noses along this coast. And they would never know now that his lionhearted ship lay buried inside the reef at Duff Head.

"Soon, quite soon, in fact, you'll be telling us everything we want to know. As will your lovely companion. And it will be a pleasure loosening both of your tongues," Hudson threatened. He raised a hand and motioned to his men to approach. "Take them. And if any one of them offers the slightest resistance, kill him. But I want Mrs. Drummond."

Cinaed's hand closed around the pistol, and he met her flashing eyes. "I am sorry that it has to end like this."

"I'm ready," Isabella told him.

She was braver than any woman he'd ever met, and she didn't deserve to die here. But he would not willingly let her be taken and broken by this blackguard.

Before he could draw the weapon, Jean's shout rang out.

"Ha, you dog-faced misery! How wrong ye are! Our lads are always keen to fight. And what a sweet, lovely moment it'll be to piss on a bunch of spineless, lowlife southlanders bleeding out in the Highland dirt."

She was pointing across the field. It took a moment for Cinaed's vision to focus. At least two dozen armed men on horseback were sitting side by side in front of the grove of trees. Suddenly, it was Hudson who was outgunned. Cinaed watched him nudge his horse back toward his men, assessing his odds.

He wheeled his mount. "Davidson. Get the woman."

The sergeant raised his pistol and spurred his horse as

he fired. Cinaed pulled Isabella's head down and returned fire.

"Go, Jean!" he shouted as Davidson dropped from his saddle. The cart took off as if a team of eight were pulling it.

Wild battle cries filled the air as the Highlanders raced across the field. The British fired, but to no effect, and rather than draw their sabers and fight to the end, they turned as one and retreated down the coach road, led by Lieutenant Hudson with the Highlanders in pursuit.

Cinaed would have liked nothing better than to go back and join in the fight. But his body was betraying him again, and it was more important to get Isabella as far away from Hudson as possible.

He waited until they were approaching a bend in the road before he let her up. That's when he saw she was covered with blood.

"You've been shot!"

The last she'd seen of the Highlanders who'd come to their rescue was the mud being kicked up by their horses as they flew after Hudson and his Hussars. A moment later, they'd disappeared around a bend in the coach road.

For one insane minute, all she could do was sit still and hold her breath as Cinaed's hand moved over her arms and the front of her dress.

"Where do you hurt? By the devil, there's blood enough." He tilted her neck to the side, wiping away the warm wetness from her skin.

His face was drawn, but he was undeterred in his search.

Weak and wracked with fever as he was, he'd still managed to present a bold and clearheaded front when facing Hudson and his men. And now, he was fraught with worry that she'd been shot.

Isabella snapped herself out of her stupor when his fingers tried to open the buttons of her dress to find the source of the blood. She'd never been struck with a bullet before, but she had enough experience with the injury to know that somewhere in her body, she'd be feeling a hot and aching pain.

"I'm not hurt. I'm fine. This has to be your blood." She pushed his hand away and pressed on his shoulder, urging him to lie back so she could find any new injury he'd suffered. Her first thought was that the wound in his chest had opened up anew.

The cart jostled them as it bumped over the road.

"If ye two're done pawing each other back there," Jean called over her shoulder, "I'd like to know which of ye is dying. And unless ye say otherwise, this nag is taking us to Inverness."

"Searc Mackintosh. Maggot Green." Cinaed's head dropped back, but another bump made him groan.

He couldn't afford to lose more blood, but it was indeed everywhere. On her clothes, on his, on her hands. It was truly a miracle he was still alive. But for how long?

She realized why he'd used only one hand to find where he thought she'd been shot. Her heart sank. Davidson's bullet had found its mark, striking Cinaed in the arm.

Isabella dove inside her bag before remembering she'd intended to use her scalpel for other purposes. Taking it from the folds of her dress, she sliced open the sleeve of his shirt and inspected the new wound.

The motion of the cart and the muscles of his arm made it nearly impossible to tell if the bullet had struck the bone. It wasn't shattered, at least, and she could see where the ball had exited, but she feared a piece of the bullet or a splinter of bone might still be lodged in there. She couldn't do anything about it here, however.

"You take off my arm, and I'll never save you again." He was watching her and, for the moment, appeared to be lucid.

His concern was hardly unfounded. In wartime, surgeons were quick to amputate a limb if a bone was shattered or a bullet or shrapnel remained embedded in the flesh. Of course, they rarely received a patient immediately after an injury was sustained. And the delays were deadly. She'd seen it herself in Wurzburg during the war against the French. By the time soldiers reached the surgeon's table, too often the wounds had already begun to fester. Untreated, the deaths were unspeakably painful. Taking off the limb could preserve a life, crippling though it might be.

But she would do everything humanly possible to save Cinaed from either of those fates.

She tried to reach into her bag for a cloth to cover and bind his arm, but he caught her hand. When he entwined their fingers, her heart swelled unexpectedly, and a knot formed in her throat.

What was happening to her? For her entire adult life, she'd been a woman of reason. She prided herself on her detached, clear-thinking approach to each patient. But this man had done so much for her. His life, his well-being mattered to her. *He* mattered. Even as she was assessing the body temperature, the firmness of the grip, the complexion of the skin, she was not only worrying about her patient, she was worried about *him*. She prayed that caring for him as a man wouldn't weaken her judgment as a doctor.

He flinched as the cart rolled over a rut and then expelled a deep breath. "I understand you. I want you to understand me." The whisper was pained. "You trusted me. And I trust you. So I'm telling you now, my arm stays."

"I understand."

As he held her hand, the impact of everything they'd gone through rained down on her. It was like hail in a summer storm, pelting her and leaving her with a confused mix of pain and awe. She tried to blink back unexpected tears, tasting their saltiness in the back of her throat. The shield she'd always been able to erect was gone. She no longer stood apart as an observer and healer. The battle was no longer surrounding her; it was inside of her.

She freed her hand and found the strip of cloth she was searching for. Binding his arm tightly, she hoped the pressure was enough to slow the bleeding.

"How does the arm look?"

She could give him a diagnosis based on her medical training. But when one considered the fever, the wound in his chest, and the physical dangers they were not yet free of, he had far more to worry about than just his arm.

Isabella had to say something, however. She took out another cloth and wrapped it even tighter. "I don't know how you're continuing to manage. One minute you're barely conscious, the next you're ready to fight a dozen men. Based on what I know of you, I'd say you should be able to fight again by the time we reach your kinsman's house."

He caught her wrist. His strength was waning, but he had something he wanted to say. She brought her face close to his.

"Searc will be no friend to you. You cannot trust him. He'll sell you to either side if he thinks he can line his pocket."

"Why are we going there, then?"

"He's a Mackintosh. And he's been true to me in the past. I trust him now to honor and protect what is mine."

Her mind raced. Isabella would need to find a different shelter for herself. They would take Cinaed to the man's house in Maggot Green and she would go.

At the inn, her reluctance to let him leave had taken her by surprise. She'd made a mistake then. Rather than consider all that could go wrong, she'd acted on what she hoped would happen. She'd wanted to trust the innkeeper. She'd wanted to believe that John would return to the inn. She'd wanted to believe the girls were safe. And she'd blindly walked into a trap.

Cinaed had not trusted in hopes. He'd stayed and put himself in a deadly position to help her. How could she *not* care for this man?

She touched his wounded arm and saw the blood already soaking through the binding. She would think as a physician *and* as a woman, for she was both of those things.

"Your kin Searc will need to find a doctor for you immediately. Someone must tend to your arm and—"

"You'll do it. You're staying with me when we get there."

A feeling of happiness billowed up within her. He wanted her with him. But there was still a problem. She had no doubts about her ability as a doctor, but she was a horrible liar.

"Tell him we're husband and wife." He took her hand again, his eyes drifting shut. "Searc will protect you if he thinks you're mine."

CHAPTER 11

The way was long, the wind was cold,
The Minstrel was infirm and old;
His withered cheek, and tresses gray,
Seemed to have known a better day.
—Sir Walter Scott, "The Lay of the Last
Minstrel"

The summer sun barely set in the Highlands, and Isabella had no idea what time it was until the church bells of the ancient port city tolled the hour. It was after six o'clock when the cart reached the muddy banks of the River Ness.

A fine stone bridge of seven arches spanned the water, but only a single row of buildings lined the far bank. Open fields, farms, and pastureland dominated the landscape beyond. For the most part, the city lay on this side of the river, and the thoroughfares were bustling with workers on foot and late-day vendors hawking their wares. The people in the street barely spared them a glance.

Isabella was relieved that Cinaed was asleep, fitful as his rest appeared. Touching his brow, she knew his fever was soaring dangerously high. And each bump on the road made him groan in pain, sharp reminders to her of the injuries that needed to be tended. She'd spread her cloak over him to avoid attention as they passed through

the city. Without it, he looked like a wounded soldier returning from the war. The abuse his body had undergone matched any battlefield injury. As for her own
blood-spattered dress, she sat beside him with her travel
bag on her lap to hide the worst of it.

Jean stopped the cart and queried a pair of women
carrying wash baskets about directions to Maggot Green.
After receiving curious looks from them, one pointed
toward a second bridge of blackened timber downriver.
Thankfully, they hadn't far to go.

Cinaed freed an arm from beneath the cloak and tried
to push the covering away. She couldn't understand his
mumbled words. Isabella imagined his dreams had
turned to nightmares, and she reached for him. His
hand closed around hers, and she stared at the contrast
between his strong callused fingers and her own pale
ones. A sprinkle of dark hair spread across sun-browned
skin. She peered into his handsome face. His labored
breathing deepened her worry. She hated the feeling of
helplessness but told herself there was nothing she could
do until they arrived at their destination.

"Look ahead, mistress," Jean said over her shoulder.
"I'm thinking these are some places ye'd be loath to pay
yer social calls. Maybe never seen alleys quite like
these."

They were approaching Maggot Green, and though
Isabella had seen neighborhoods nearly as bad as these
in Edinburgh, she understood Jean's words. And she
now grasped the meaning behind the washerwomen's
looks.

The twisting lanes grew narrower and muddier, and
the stench from the river grew stronger. It seemed as

though half the buildings were deserted. Many of them had collapsed, and their crumbling walls had fallen into the lanes. Cottages and houses that offered any shelter at all were crowded with poor folk, who stood in the doorways and the alleys and watched them suspiciously as they passed.

"What happened here?" Isabella wondered out loud as Jean negotiated the cart around a pile of rubble.

"The earthquake two years back," the older woman told her. "Never felt anything like it. It was like yer insides were all aquivering. It was worse here than at Duff Head, they say. The steeple of the High Church back there twisted and nearly fell in."

Larger buildings of red stone crowded the banks of the river. They also seemed empty, even those that appeared intact. Of course, there was no telling who might be living in them.

Jean noticed where she was looking. "Some of them's warehouses. Some, auld malt houses." She gestured downriver. "The port is moving toward the firth. When they open the canal, if they ever do, all this'll be left to rot."

"How do you know all this?"

"My husband came to Inverness to sell his fish." The older woman's lips thinned. "Back in the day, that is."

Jean looked away, and Isabella saw her bat away a tear. The two of them, she thought, had been thrown together for a reason. They sat quietly for a few moments, and then she broke the silence.

"What will happen to the poor who are living here? When they open the canal, I mean."

"From what I've seen in my life, no one cares much

about the poor." Jean shrugged. "I don't know why it'll be any different then."

When no one cared about them, people were forced to take control of their own future. If there was one thing Isabella had learned since coming back to Scotland, it was that people would only stomach so much suffering.

Not too long ago, forty thousand Scots made their voices heard at a meeting on Glasgow Green to end the Corn Laws that kept the grain prices high and to demand a more representative government. A week of rioting rocked Paisley. Protest meetings stirred the hearts of folk in Ayrshire, Fife, Stirling, Airdrie, Renfrewshire, and Magdalen Green in Dundee. The riots in Glasgow and Edinburgh this past April. She knew every name Cinaed had mentioned, but she couldn't admit it to him then.

The aristocracy feared the kind of revolutionary turmoil that had been seen in France and Ireland could take place in Britain. But they did nothing to help people or give them a voice in Parliament. Instead, they passed laws that made public gatherings criminal and speaking out in protest sedition. South of the border last August, sixty thousand people had been peacefully protesting in Manchester when government forces attacked, killing and injuring hundreds of innocent citizens. The newspaper called it the "Peterloo Massacre" in spite of the authorities' efforts to suppress information about the event.

The hypocrisy of the elite and the repressive efforts of those in power were only stoking the fires they sought to extinguish.

Isabella took a deep breath and tried to calm the rush of temper heating her veins. For all these years, she'd told herself she wasn't listening. She wasn't interested in politics. Reformers and radicals had a job to do, and she had a job to do, and a solid line existed between them. She'd worked hard not to cross it. But sometime during these recent weeks, the line had been erased.

"Maggot Green, mistress," Jean announced, breaking into her thoughts. "Though it looks to be more maggot than green."

She was right. Maggot Green was a flat, muddy field at the edge of the Ness, empty except for wrecks of boats and broken casks and crates along the shore. Ragged children were sorting through the trash for anything of the least value. Next to the field, a distillery appeared to be operating, and smoke from its chimneys had coated the crowded buildings around the green with heavy, black soot. To Isabella, the area smelled like a combination of barnyard and wet dog.

A young lass steering a pair of filthy boys along the lane pointed out the house of Searc Mackintosh.

"The Shark," one of the little ones whispered to Isabella before they moved on.

Searc's house appeared to be as dilapidated as the rest of the area. It was set back a little from a busier main road, behind a high wall. They followed a narrow lane down one side of the wall until they reached a gated opening. Farther on, the lane appeared to drop off into the river. She studied the house. It was large and appeared to be attached to a warehouse of some sort. Inside the gate, she could see a yard and neglected gardens, and a small stable standing at the end of the yard. A round, tower-like structure had been added to the front at some time, with a square block of a room perched on top.

"Not too inviting, I'd say," Jean noted as she reined in their horse.

Isabella remembered Cinaed's warning. Taking her wedding ring out of her purse, she slipped it on her finger.

"Why don't you go and ring the bell at the gate, if it has one, and tell this Mr. Mackintosh that Captain Mackintosh is in grave need of assistance. He is here with . . . with his wife."

Stony-faced, Jean had no reaction to Isabella's mention of the word "wife." One might have thought the old woman had even been a witness at the wedding.

Before walking away, Jean looked back up the lane, where a group of tough-looking men were staring down at them. She nodded in agreement. "To survive around here, mistress, a body needs to be spoke for. And don't forget, I'm spoke for by ye."

She shuffled wearily to the gate. Isabella was grateful for how strong Jean was, in spite of her age and affliction.

Peeling the cloak off Cinaed's body, she turned her attention to him. Between the blood and the sweat, he was soaked to the skin. His pulse was rapid, his breathing heavy. She pushed the hair back from his forehead. His eyes were closed, his body jumping as if he were caught in another nightmare. She didn't want to look too closely at the wounds on his chest or his arm for fear of not having any way of stopping the bleeding if it started again.

"Soon now," she murmured. "We'll take you inside soon."

"Who are you?" The gruff voice made Isabella jump.

She'd heard no one approach. "What have you done to him?"

Black eyes were peering at her from beneath bushy dark brows that formed a solid line across his face like an overgrown hedgerow. He was stocky and short, but even standing still, he seemed to be constantly in motion. His clothes were not shabby, but they were not new, by any means. He had one hand inside his coat, and she half expected him to draw a weapon at any moment.

Without waiting for an answer to his question, he leaped with unexpected agility onto the cart and studied Cinaed's face and the bloody shirt.

"He was shot. Twice." Her words drew only a quick glance. "The wound in his chest has been tended to, but it needs to be sewn shut again. I fear the hole in his arm may still have a piece of the musket ball lodged in it."

He was back on the ground with the same abruptness as he'd climbed up, barking orders at a servant standing in the open door. A moment later, two burly serving men ran down from the house, and a stable boy was running up the lane to fetch a surgeon. No formal introductions were made, but from the servants' responses, she knew this was Searc Mackintosh.

Cinaed was gently lifted off the cart, with Searc bearing the bulk of the weight as they carried him inside.

"I'll get the bags, mistress," Jean told her, gesturing with her eyes. The pistols had been stored there. "Ye stay with them."

"My medical instruments."

"Ye'll have them soon enough," she replied, lowering her voice. "But let them get used to ye a wee bit before ye start flashing all them fine, shiny things of yers."

Isabella saw the wisdom of Jean's suggestion. Searc had already accused her of wounding Cinaed. She had no doubt he'd be horrified to find out she was a doctor. She hurried after the men.

A housekeeper and a woman wearing a cook's apron leaped into the fray as soon as they passed through the front door. With each of them shouting unintelligible directions at Searc and the men, they added more confusion to exactly where the wounded man should be taken. The master of the house ignored them entirely, however, and he was carried through a dimly lit hall up an even darker stairwell.

Isabella saw almost nothing of their surroundings, though, keeping her eyes on Cinaed's face and the uneven rise and fall of his chest. He was in his prime and strong, but what he'd gone through and how much blood he'd lost since last night was enough to kill any man.

They laid him on a bed in the square room at the top of the tower. In the lane below the window, she could hear Jean exchanging words with a stable hand.

Isabella wasn't waiting around for an invitation to help. "I need pitchers of cold water and clean cloths I can use for bandages," she ordered. "And more light."

Hearing no response, she looked up and found the men staring at their employer.

"The surgeon is coming," he said curtly.

"Do you see his arm? The wound must be cleaned of the blood to prepare him for your surgeon."

The hedgerows tilted to one side. "Have you any idea what you're doing, woman?"

She rolled up her sleeves. "I know what to do, and I won't hurt him. I promise."

A long pause followed. Then, to Isabella's relief, Searc ordered the men to go and send up the housekeeper with what she needed.

He stood at the foot of the bed, and she saw his hand move inside his coat again when Isabella took the knife from Cinaed's boot. Ignoring him, she used it to cut the sleeve from the injured arm. His shirt was already torn, and it took only a moment to remove it. She inspected the bandages on his chest.

"Who are you?"

She unwrapped the bloody strips from Cinaed's arm. Her attention focused on the wound, but she was aware of the man watching her every move. For every question he asked, she had no doubt there would be ten more.

"Who are you?" he repeated, sharper than before.

His wife. She was Cinaed Mackintosh's wife. The words wouldn't leave her lips. What did she know about him if Searc didn't believe her? He was owner and captain of the *Highland Crown*. His brig sank off Duff's Head. But what else did she know? He was fast with a knife and braver than any man who ever lived. But that wasn't enough. What if he asked when had they met? Or wed? Or anything else, for that matter?

"Do you have a name, woman?"

The housekeeper barreled into the room, carrying a pitcher and basin. A serving girl carried a candle and cloths. Isabella motioned to put them on a table beside the bed.

"Could you bring him something to drink?" she asked the housekeeper. "And perhaps some broth, if the cook can manage it."

"And whiskey," Searc ordered, sending the two women scurrying from the room.

She held the candle where she could see the wounded arm better. Thankfully, the ball traveled through the fleshy part of his bicep. She carefully shifted the arm and peered at the bullet's exit.

"It missed the bone entirely," she said, relieved. "The ball went straight through."

Wetting a clean cloth, she washed the dried blood from around the damaged flesh.

"You can't stay here unless you tell me this minute who the devil you are and what business you have tending to him," Searc threatened. "For all I know, you could be the one who shot him. You could be a blasted spy sent here to meddle in my affairs."

Isabella recalled Cinaed's warning that Searc would be no friend to her. "If you please, I know and care *nothing* about your affairs. Now you will kindly remain silent and let me focus on what I have to do."

She was pressing hard with the cloth near the wound, and Cinaed gasped. He blinked a few times, staring at the ceiling.

"Your arm stays," she whispered to him. "I'm cleaning it now."

"Isabella?" His head turned, and his eyes slowly focused on her face.

"You need to lie still."

"Come closer."

She leaned over him.

"Closer."

His voice was weak. She decided whatever he was going to tell her was for her ears only and not for the bulldog standing at the foot of the bed. But before she could speak, Cinaed reached up with his good arm. His hand slipped around the nape of her neck, and his lips closed on hers.

His lips were parched and hot from the fever, the texture of his whiskers rough on her chin. Despite it all, her heart leaped, and she reveled in the touch of their mouths. His head dropped back too soon, ending the kiss.

"Whatever you do," he said wearily. "When our bairn is born, don't name him Searc."

CHAPTER 12

Respect was mingled with surprise,
And the stern joy which warriors feel
In foeman worthy of their steel.
—Sir Walter Scott, "Lady of the Lake,"
Canto V, stanza 10

In the medical chain of being—the rigidly structured hierarchy of practitioners—the physician occupied the highest rung on the professional ladder, far above the lowly surgeon. In the British mind, conditioned as it was to the benefits of class structure, the system made perfect sense. If one wished to compare the physician with the surgeon, one might as well compare the archangel with the honeybee. But if the physician were a woman, Isabella learned long ago, she had no place in this order of beings, regardless of her education and her training. It was only due to the open-mindedness of her father and husband that she had practiced at all.

Or so the men around her believed.

Her life in medicine had taught her that the privileges of gender or title or even education, in some cases, were meaningless when it came to the ability to save a life. When it came to treating patients, talent and dedication and sincerity always took precedent. So as she looked over the shoulder of the surgeon Searc brought in to tend to Cinaed, she was relieved the man seemed to encompass all those qualities.

Mr. Carmichael wore a perpetual frown on his face, as if the weight of the world were on his shoulders. But he immediately got off on the right foot with her when he arrived, removed his coat, and washed his hands before removing the dressings from Cinaed's chest and arm. That alone set the man apart from most others. After that, as he stitched the wounds, his speed and deftness of touch impressed her even more.

As the needle and hempen thread drew his broken flesh together, Cinaed never stirred. Isabella was thankful for that. He didn't need to withstand any more pain right now. The healing process would be difficult enough, and she prayed once again that he could outlast the fever. Prior to Carmichael's arrival, Isabella had removed the rest of Cinaed's clothes and washed him with the help of a footman. That had helped cool him a little.

Once he was done with the arm, the surgeon turned his attention to the chest wound. There was discoloration and swelling around the place where she'd stitched it. Cleaning it earlier, she knew exactly which sutures had burst.

"When did this happen?"

"Last night."

"And *you* removed the bullet?"

"I had no choice. He was bleeding badly."

Searc Mackintosh had introduced her as Cinaed's wife and then made a vague comment about midwifery. She couldn't recall exactly if she'd told him that or if he'd made the information up.

"You could have killed him digging about in his chest for a musket ball."

"I was sure he would die if I didn't."

She could feel the surgeon's searching gaze. But Cinaed's sleeping face was also turned to her, and that sight buoyed her. Isabella couldn't believe she'd found him on the beach at Duff's Head only last night. Or was it this morning? The sequence of events, what happened and when, all swirled about in murky waters. Lack of sleep was catching up with her. She feared she'd soon forget her own name.

"How was he shot?"

She jerked around at the sound of Searc's barked question. She'd forgotten he was still in the room. He hovered restlessly by the window, and Isabella was reminded of a similarly stocky vampire bat from the jungles of the Amazon. She'd seen it when Wombwell's Menagerie came on tour to Edinburgh. A hideous-looking creature. It was, perhaps, wishful thinking on her part that he would fly out the window. If Searc were a vampire bat, he'd be more likely to clamp down on her throat and suck her veins dry.

She'd narrowly escaped his inquisition when they'd first arrived. Cinaed had come to her rescue. Once again, she feared she would utter the wrong words and give herself away.

"I *did* hear you say that the wound is from a gunshot. Did I not, Mr. Carmichael?"

The surgeon had to be within the circle of trust, she surmised. If he weren't, Searc would never ask such direct questions in his presence. She'd already learned the military barracks at Fort George and the soldiers stationed there were closely connected to life in Inverness. Even the whisper of a bullet wound could bring Hudson and his troops to this door.

"Two wounds," Mr. Carmichael stated. "One in the chest and one in the arm. The bullet that struck him in the chest is the one to worry about."

Searc's eyebrows bristled as he scowled at Isabella. He had been trying to intimidate her since they'd arrived, and she hated to admit it, but he was succeeding. And she could count on one hand the number of people who'd successfully done that.

"In all the years I've known the blasted scoundrel, he's never been shot. You must be bad luck for him."

Isabella had a strained relationship with luck, to say the least. As a scientist, she'd always studied and worked hard and told herself she created her own luck. But as a woman, she'd come to realize that chance played an unavoidable role in people's lives. But this was not the moment for philosophizing.

She pointed to a scar near his hip. "This bullet wound occurred before he ever met me."

Searc glanced at the old injury and huffed.

Isabella moved to the other side of the bed and sat on the edge of the mattress and took Cinaed's hand. Perhaps it was involuntary, or perhaps he was in the midst of another one of his dreams, but the strong fingers closed around hers.

"We take care of our own." Searc wouldn't give up. "I need to know who shot him."

"He can answer for himself when he awakens," she said tiredly.

"You brought him here. You must know."

"I brought him here because he said you're kin. He told me he trusts you and you would protect us and keep us safe until he heals."

She planted her elbows on her knees, clutching his hand, unwilling to let go. He had to heal. But what if he didn't? Fever behaved unpredictably. It could kill him.

Cinaed's hand twitched. His face was turned toward the doctor. She studied the cords of muscle in his neck, the wide powerful shoulders that bore responsibility for others so selflessly.

He would survive this. And he owed her nothing. Whatever she did for him in pulling him out of the sea, he'd returned tenfold in coming to her rescue at Stoney-field House.

His muscles twitched again, and the surgeon noticed it too. He paused until Cinaed's breathing proved he was asleep.

"I gave him some whiskey," Isabella told Mr. Carmichael. "For pain and to help him sleep."

"You've done well by him."

She was glad to know there was one person in the room who could give her credit for doing the right thing.

"You're certain that nothing else was lodged in the chest before stitching it shut?"

"None. I made certain of it."

The wound wouldn't kill him. He'd be fine, Isabella told herself. But what about her? John Gordon was in the custody of the British authorities. She had no means of finding the girls. Each time she thought about it, the cold, sinking feeling of desperation that pervaded her body was paralyzing. It was even worse now than the days when they'd been hiding in that dank room in Edinburgh, fearing that any knock at the door or voice on the street meant imminent doom. At least the three of them had been together then. Now she had no one.

"By the devil, where is the *Highland Crown*?"

Searc's tone was a sharp scalpel poking *her* wounds. In spite of her exhaustion, Isabella raised her chin defiantly. "That is for Cinaed to tell you."

"But you claim to be his wife. You should know."

"And *you* should know I'd never tell you about his ship, considering the . . . the special cargo." Cinaed had blown up his own ship, and the explosions indicated he was carrying gun powder. A great deal of it. Searc's interest told her he knew, or at least suspected, the nature of Cinaed's business.

His eyes were shining black stones beneath the hedgerows. "Is the cargo secure?"

She wasn't about to be the bearer of bad news. "You'll need to wait."

"When did he arrive?"

"Last night."

"You said he was shot last night."

Isabella let go of Cinaed's hand and rubbed at the painful ache in her temples. They weren't safe here. She wasn't safe here. But she had nowhere to go. She couldn't tell this man the truth, but she couldn't lie either.

"*Where is the—?*"

"If you please . . ." the surgeon interrupted. "It's critical that my patient receive our full attention *now*. I need Mrs. Mackintosh to assist me here in tending to the chest wound."

His request was direct and firm without openly challenging Searc's authority.

For a moment, the outcome hung in the balance. She didn't know how close Carmichael's relationship was with their host. When Searc jammed his hand into his jacket, she wondered if the surgeon was jeopardizing his life in standing up for her.

Searc took a few paces toward the door, only to wheel and stomp back to the window. He was muttering incomprehensible words into the murky twilight. Then, abruptly, he turned and charged from the room, slamming the door behind him.

Isabella waited a moment before letting out a breath. "Thank you."

A slight nod was his only response. He'd already gone back to work on the chest wound. He was tying off the last stitch. He needed no assistance.

"You use a continuous locking stitch," she said absently. "The stitches are exemplary."

"So are yours."

She was speaking before thinking. Her unguarded observation only encouraged him to question her. It would be better to get the man talking about himself. "Where did you train, Mr. Carmichael?"

"I served a five-year apprenticeship in Glasgow. Before I could be licensed as a surgeon, I needed further training. So I spent six months in Edinburgh."

Isabella suppressed her curiosity about where in Edinburgh he'd trained. She watched him collect his instruments.

"Most of my practical training, however, came from working on several ships of the line during the war with Napoleon." He used a wet cloth and dabbed the skin around the stitches, inspecting them all closely. "I did that for a decade."

Isabella wondered vaguely if Cinaed had a surgeon on his ship. She'd traveled several times between Scotland and the continent, but so much of that life was a mystery to her.

"Why did you give up that career? It must have been lucrative during the war."

"It was . . . fairly. But I have a wife and three children now."

Her thoughts turned to Cinaed again and how much of his personal life she didn't know about. Most seafarers must have families. He was a Mackintosh, but what did he call home? And did he have a woman or even a wife there?

The memory of his lips pressing against hers brought back that momentary thrill, but she immediately buried it deep within her. Any repeat of that instant was beyond the realm of fantasy, and she understood his motivation for kissing her.

"His fever?" the surgeon asked.

"It came on today." She searched for the right words. "He's certainly overexerted himself since being shot."

He frowned, pressing the back of his hand to Cinaed's temple. "I don't recommend bleeding him. He's already lost too much blood."

Isabella silently agreed. Treating fever commonly included cutting a vein and draining blood from the patient. In a situation where the fever was this high, a good doctor was expected to cut deeply and allow the patient's blood to spurt into the air with every beat of the heart.

Archibald had been a believer in the method, but she'd never seen evidence of its effectiveness.

"Perhaps leeches," Carmichael mused aloud. "Just to be safe."

She ran the back of her hand across her brow, brushing back an errant lock of hair. When a feverish patient was too weak for bloodletting, leeches were considered useful. Rubbing the skin with sugar water, milk, or blood would persuade the leech to bite and suck blood until gorged. She was more open to such a controlled approach, but she still thought Cinaed would be better off without it.

"Perhaps we should give my husband a chance to battle the fever on his own, without the loss of more blood."

Mr. Carmichael checked Cinaed's pulse and brought his ear close to the chest to listen to the heartbeat. "Very well. I may send for the apothecarist to suggest a potion to help reduce the fever."

She'd had no faith in the potions she'd seen mediocre apothecarists produce in Edinburgh: tinctures, poultices, soups, and teas made with water or alcohol-based extracts of ground or dried herbs, animal bone, and whatever minerals the maker had at hand.

"Why don't we wait?" she suggested gently. "Considering his condition, the distinction between a medicine and a poison is hazy at best, wouldn't you agree?"

She'd read deeply on the subject when she was studying in Wurzburg and recalled Paracelsus declaring the only difference between a medicine and a poison was the dose. All medicines were toxic. It was cure or kill. And in her experience, very few apothecarists—even the good ones—took into account the particular patient when determining the right dosage.

Mr. Carmichael pulled at his ear and began to say something but stopped. He turned his back and carried his instruments to the table.

"Searc won't be satisfied if I suggest we wait a few days to see how our patient does with his fever. As you've already seen, he demands answers and solutions. He wants everything to be done for your husband now. If he thinks I'm not doing the best job, he won't hesitate to fetch another surgeon."

Isabella rubbed at the throbbing pain in her head. She wished she could explain to the bulldog downstairs that Cinaed was getting the best medical care possible. But it was impossible.

"What do you suggest we give him?" the surgeon asked quietly.

"Willow bark. Or the distilled water of the blackberry bush. Both are effective. Devil's bit might be another good choice," she added. "I'm certain they must have it here. The boiled root can be very powerful against . . ." Isabella stopped, realizing she'd said too much.

For what felt like an eternity, silence filled the room, broken only by the sound of Cinaed's breathing.

"I see. Where did *you* train, Mrs. Mackintosh?"

For a moment, she was speechless. Isabella squeezed Cinaed's hand with the hope of gaining even an ounce of his courage. "Well, midwifery requires—"

"Becoming an expert in surgery?"

"Hardly an expert, Mr. Carmichael. Not even a novice. Only a wife trying to save her husband's life."

Isabella stood and pulled the clean linen sheet over

Cinaed's chest. Turning around, she found the surgeon taking his time as he wiped his instruments and placed them in his bag.

"I've known no novice, and certainly no untrained wife, who could perform as precise and complicated an operation as the one you conducted removing the bullet from his chest. In fact, I'd say it was brilliantly done, no matter who did it."

Isabella wrapped her hands around her waist and told herself he wasn't accusing her. He was complimenting her.

"And as to your knowledge of apothecary . . ."

What got into her to offer so much information?

"How did you gain that knowledge?"

"I am four and thirty." That was the truth. She forced herself to think. "And prior to marrying Cinaed this spring, I'd never been married." That was a lie. She paused. "I've had many years of watching and learning and practicing."

"And where did you do all this watching and learning and practicing?"

Isabella took a deep breath. "Are you a spy for Searc, Mr. Carmichael?"

"Thankfully for your sake, I am not." He dropped the last of his instruments into the bag.

Isabella waited, not sure what he was after. The truth, of course, but she wasn't willing to make him a confidante simply because she admired his surgical skills.

He closed his bag. "I've worked at this long enough to recognize expertise and education. And I'd say you have both, mistress. But I've also had enough experience dealing with people to know when someone is lying."

Her chin rose. Isabella was ready to defend herself, but he held up his hands in a conciliatory gesture.

"I don't fault you for it. This is not a house to expose one's secrets."

She'd known that much from Cinaed's warning.

The surgeon picked up his bag and walked toward the door but paused before opening it.

"So, I'll share this with you. Most Mondays, Searc entertains the British commander in charge of the port, as well as his staff. On Tuesdays, the government exciseman is invited to dine. Wednesdays are generally dedicated to entertaining politicians. And every second or third Thursday, Searc hosts a squire from the foothills who coordinates the whiskey smuggling in the region. Shall I continue or is that enough to get a taste of the household?"

No wonder Searc was suspicious of Isabella. "He deals with friends and enemies alike."

"He has no friends. He has business partners."

"But he does business with British officers."

"So long as there is a profit to be made."

She understood clearly now why Cinaed insisted Searc think they were married.

"Thank you." She nodded. "Will you be coming back tomorrow to check on my husband?"

"I may stop by," he said. "But I know he's receiving excellent care by someone far more qualified than me."

Isabella was grateful for the man's confidence and she told him.

"Before I go," Carmichael said with his hand on the latch. "Don't trust the days of the week as I recited them. And know this: Real danger lurks inside this house, and it doesn't only come by way of Searc's dinner guests."

CHAPTER 13

She look'd down to blush,
and she look'd up to sigh,
With a smile on her lips,
and a tear in her eye.
—Sir Walter Scott, "Lochinvar," Canto V

As he awakened, the first place he looked was at the bed of blankets on the floor. She wasn't there. Immediately worried, Cinaed half rose, ready to push himself out of the bed. Then he spotted her at the window.

The perpetual glow of the summer night spread its gentle light around her, crowning her head and the long hair cascading over her shoulders with a halo. Her forehead pressed against the glass, and her attention was fixed on the street below.

He relaxed and lay back. The fever had broken, and he no longer burned. He took a deep breath and rolled his shoulder. It was stiff, but the pain in his chest was manageable. He flexed his arm, and hell fire shot into the muscles of his upper arm. Still, he could move it. Appreciate every blessing, he told himself. Clean bandages covered whatever damage had been done.

Cinaed guessed a week had passed, though it may have been less, he supposed. It seemed like it'd been a devil of a long time. For most of it, his body had felt as if he was lying one minute on a bed of ice and the next on a brazier of red-hot coals straight from the fiery pit. And when he was able to sleep, his mind had been tormented by a single nightmare that came back time and again. He couldn't escape it. Trapped in the maze-like streets of a burning city with battered buildings looming over him, a thousand men and women and children followed him. Thick smoke at the end of an alley hid them from the enemy, but the sound of war drums was getting closer. He was the only one armed with a single pistol. The fate of all these people depended on him, and the smoke was growing thicker. There was no escape. Each time, he'd wake up in a panic. If it was the dream or the fever, it didn't matter, he was chilled to the bone.

Isabella was his salvation. He recalled her feeding him broth to quench the thirst. During other brief moments of awareness, he'd be watching her as she changed the dressings on his wounds. Even now, he could feel the feathery caress of her fingers when she washed his scorched skin.

She was there with him the entire time. She never left his side. During the day, he heard her talking to Jean. When Searc's voice filled the room, she became cautiously silent. At night, he opened his eyes and always found her curled on the bed of blankets on the floor, within reach of him.

Those were the times when guilt cut into him. What kind of a man was he to lie helpless in bed while she slept on the hard floor? He wanted to give Isabella his bed, give her his protection. No one took care of him; he took care of others. But here she was, turning the tables. Saving him.

He was whole again because of her, and a warm sense of gratitude filled his heart.

Cinaed tucked his good arm under his head and watched her as she gathered her hair over one shoulder and ran her fingers through the thick mass. She looked uninhibited, free, lost in her thoughts. She also looked beautiful.

He sat up slowly and swung his legs off the bed. It was good to feel the solid wood floor beneath the soles of his feet. Sometime after arriving, he'd had all his clothing stripped off. He was now wearing only drawers, tied at the waist and the knees. Not his, by the devil. He was no dandy and never had been. He had a vague recollection of a conversation between Isabella and a servant that she'd asked to help put Cinaed into the garment.

He wondered what the staff made of a wife demonstrating such modesty in her treatment of a sick and injured husband. No wonder Searc kept coming up here and questioning the veracity of their marriage claim.

Something beyond contentment stirred in him as she started braiding her hair. "Would you wait to do that until I have a good look at you? This is the first time I've seen my wife with her hair down."

Isabella whirled. Seeing him sitting in bed, she smiled. "You're awake."

It was the first time he'd seen her smile. In every lucid moment, he'd found himself admiring her beauty. Each time he opened his eyes, her face was the only one he wanted to see. He'd come to know the perfect arch of her eyebrow, the length of her dark lashes, the color of the full lips that pursed when she was concentrating. Cinaed didn't think he'd ever seen skin as smooth as Isabella's.

She walked toward him, and he paid homage to the waves of lustrous hair falling to her hips. Her shining eyes and her smile dispelled the gloom and made this grim chamber a palace. Cinaed adjusted the blanket on his lap, realizing his mind wasn't the only thing affected by her. She was an enchantress who had cast a spell on him, body and soul.

"I'm whole again."

"You are not whole again," she corrected. "Your fever broke yesterday evening, but you are far from healed." She went to the bedside table and lit a candle before coming to him.

She checked his pulse, touched his forehead, carefully lifted the dressing away from his shoulder, and inspected the wound. Cinaed inhaled the scent of her hair as it brushed against his chin and fought the urge to thread his fingers into the soft, silky tresses. Her hair was damp. She raised his arm to check the shoulder joint and his hand brushed against the curve of her breast. Her lips were so near.

"You've taken a bath." He stopped fighting his impulse and pressed his face into her hair.

She drew back slightly, but she didn't release his arm. "I had to. I couldn't stand myself."

"Where did you bathe?" He needed to keep himself distracted. His hands itched to gather her in his arms.

She motioned to the tall, wooden screen that partitioned off a corner of the room. "The housekeeper had a tub sent up and they put it there for me. And Jean somehow sweet-talked the stable hand into carrying up buckets of hot water."

"Jean must have a diplomatic side to her that I haven't seen," he said. But his mind was envisioning Isabella sitting naked in a steaming bath and washing herself as he slept on this side of the thin wall. Why the deuce hadn't he woken up sooner?

Not wanting to frighten her off, he arranged the blanket discreetly on his lap and forced his attention on their surroundings.

This was the room he always stayed in whenever he came back, and he realized how little it had changed from the first time he'd slept here as a lad. Except for the tub, of course. There had certainly been no thought of a tub for him when he came down from the hills. Searc had dragged him to the river and thrown him in to "wash the cow shit off." Cinaed was sure he'd emerged from the water dirtier than when he went in.

The room had two ill-fitting windows, one facing the lane and the other facing the river. In the winter, the wind would howl through the chamber, and if Searc was withholding firewood for some boyish transgression he'd committed, the tower room would get colder than a witch's teat. He'd only been here the one winter, though.

Curious, he thought, how the chamber's contents had taken on a nostalgic quality. By the river-facing window sat the same scarred table and rickety chair. And next to the screen, the wee fireplace that wouldn't draw if you built a bonfire in the tiny hearth. His eyes moved to his favorite feature in the room, the shelf above the clothes pegs.

It was here in this chamber and in Searc's study that the world opened up to Cinaed. The shelf still held the books that he read over and over. Reading Macpherson's tales of Ossian was like reading of his own ancestors. Sitting on the bed, he ploughed the fields of the Lowlands with Robert Burns and laughed with him at the church-going louse striving to reach the top of Jennie's bonnet. And in the books he carried up from downstairs, he traveled the roads with Roderick Random and Matthew Bramble, reveling along with them in the adventures they found. He sailed the seas with Robinson Crusoe, escaped with him from slavers, and walked beside the unconquerable seafarer the fateful day he'd found those footprints in the sand.

"This place never really changes," he mused.

"And Mr. Mackintosh is everything you warned me about."

He put a hand on top of hers, stopping Isabella as she began to remove the dressing from his arm. "Has he been hard on you?"

She shrugged and the furrow on her forehead deepened. "After four days of it, I'm learning how to deal with him."

He'd wondered how long he'd been delirious. Now he knew.

"You've learned to ignore him."

A smile tugged at the corner of her lips. She took the used bandages and walked to the table where she kept her clean cloths and ointment.

The dress was baggy and draped from her shoulders. He assumed she'd borrowed it from the housekeeper or one of the servants. He truly thought she'd never left the room at all while he was going through the duration of his illness.

"He doesn't know what to make of me. At first, I believe he didn't trust me with your life. In fact, I think he was somehow convinced I shot you. Now, why I would bring you back here after shooting you involved some logic I couldn't understand. But since Mr. Carmichael's visits and his good words to Searc about my abilities, he's eased up in attacking me. Still, I doubt he believes we're married. When he glowers at me from beneath those eyebrows, I know he cannot see any reason *why* you would marry me."

An old bachelor, Searc was blind to real beauty and goodness and talent. He would state outright that he had no room for feminine influence in his life. His women were bought and replaced with as little concern as a pair of gloves. When he wanted one, he simply went across the river to a brothel he owned with several partners. He could only remember the topic of marriage coming up a few times, but when it did Searc always spoke quite disparagingly about the institution. On the other hand, Cinaed couldn't imagine he'd ever met someone like Isabella.

If Searc only knew what she had to offer. In truth, it was Cinaed who was not worthy of her. If the dire circumstances that had thrown them together had never occurred, he didn't think she'd even acknowledge his existence. She was a university-educated doctor, he a mere self-taught man of the sea who did whatever he needed to survive.

She was the noble mainsail, he the fouled anchor.

"Who is this Carmichael you mentioned?" Since he'd been carried up here, faces coming in and out of the room had been only vague and fleeting images.

"The surgeon. Searc brought him in the first night to see to your injuries." She brought clean bandages and ointment back to the bed. "He's pleasant and honest. I like him."

She started to put the salve around the sutures, and he caught her wrist. "Don't trust anyone who comes to this house."

Their gazes locked. "That's what *he* told me."

Cinaed knew he had to have faith in her judgment, but he was still not completely satisfied. Years ago, he'd learned that in the murky world in which Searc existed, a thin line existed between friends and enemies. And it was a line that was constantly crossed.

Isabella freed her hand and spread the ointment. His skin warmed beneath her fingers. He tried not to think of how close she was standing. The pressure of her arm against him, the brush of her skirt, a dozen inadvertent touches . . . he noticed them all.

She moved on to his arm. "Who were the Highlanders who came to our rescue that day at Stoneyfield House?"

He'd asked himself the same question. He didn't know them. Outlaws perhaps, down from the hills to steal cattle or horses. Reckless as it was attacking British soldiers, they'd shown admirable courage. He intended to ask Searc about it. The Innes and Ross clans, as well as the Frasers and others, were all increasingly eager buyers for weapons he smuggled into the Highlands. But Searc and his agents handled the business side of those transactions.

He shook his head. "I wish I knew. But I'll find out. I owe them a great deal for what they did."

"That wasn't the only help they've given us," Isabella said, wiping her fingers on a piece of cloth. "They've been here."

"The same men? In this house? Are you certain?"

"They keep to the shadows outside. I didn't know who they were, but I began seeing them right after we came here. When I looked out the window, they'd be watching the house, standing in pairs or alone."

Cinaed wondered if they were members of the army of men Searc employed to keep his house safe. If not, he had to already know about them. Nothing went unnoticed by him.

"That changed yesterday. One of them came forward."

He waited for her to say more.

"Yesterday was market day in town, so Jean went up to High Street, thinking she might hear something. Talk of what happened at the inn, rumors, news that might be coming from Fort George about John. Anything." She backed away from the bed and leaned against the table, facing him. "While she was at the market, a man approached and gave her a message about John and about my family."

He recalled Isabella's hesitation to leave Stoneyfield House without learning more about John Gordon. She wanted to know where her sister and stepdaughter were hidden. "The man gave Jean a letter?"

She shook her head. "According to Jean, he said that John Gordon is still at Fort George. He's only told the authorities that he shared a coach to the Highlands with a woman who called herself Mrs. Murray and he knew nothing else about her."

He knew this was only the start. The soldiers interrogating the man would torture him until they'd forced whatever confessions they wanted out of him. Cinaed had been barely alive, but he remembered promising the old woman that he'd help to free her nephew.

"I need to talk to Searc. He can gather together enough men for me to—"

"John is being moved," she interrupted. "The Highlander told Jean that her nephew was being sent to Edinburgh next week."

"What day?" he asked, already relieved. It would be far easier attacking a prisoner escort than breaking into Fort George.

She shook her head. "He didn't know."

They could find out. Searc had ears in every corner of Inverness. British officers, merchants, men at the courthouse, dock workers at the new harbor—information was eagerly bought and sold. And like a crate of oysters, the fresher the merchandise, the more valuable to the buyer.

"You said he had some news about your family?"

"Only a message for me." Isabella's voice quavered slightly, but she cleared her throat and continued. "He said, tell the doctor the lasses have been moved, and they're safe."

"Where were they moved? Who took them?"

She hugged her hands around her middle. "He didn't say."

"Why trust *anything* he said?"

"The man was a Highlander, Jean said, and no Englishman. He told her he was one of those who'd chased off the blue-backs on the coach road near the Stoneyfield House. They followed us here."

A dozen questions arose in his mind. No one helped anyone here, unless they wanted something in return. Cinaed's weapons smuggling was beneficial to the clans. He was worth keeping alive. But no one knew to connect him with the trade, and they couldn't have known he had anything to do with John Gordon. He'd given no name at the inn. They couldn't know he was involved. It had to be Isabella they were interested in.

The most troubling thing was that they knew she was a doctor. They knew her identity, which meant they also knew about the reward. And now they knew where she was staying. But if the reward was their motive, why had no one shown up to take her? And why move the two young women to a "safe" place?

He ran a hand through his hair. "I'm grateful for what they've done. But I don't understand why they're doing it."

"Neither do I," she admitted. "Tonight, I decided to stay by the window and watch for them."

"Are they out there?"

She shook her head and glanced at the window. "If they are here, I haven't seen them."

He stood, and for a moment the room swung around his head. He put out a hand and she was there to take it.

"You've hardly eaten anything for four days. You need time to regain your strength. I can call for one of the servants if you need to use the water closet or—"

"Just help me to the window."

The dizziness went away as quickly as it came, but Cinaed put an arm around her shoulder, savoring the feel of Isabella against him.

She helped him pull the blanket around him as they walked.

The lane below was quiet. In the shadows, a movement drew his eye. And then another. "They're still out there."

"I don't see anyone."

"Beyond the cart toward the river. A man is crouching by the stack of lumber, watching the gate." He pointed up the lane. "Look in the shadow of the deserted cottage halfway up the lane. Two more."

Isabella's body went tense and her hold on him tightened. "This is what I feared. If they simply wanted to deliver that message, then why are they still here? What do they want?"

He didn't know. He didn't have much faith in faceless informants, even those who seemed to know so much. At the same time, he didn't want to destroy Isabella's confidence that these men might be protecting her family. Something was amiss. They could be the same ones who'd come to their rescue, but he couldn't be sure. And even if they were, Isabella's question echoed in his head. What did they want?

The news of a British soldier being shot while members of his regiment were run off by a gang of rogue Highlanders had to have spread far and wide. But the reward of a thousand pounds for handing Isabella over was even bigger news.

"For as long as we stay here, you must never venture outside these walls." He took her hand and drew her

away from the window. "And don't worry about the de-
crepit and tumbledown look of the house. Because of his
business, Searc has made this place a fortress. The walls
and doors are thick and the window shutters on the
lower floors are reinforced with iron bars. He's built an
underground tunnel that leads to a dockyard downriver
by the old pier, and another that leads to a stable inland
beyond the ropeworks. At any time of the day or night,
he could snap his fingers and have more than a dozen
armed men here ready to fight off any invasion of the law.
The city authorities know this, and the British are aware
of it. He lines their pockets handsomely to leave what is
his alone."

"What is his," she repeated. "Unfortunately, I have yet
to prove to him I'm worth protecting."

"Then we need to change that."

"How?"

"Let me show you." Taking Isabella's hand, he led her
wide-eyed to the bed. "After tonight, Searc will never
question that you're my wife."

CHAPTER 14

Thy hue, dear pledge, is pure and bright
As in that well-remembered night
When first thy mystic braid was wove,
And first my Agnes whispered love.
—Sir Walter Scott, "To a Lock of Hair"

As Cinaed seated her on the bed, expectation surged within her, and Isabella's insides warmed and then liquefied. Although she'd been married for six years, her marriage to Archibald was one of convenience, not passion. He was twenty-six years her senior, but as a widower in perfect health, he wanted to enjoy the physical side of the marital relationship. She tolerated their occasional time in bed. It was her duty. But thinking back on it now, she recalled no anticipation. No excitement. No glowing aftermath. None.

Tonight, she had no idea what Cinaed intended to do when he eased himself down on his knees beside the bed, but she felt light-headed imagining the possibilities. The blanket had slipped from his shoulders, and the muscles of his back rippled in the flickering light of the candle. In her mind's eye, she saw herself reaching out, boldly grasping the curls of his dark hair, and guiding his face to her . . .

"Candle. Would you kindly bring it closer? And hand me my knife?"

Isabella realized her daydreaming was for nothing when he turned to the bedding on the floor and tossed it to the side. She did as she was asked and crouched beside him.

"What are you looking for?"

He was running his hand over the wide floorboards until he found what he was looking for. Slipping the blade of his knife into a nearly invisible slot, he pried gently. The board popped up, and he reached into the dark space beneath.

A satisfied smile lit his face. Cinaed withdrew his hand and held up a small box, covered with dust. He must have concealed it there a long time ago.

He sat against the bed and patted the floor next to him. She sat beside him, hip to hip, shoulder to shoulder, their legs stretched before them. She put the candle on the floor as he wiped away the dust from the box.

"When did you hide this?"

"When I was nine years old."

Cinaed and Searc were both Mackintoshes. And although they looked nothing alike, he'd called the older man kin.

"Were you visiting Searc then?"

"Not exactly a visit. I had nowhere else to go. I was essentially dumped on his doorstep. And he took me in."

Surprised, she turned to him. Cinaed was studying the grain of the wood on the small box. He was in no hurry to open it. His beard was getting long, hiding much of his face and chin. His hair was wild as a lion's mane. Despite the recent days of being bedridden with fever, he exuded strength and energy. But he'd not always been the man beside her. She thought of the boy that no one wanted.

As the silence settled around them, Isabella heard the mournful call of an owl. A moment later, a second one in the distance answered. Cinaed rubbed the box with his thumb, and she could see him traveling back in his mind over the years. She tried to recall her own life at nine years old. She and her father were living in Wurzburg. By then, her mother was a cherished memory she clung to. It would be three more years before her father married again.

Isabella had already become his shadow. When he'd met with his students at the university, she was there at his heels. When he'd traveled to visit his patients, she stood beside him. He'd allowed her into the operating theater, and she'd trailed after him when he went to consult with the anatomists in the dissection rooms. At nine years old, she could already read German and French as well as English, and she'd pored through his medical journals, devouring them like adventure novels. It was during those years that she decided to become a physician. She'd led a very different life from Cinaed.

She put her hand on top of his. "Why did no one want you?"

"I had no parents."

"What happened to them?"

"I was told my father went to sea eight months before my mother gave birth to me and never came back. My mother passed away when I was six years old."

Isabella tried to imagine this man beside her a forlorn orphan waif, and her heart began to ache. "Who raised you after your mother was gone?"

"Aunts. My uncle. The folk in my uncle's castle and in the village brought up not only their own bairns, but all the clan children. This was the way of things in the Highlands then. I suppose it's the same now." He tapped the lid of the box but didn't open it. "I lived at Dalmigavie Castle, and I was no distant relative of the laird. Lachlan Mackintosh was my uncle, the brother to my mother, but one day he decided I was no longer welcome there."

Many boys were sent away at such a young age on the continent and in the south of Scotland to be educated. But this didn't seem to be the reason for Cinaed's expulsion.

"Were you trouble to them?"

"Not more than any other boy my age."

"Did Lachlan see you as a threat in some way to his position as laird?" she asked. She wasn't familiar at all with clan society or rules of inheritance.

"I was only nine. I was no threat to anyone."

Isabella's fists clenched involuntarily as the anger in her flared at the injustice done to that boy. She took a breath to calm herself. "Did Searc raise you then?"

"Nay. I lived with him over the fall and winter of that year, and in the late spring, he signed me on to a merchant schooner going to Halifax. I worked as a ship's boy."

"Did you have family there?"

"None," he told her. "But it was time for me to learn a trade and become a man."

Searc was no better than the uncle. And what was the purpose of family if they didn't take care of their own?

Cinaed had to sense her frustration as he pushed a strand of hair gently out of her face and looked into her eyes. "I don't care to talk about my past anymore. I made myself the man I am today and am obliged to no one."

Isabella's heart still stung for the boy who'd had to grow up too fast.

"What I left, however, better be here still."

She watched the slow and deliberate movement as he slid open the top of the box. Inside, a woman's embroidered handkerchief lay neatly folded. He felt for whatever it was hidden within it.

"This is all I have left of what belonged to my mother."

If she'd been hurting for him before, the feeling became ten times worse now. At the same time, she thought of her own life and what little she had left of it. What she wore and traveled with were all she possessed.

He unfolded the handkerchief. A silver ring lay at the center. He held it up for her.

The ring was elegant and demonstrated the work of a master craftsman. Within a delicately wrought heart, two leaves surrounded a thistle in bloom. At the top of the heart rested a crown.

"It's beautiful," she whispered. "Breathtaking."

"My mother wore it on a chain around her neck and gave it to me on her deathbed. She told me it had been a gift from my father."

"A thistle and a crown."

"That's the reason I named my ship *Highland Crown*. I hoped it would be a fitting tribute, though I knew but little about him." His thumb ran across the emblem. "He was a seafarer like me."

There was so much that she wanted to say to comfort him, but words failed her. She began to understand Searc's defense of him now. No matter how short the time he'd sheltered Cinaed, there seemed to be a protectiveness that still ran in the man's veins.

He took her hand and spread her fingers across the palm of his hand. A tingling sensation raced through Isabella's body. She stared at the contrast of her pale skin against his darker hue. She was still wearing her wedding ring.

"Would you mind wearing this, instead?"

Emotions churned inside of her. She was no fool. She understood what was behind the offer, just as she'd known why he'd kissed her in front of Searc that first night.

"I promise to give it back to you the day we leave here."

She pulled off her wedding ring and tucked it into the pocket of her dress. As she reached for his mother's ring, he took her hand.

"Searc knows I left the box in this chamber. And I warned him that I'd kill him if it went missing. He knew this ring was intended for my wife."

He tried to slip the ring onto her finger, but it got stuck at the knuckle.

"I guess it was not meant to be."

"Give me a moment." His eyes danced with mischief as he brought her hand to his lips.

Isabella let out a gasp when his mouth unexpectedly closed around her fourth finger. His lips and tongue laved her skin. Warmth and excitement pooled in her belly and moved lower. She didn't even realize she was holding her breath until he ended the delicious torment and slipped the ring on her finger. The fit was snug but perfect.

"Be my wife?"

Her throat was dry. She nodded. "In name. Of course."

His blue eyes caught the candlelight as he pressed a hand to her brow. "Now you're the one who is feverish."

"I . . ."

He kissed her. Or was it that she kissed him? Isabella's wasn't too sure. What she knew was that she did not pull away, but rather leaned into him and clutched his shoulders gently. His weathered lips were surprisingly soft and giving. He angled his mouth over hers and was about to deepen the kiss when sanity quickly returned, and she dragged herself away and sat back. The heat in her face was scorching, her hand pressed to her mouth. Her lips tingled.

Kisses weren't supposed to undo people. Or at least this was the way she'd always lived her life.

"I . . . you're not well enough for such things. I should wrap your shoulder and arm again. Jean will be coming up soon. She warns me when the kitchen is hard at work and the rest of the household is stirring."

She didn't wait for him to say anything but picked up the candle and put it on the table. Grabbing the blankets off the floor, she became a whirlwind of movement, folding her bedding and storing it away, trying not to look at him. Cinaed said nothing, but she heard him push to his feet.

Going to the table, she chose the cloths she needed to

bind his shoulder and turned around. He sat on the edge of the bed, exactly as she'd found him before. She thought he must be Adonis, sent by the gods to tempt her with his beauty and fan her desire.

She forced herself not to admire his body and stared at the dark beard. The long lashes framed the blue eyes that looked so dark in the candlelight. Her gaze fell on his lips. She ran a hand down the front of her dress and wondered if he would ever kiss her again.

"I'm ready." He tilted his head and smiled. "Whenever you are."

Oh, was she ever ready, Isabella thought, approaching him. She went to work on his arm first.

"Your wounds are healing nicely. But to be safe, I'll wrap them for another couple of days."

He caught her hand, and the bandages dropped onto the bed.

Their gazes locked. Isabella didn't know what was happening to her, but she was uncontrollably drawn to him. He pulled her between his knees. Her fingers were on his skin, working a slow path up his neck. They were eye to eye, lip to lip. The memory of the kiss from a few moments ago filled her mind. She wanted it again. Now.

Wordlessly, she brushed her lips against his—once, softly, gently, and then again. His lips were warm, inviting. He patiently waited, leaving Isabella in charge of what she wanted to do.

Summoning her courage, she let her mouth linger a bit longer. Her tongue hesitantly teased the seam of his lips.

His hand slipped around the back of her head. Isabella felt his mouth open beneath hers, drawing her in. Enthralled with her position of control and by the heat that was spreading through her, limb by limb, she deepened the kiss. Their tongues danced and mated.

A hungry groan escaped Cinaed's lips, and his fingers delved and fisted in her hair. She answered and matched his urgency with hers.

He inched back farther on the bed and she followed, climbed up and moved on top of him, straddling him. Her hands caressed his face, and she threaded her fingers through his hair. She was lost in the play of their lips and tongues and the power of a kiss that continued on and on.

Thirty-four years in age, six years of marriage, and she had never kissed anyone like this. The joy of this one act far exceeded any physical encounter she had yet experienced in life.

Her head tipped to deepen the kiss, and Cinaed's passion surged. Suddenly his arm tightened around her. He was cupping her breast, feeling the nipple hardening through the dress. Her body and her hips moved restlessly, instinctively seeking a better fit. His hand found the hem of her skirt and slid upward along her bare leg.

The tap on the door was sharp, and Isabella, breathless and mortified, tore her mouth away and jumped off the bed.

An instant later, the door swung open and Jean came in.

"Yer fever's gone only a few hours, and here ye are restless as a salmon running upriver," Jean declared, seeing him sitting up in bed. "Damn me, but I'm thinking yer a man who can't wait to be up and going."

Carrying the pitcher of water she'd brought up, she disappeared behind the screen.

Cinaed's attention was only on Isabella. She had her back to him, her hands busily cutting strips of linen while more of it was scattered across the bed. But he knew her mind was caught up in the same excitement that had taken hold of him. Her body had to be as affected as his. If Jean had come ten minutes later, the two of them would have had more than their mouths to untangle.

He pulled the blankets across his lap. Watching Isabella, he took a deep breath, remembering the scent of her hair. He wanted to taste the sweetness of her skin, feel the texture of her willing mouth. Her tempting blend of innocence, experience, and desire drove his need. He wanted her. He wanted to make love to her. He couldn't recall ever wanting a woman so much.

Cinaed ran a hand down his face to shake free of the lust that was keeping him hard. He needed to think of something else besides the woman across the room. He reminded himself Isabella wasn't one you made love to and then left. She was a prize, a love-and-cherish kind of woman.

So what was he doing? Both their lives were complicated right now. She deserved better than what little he had to offer.

"This one's kinsman is pacing about down there like a mad dog, waiting to see him," Jean said, addressing Isabella as she came around the partition. "He says to tell ye to get presentable, mistress. He can't wait much longer, says he."

Isabella turned around and started braiding her hair as quickly as she could.

Cinaed swung his feet to the floor. "Tell him he's not wanted up here. I'll go down to him."

Isabella turned to him for the first time since Jean

entered the chamber. "Do you think you're well enough to go downstairs?"

"Well enough?" Cinaed arched a brow at her. She immediately blushed and looked away. "My clothes. Are any of them here?"

Isabella walked the older woman to the door. "He'll need a shirt to go with the rest of his clothes. The housekeeper said they'd all be ready for him this morning."

"And a manservant to help me wash and dress," Cinaed added.

After Jean went out, Isabella pressed her back against the door.

"I'm appalled at my behavior. The way I acted. I practically attacked you. I had no right to behave—"

"Stop." He pushed to his feet and went to her. As much as he wanted to take her in his arms, he kept his hands at his sides. "You're a woman. I'm a man. You saved my life, and I saved yours. We have a bond between us now. We've weathered more danger side by side than most people experience in a lifetime. Perhaps that has something to do with how we feel about each other. And how we both have behaved."

There was more he wanted to say, but he didn't trust his heart not to interfere with the cool logic that was called for in this moment. It required great effort, but he walked back to the bed, picked up the bandages, and stretched out his hand to her.

"Would you kindly do the honors, Mrs. Mackintosh?"

She approached, and he sat on the bed. Her focus was exemplary, the furrow in her brow reminding him of the first time he'd opened his eyes to see her working on the wound in his chest. But her hair was delightfully disheveled from his fingers pushing into it. Her lips were swollen from their kiss. The fair skin on her cheeks and chin bore the marks of his beard. He'd be shaving that off as soon as the servant came up.

He fisted his hands on the blanket at his sides so he wouldn't reach for her.

"What do you think Searc wants so early in the morning?" she asked.

Cinaed looked down at her fingers expertly bandaging him. "I'd guess he's heard about the loss of the *Highland Crown*."

"But that was your ship, was it not? Why should that upset him?"

"The sinking affects him as well. It was my ship, but he was the middleman for the cargo I was carrying."

"Guns? Powder? Shot?" she asked, her eyes meeting his briefly.

He knew the British charges against Isabella. It was just as well she knew his.

"The *Highland Crown* could make the crossing to Halifax and to Philadelphia in six to eight weeks, sometimes taking up to twelve weeks to return. I try to bring a cargo of arms in twice a year, sometimes if the wind is good, three times."

She let out an unsteady breath and focused her attention on his arm. "A dangerous business for you."

"You say dangerous." Cinaed lifted her chin and looked into her beautiful face. "And yet, you don't say it's wrong."

A thoughtful, mirthless laugh escaped her. "Six years ago, I would have been horrified. Two years ago, I would have had a slightly better understanding, but I still would have lectured you and reminded you of the pain and suffering armed conflict causes. But now?" She shook her head.

"What do you say to me now?"

She placed his hand on her shoulder, a better position to bandage. "The British pretend the Scots are equal to them in the eyes of the king. But it's a lie. They have their armies here as occupiers of a conquered land. For fifty years, the British kings have been giving land and power to men who are more English than Scot, men who have sold their souls for profit. In the six years I've lived in Edinburgh, I've tried to be an objective observer, but sooner or later, even a blind person must see the hardship that poor and working folk are being forced to endure."

Cinaed heard the notes of anger and shame in her voice.

"And if they speak out against the laws that make it impossible for a farmer to sell his crops at a fair price," she continued, "or if they try to organize and protest that their wages are too low or that they are being governed and taxed and denied the ability to vote for their representatives in Parliament, they are portrayed as radical extremists and traitors, and cut down in the street or imprisoned by monsters in British uniforms, men like Lieutenant Hudson."

"You've been more than an observer, I think," he said, impressed. Hudson's accusations had been about the husband, but Cinaed felt Isabella was a crusader for the same causes. "This is the kind of thinking that leads to change."

"Unfortunately, it's also the kind of thinking that gets innocent people killed." Isabella lowered his arm from her shoulder. "But why did you get into it? This is not Edinburgh or Glasgow or Aberdeen. Certainly, there must be profit in shipping without making yourself an outlaw or an enemy of the Crown."

"What you say about soulless men being installed in positions of power is true in the Highlands, as well. And in the name of economic progress, they have been clearing the land and gutting the power of the clan chiefs. They say it is for the benefit of the people, but it is actually only for the benefit of the Crown and those absentee landlords who build their palaces in England from the profits of wool and the blood of the dispossessed."

"So, it's the same here as it is in the south," she said quietly.

"About six years ago, on the northern coast, Lord Stafford ordered the clearing of his lands in Strathnaver. A man named Patrick Sellar was his factor. He used violence of the worst order to turn out the tenants whose families had farmed the land for generations. Over forty villages were burned and pulled down. Men and women were brutalized and even murdered. Eventually, Sellar was indicted for his crimes and tried here in Inverness. He told the court his actions were benevolent and intended to put what he called 'these barbarous hordes' into a position where they could become more industrious, educate their children, and advance in civilization. But the truth was that those who were unwilling to be starved on tiny plots were forced onto ships with only the clothes on their backs and sent across the sea to unknown lands."

"What happened in his trial?" she asked.

"He was acquitted in a legal system that protects those with money and power." Cinaed stood and went to the window. That wasn't the end of it. Searc's men caught up to Sellar about a year later and made him suffer.

The Highlanders were still out there. He was certain of it. He turned and looked back at her. "And that is why I bring arms to the Highlanders who refuse to give up the fight. I'd be a liar if I said I don't do it for profit, but I have good reason for doing it."

Chapter 15

*One hour of life, crowded to the full with glorious action, and filled
with noble risks, is worth whole years of those mean observances of
paltry decorum, in which men steal through existence, like sluggish
waters through a marsh, without either honor or observation.*
—Sir Walter Scott, *Count Robert of Paris*

Cinaed descended the stairs from the tower room. The
chamber on the floor below had always been reserved and
ready for special guests. He'd never known there to be
any, but the room was made up as it always was, neat and
tidy, as the master of the house demanded.

A curious fellow, his kinsman. And as tough and tight
as sharkskin.

In his gruff and surly way, Searc enjoyed his reputation for frugality. In the eyes of his business associates,
he operated his household on a skeleton staff. But aside
from the few required workers, in truth he had more
than a score of men who came and went at all hours of
the day and night. They not only performed various
functions in the household, they were his own private
army. Searc's men protected the place, watched over his
business holdings, collected money owed to him, and
applied muscle when needed. Indeed, this company of
"manservants" and "kitchen help" had responsibilities

that extended far beyond mopping floors, polishing silver, and delivering meals.

It was one of those men who met Cinaed at the bottom of the stairs. Another member of Searc's gang stood in a doorway across the great hall, a pistol in one hand and a cleaning cloth in the other. Searc, Cinaed was told, was waiting to see him in his study.

As always, the ground floor was dark due to the shuttered windows that were opened only on rare occasions. Crossing through the great hall past a staircase that led up to the dining and drawing rooms, he made his way down narrow corridors that snaked past the kitchens and storerooms. Doorways leading to wine and root cellars also led to other corridors and other doors that gave access to tunnel entrances. Searc had always used only the wine cellar entrance for guests who needed to avoid notice when they entered his home, but every entrance was well guarded. No one came in without an invitation.

Passing the kitchens, Cinaed climbed a set of stone steps into a second, rectangular-shaped tower at the back of the house. Outside the study door, he knocked twice and opened it.

In his life's travels, Cinaed had seen great cities, cathedrals that pierced the skies, circles of standing stones, and castles built to last a thousand years. Nothing, however, matched Searc's study for the rich and wondrous curiosity it engendered. As an awestruck nine-year-old boy, Cinaed remembered thinking the entire world had somehow been shrunk and fit into this room.

Shelves filled with books rose to a ceiling so high a special ladder on wheels had been installed just to reach them. Maps depicting the seas and coastlines and nations of the world covered an entire wall, and more lay on and under a work table. Navigation and charting instruments, clocks, a barrel filled with walking sticks and swords were scattered around the room. In one corner in a tall locked cabinet, Cinaed knew shelves held dozens of muskets, pistols, powder, and shot. In another corner, some of the most beautiful paintings and portraits he'd ever seen stood lined up like chops on a butcher's tray. Piled on top of an iron strongbox as tall as a man, stuffed animals and brightly colored tropical birds stared blankly out at dust motes floating in the morning light.

Searc's desk was situated at the center of it all. It was piled high with stacks of ledgers and even taller mounds of paper. Letters, contracts, bills of lading, newspapers—all threatening to avalanche onto the floor at any moment. But for all the times Cinaed had been in this room, he'd never seen Searc sitting in the chair behind that desk. Like that killer fish whose name he'd taken, Searc was incapable of being still. Today was no exception.

A surly clerk who looked as if he could cut a man's throat as easily as add a row of sums, stood over an open ledger at the desk, taking directions from his master. Searc motioned to Cinaed to help himself to the breakfast dishes that had been set out at a side table.

He filled a plate and sat. He didn't know how hungry he was until he took the first bite.

Searc dismissed the clerk with the same abruptness that marked everything in his life. He looked even more like a bulldog than usual this morning, Cinaed thought. When the clerk left the room, Searc came and stood by the window.

"I know the *Highland Crown* is gone."

He wasn't surprised the news had reached Searc. The ship had been expected to arrive at Inverness the morning after it was sunk. Cinaed had showed up at his door badly wounded. That was enough to surmise the truth.

"My crew. Have any of them made it to Inverness?"

"Your first mate and two longboats landed near Nairn." Searc began to pace. "They sent on news of the sinking. They didn't know what happened to you. They'd seen nothing of your second mate and the rest of your crew."

Cinaed wasn't about to lose hope. The men in the last boat must have assumed he was dead after he was shot and went overboard. They knew Duff Head was no safe place for them. If they cleared the rocks, they could have come ashore at a less hostile point along the coast.

"And I should live, by the way. Thanks for asking."

"The indestructible son of Scotland?" Searc scoffed. "What happened to the ship?"

"The storm pushed her up on the reef." He shoved the food away. His stomach wasn't ready for a large meal. "She was gone in a few hours."

"Who shot you?"

"Some villager you shouldn't have sold a musket to," Cinaed snapped. Searc almost smiled. Irony had always appealed to him. "The bloody sandmongers felt they'd been cheated because so little was washing ashore."

"Was all your cargo lost?"

"Gone. I blew it up. I wasn't about to let anything fall into the hands of the local authorities. No evidence remains of what the *Highland Crown* carried." He was left with nothing. "I need to start over."

Cinaed quaffed some small beer and sat back, stretching his legs out. He remembered another time in his life, sitting right here in front of this man, when he'd had nothing to his name. Albeit, he'd been a boy then.

"You think you're poor, is that it?" Searc stopped moving and faced him.

Cinaed shook his head. "I have no money, but I'll never be poor again. I have skills and I have experience. I've sailed every type of ship seen on the Atlantic. I can command anything from a sloop to a brig to a barquentine. I know there are ship owners along the coast who are looking for an able captain to—"

"You're *not* poor," Searc interrupted, stabbing the air with a stubby finger before going back to his pacing.

Suddenly, he didn't like the direction this conversation was going. "I'll not borrow money from you. You're still a Mackintosh. Even though I rank you far above that dog-faced clan of ours, the business between us is still just that. And I refuse to put myself in debt to a—"

A pudgy hand shot up, stopping him. Searc leaned on the back of a chair and pointed his bushy eyebrows at him. "*You're not poor, you bloody fool.*" He enunciated each word slowly and clearly.

Cinaed's eyes narrowed. Since he'd started smuggling arms, he'd procured weapons in New York or Philadelphia, and Searc always handled this end. The clan chief who was to receive each shipment was arranged here. Searc's men met the *Highland Crown* with boats to transfer the cargo when they arrived, so he'd had no worries with customs house officials when the tow horses hauled her upriver to her berth at the pier. Searc took care of all of it, including any bribes that were needed for the excise men to look the other way. Prices were agreed upon in advance, and Cinaed's share provided ample capital for fitting out the ship and investing in cargo for the next crossing.

He liked the arrangement. He kept his independence. He didn't want to be under Searc's thumb by borrowing from him. But that didn't seem to be what he was saying.

"I know what is mine back in Halifax. I know what I've lost." Cinaed sat back, crossing his arms. "But I'm not about to guess at whatever it is you're trying to tell me. So, out with it."

Searc's restless nature wouldn't allow him to stand still long enough to explain anything. He paced back and forth a few times, then came to a sudden stop by his desk, glaring at Cinaed.

"Just know that what I did was for your own good."

Already, he didn't like the sound of this. "What exactly did you do?"

"I invested it. All of it. For you."

The words tumbled out and lay stinking between them like month-old herring. Searc had been holding out on him. Despite knowing how the man dealt with others, Cinaed believed Searc treated him differently. They needed to trust each other when Searc laid out their business arrangements. But he'd been lying.

"Invested?" The word left a nasty taste in his mouth. If this were any other man, Cinaed would have already had him by the throat. But because it was Searc, he waited. The man was pacing again, his hand inside his coat. He was taking no chances.

"You've always been too free with your money to be a good businessman. I've seen how you've wasted it, sharing more with your crew than they deserve. You take risks for Scotland. That revenue cutter you stole and sank. All those rebels you transport back and forth, charging them nothing for the crossing. You're all heart and no head."

"I've done well enough doing business my own way," Cinaed said. "So, you've been keeping the lion's share?"

Searc stalked to his desk and began pawing through the pile of ledgers. "Not keeping it for myself."

Cinaed thought he was broke, having lost his ship. Now he wondered if Searc had kept enough for him to start again. "How much have you *invested*?"

The dark brows drew together. "Calm yourself."

"This is as calm as I plan to be right now," he threatened.

"Well, you need to hear and agree to my terms."

"Terms?" Cinaed growled. "You steal money from me, and now I have to agree to terms to get my own money back? If someone pulled this on you, their body would wash up in pieces on the banks of the river."

"I didn't need to tell you," Searc barked. "I could have kept it and never said a word."

"But you did. So, out with it before my patience gives way."

Searc pulled out a ledger from the pile and laid it on the desk. A folded paper was visible between the pages of the book. Cinaed glared at the man. He knew nothing would make Searc divulge anything until he was willing.

But the most important thing was, he wasn't completely ruined.

"This Lowlander you've brought into my house. Who is she?"

He knew he'd need to explain sooner or later. The time had come. "That Lowlander is my wife."

"Does the woman have a name? Family?"

He had no time to come up with a name other than the one she'd already chosen herself. "Isabella Murray. But she's Mrs. Mackintosh to you."

The sun, which had hovered just beneath the horizon for only a couple of hours during the night, was now beginning to rise high enough to brighten the chamber. Still, from this distance, Cinaed couldn't read the look in Searc's eyes. He didn't like lying to the man, but he had no idea how he'd explain having a wife one trip and none the next. He figured Isabella's future and his were murky enough. The time for explaining might never come.

"When did you marry her?"

"In Aberdeen, not a fortnight ago."

"Why? She's hardly a lass."

"Because I wanted her in my life. What of it?"

"Is that all?"

"I feel deep affection for her. I have no desire to be apart from her. She's mine now, and I'm a much better man for it."

The words were spoken without forethought or pretext. Cinaed's mind flashed to Isabella and the kiss they'd exchanged this morning. He was attracted to her physically, but there was so much more he wanted to know about her. Her life. What she enjoyed doing. What she dreamt of. What could he do to erase the permanent furrow in her brow? But beyond all that, what would become of her now was even more important to him than replacing the *Highland Crown*.

"How long have you known her?"

Cinaed understood Searc's distrust of strangers. They both had too much at stake. He'd put into port in Aberdeen for only a few days. Short enough for romance, but hardly long enough for marriage.

"I met her last summer when I docked in Aberdeen to have the hull scraped. I've made a point of calling on her the last two times I've stopped there since."

"What do you know about her family?"

"Enough," Cinaed barked. "We are not going to ferret out whether her third cousin's husband might be distantly related to some exciseman who wouldn't take a bribe from your partners in Aberdeen. She's more trustworthy than you, apparently. She saved my life. She'll not do anything to jeopardize your business dealings or bring danger into your house. Let it lie at that."

Searc's eyebrows pumped up and down as he stomped about and wrestled with the answers, but after a minute, he stopped abruptly at the desk.

"She's a woman of quality?"

"She's a woman of quality," Cinaed repeated.

Searc nodded curtly. "I want her down with us tonight for dinner."

This had to have something to do with Searc's terms. Cinaed knew it'd come out sooner or later. "Why? Who are you trying to impress?"

Searc ignored the questions. "And clean up, both of you. I'll have clothes sent up."

"Who are your guests?" he demanded.

"The organizers from the local weavers, their wives, and some others."

The weavers were the heart of the radical reform movement in the south, and in England. They'd been organizing for better wages and working conditions for years. To the chagrin of the manufactory owners, they controlled the workforce. But they were also the people who'd put a price on Isabella's head. Cinaed kept his face impassive.

"I thought they kept themselves clear of your influence. 'Unbribable' was the word you used less than a year ago. What are they doing here?"

Searc went to the window and looked out before answering. "They're calling for a day of strikes in Inverness. The same as they've done in every bloody town and city south of here."

"What does this have to do with you?"

"They want my protection." Searc went back to his desk. "Nearly everywhere else, when they've shut down the work and gone out to protest, they've been attacked by the British and the local authorities. They know I have my own men. They know I entertain officers here from the port and from Fort George. They don't want it going bad here the way it has in other places."

Cinaed didn't want to know what Searc was getting in return for such intervention. He doubted he was doing it for any noble reason.

"You don't need me or Isabella for this dinner."

Searc's dark visage became as fierce as Cinaed had ever seen it. The look had been fairly intimidating when he was a boy, but it had no effect on him now.

Cinaed returned the look. "I'm still waiting to hear

about this money you stole from me, but I'm not about to become your dancing bear to get it back. You'll give me what's mine."

Searc huffed and stormed back to his desk again. Yanking the folded paper from the ledger, he stalked back and tossed it to him. "That ledger accounts for every ha'penny, but you need to look at this first."

Cinaed opened the sheet of paper and stared at it for a moment. It was a flyer, advertising the sale of a ship, a cargo-carrying schooner of 280 tons. Apply to Captain P. Kenedy, Citadel Quay, New Harbour.

"Two hundred eighty tons at £25 per ton. The seller wants £6800. I can get him down to £4000."

Cinaed waited, assuming the negotiated price was what he could afford.

"Captain Kenedy will be dining here tonight with his wife."

"I don't know him."

"Well, I do," Searc scoffed. "The man's a bloody bore, but he owns that ship and a dozen others. Wants to 'slow down,' he says. After me, Kenedy is the richest man in Inverness, and I've done him a few favors over the years."

Cinaed didn't care to know any more details about how the man made *his* fortune.

Searc snapped the paper out of his hand. "You and your wife will come down to dinner."

He didn't know how he was going to convince Isabella to show her face at a dinner hosting the leadership of the local weavers. She'd probably suggest inviting Hudson and his men and let them fight it out for her head right here.

So far as he could tell, the people she knew were in

Edinburgh. Inverness was a long way from there. The chance of anyone recognizing her was almost naught. She was also being presented as his wife, an added layer of concealment. Still, the decision was hers to make.

"While we're making deals and calling in favors," Cinaed stated, knowing he needed to get everything on the table before Searc decided they were somehow even after his deviousness. "I'll be needing the assistance of your men next week for a private matter of my own."

Searc stuffed the flyer back into the ledger. "Getting shot twice in one day wasn't enough for you?"

"I tried to do it alone last time. This time I'll have your help."

"What needs doing?"

Cinaed was going after John Gordon, but there was no reason Searc had to know. "Perhaps, if you're hesitant, we should take a look at that ledger you've been waving about like Moses and his tablets. I have a notion there's not a deuced word or number written in that book."

As he pushed to his feet, Searc waved him off. "When do you need them?"

"One day next week. I'll let you know exactly which day."

CHAPTER 16

So wondrous wild, the whole might seem
the scenery of a fairy dream.
—Sir Walter Scott, "Lady of the Lake,"
Canto I, stanza 12

The dress of yellow-gold brocade, with its short, puffed sleeves and its patterned satin shawl, was more elegant than any gown she would have thought to order or wear in Edinburgh.

Isabella stood in front of the mirror as the early evening sunlight played over the subtle shades and contours of the material. She pulled up the top of the bosom gently, without success. It was far more revealing than she would have wanted, but it was truly a beautiful dress.

Since their arrival, no one had thought for a moment that Jean might be a servant. So, to get ready for this evening's dinner, a seamstress was brought in by the housekeeper to help fit and dress her. As it turned out, the garment fit her almost perfectly, and the few required tucks were dispensed with in no time.

Isabella didn't ask where the dress came from or to whom it belonged. She definitely had no interest in finding out more about Searc's business dealings than she needed to.

Cinaed had explained to her who would be at dinner. One of the guests was a man named Kenedy, who was attending with his wife, and a possibility existed that he'd sell Cinaed a ship at a good price. When he told her the leaders of the weavers would be there, as well, Isabella stifled her nervousness. She was being introduced as Mrs. Mackintosh, and she agreed it was highly unlikely anyone from Inverness would recognize her as the wife of Archibald Drummond.

She knew all of her husband's friends in Edinburgh, and many in Glasgow, as well—their names, their trades, their families, where they lived. These were the names that Lieutenant Hudson and his people wanted from her. It was information she would never reveal, despite the radical reformers' distrust of her. But whether they were weavers or tinsmiths or carpenters or lawyers, all of those activists she knew were Lowlanders, and none of them would be here in Inverness.

She would go along with Searc's request—or was it a demand?—if it helped Cinaed get the ship he needed.

Long before it was time to go downstairs, Isabella was dressed and had her hair gathered up in a fashion that was simple and comfortable. Earlier, Cinaed had given her some needed privacy—a gesture she found touching—by offering to bathe and dress in a guest bedchamber one flight below her in the tower.

After he left, however, questions began to edge in. She glanced at the bed where he'd been fighting through the fever and wondered if he'd be sleeping elsewhere. Many married men and women slept separately, but would he draw undue attention to their relationship, especially when they were still supposedly newlyweds? Could the two of them be in the same room and not continue what they'd begun this morning?

She was relieved when Jean arrived to rescue her from her thoughts. Coming over to the mirror, she circled wordlessly around Isabella, studying the dress carefully. It seemed today that the older woman's back was a little more stooped. She was more unsteady on her feet than she had been, and her hand shook more severely. No surprise. Jean had been indispensable in caring for Cinaed during the fever. She had to be exhausted from the ordeal, especially since it only added weight to her constant worry about her nephew.

Jean cast a critical eye over the dress and wearer as if she were some Parisian modiste.

"Damn me, but yer a bonnie lass." She flared the skirts out to get the full effect of the brocade, then pulled down on the bodice, revealing a little bit more of Isabella's breasts. "When ye go to market with the halibut, mistress, ye don't hide 'em in the sacking."

"I'm not taking anything to market, Jean."

The old woman shrugged and held up the shawl to inspect.

"I just saw yer handsome husband. He's a fine braw man, to be sure. Ye won't be recognizing him."

Isabella pressed a hand to her fluttery stomach. She, too, thought him handsome, with his broad shoulders and his blue eyes and his hair like a lion's mane. Recognizing him would never be a problem.

"He's not my husband," she replied.

"Hush now." The old woman looked over her shoulder as if afraid the walls might have ears. "Have ye forgot what I told ye the first day we come here? Ye need to be spoke for to belong. And there's no better person to belong to around here, that I can see, but yer handsome sea captain."

It wasn't belonging that worried her. It was the future, and it terrified her. Death was dogging her steps, and she feared taking him down with her.

She didn't want to think about this idea of husband and wife and the charade he'd started as another way of protecting her.

Isabella faced the mirror. Still, the woman looking back at her was a different person from the one who had, little more than two months ago, fled Edinburgh. A single-minded, dedicated physician had grown into some new creature, a person with the courage and the desire to play a part in a larger world.

Her gaze involuntarily wandered to the bed reflected in the mirror. But she blinked it away.

"Have the guests begun to arrive?" she asked.

"Can't say. I was down by the pier, milling about with the workers on the docks, hoping one of them Highlanders would come to me again."

"Did they?"

"I saw a couple of lads that could've been the same ones, but when I tried to talk to them, they just moved off." Jean shook out and refolded the blankets Isabella used at night to sleep on. "Coming in just now, I saw no guests, but that means nothing. This house doesn't have one door. I swear it has ten. Leastwise, that's how it seems."

Isabella hadn't been out of this chamber since she'd

arrived, but from what Cinaed told her, Jean might not be wrong.

"I can't tell ye how many times I'd be down by the kitchens and hear someone's in a private meeting with that shark when I *know* his men have answered no door. So where did they come from?"

"Cinaed says this house is a fortress, with all sorts of hidden passageways and secret doors."

Isabella walked to the window to see if she could see any arrivals from this vantage point.

In the lane below, a tall man impeccably dressed in black coat and trousers passed under her window. A pure white cravat was just visible as he walked across the way. Wide shoulders filled the coat to perfection. He was dressed formally for dinner, but he wore no hat and his dark hair curled over his collar. She wondered if he might be one of the guests.

Before he reached the far side of the lane, he turned and looked up at the window. He nodded, and Isabella's heart took off like a flock of birds. She flattened her hand against the glass. It was as if Cinaed knew she was watching.

"Didn't I tell ye? All clean shaved too. The man's a handsome dog, is he not?" Jean asked, standing beside her. "Who'd not want that one for a husband?"

Cinaed came out for two reasons—learning who these fellows were and what they wanted. The message they'd passed on through Jean wasn't enough.

He felt Isabella's eyes on him, and when he looked up at the window, he caught a glimpse of her. Even though he'd stressed the safety of the house and the value of

Searc's protection, he still worried about her. He'd convinced Searc that she was his wife, but these men outside knew the truth.

Two tall figures melted into the shadows of a ruined malt house that had been deserted since he was a boy. He passed them without a glance and continued up the lane to the corner. It was somewhat troubling that Searc, with a gang of ruffians at his disposal, didn't mind their presence. Cinaed hadn't mentioned it this morning. He wanted no attention brought to them until he had a chance to learn who they worked for and what they wanted.

The road that ran in front of Searc's house bustled with traffic. Carts and wagons loaded high with barrels and crates were making their way in the direction of the harbor or back toward the center of Inverness. A flock of sheep was being driven to town, and a ragged family, carrying all their worldly possessions, circled wearily around the animals. One of the children, a scruffy lad with a dirty face, pulled a small but resistant yellow dog along by a cord. They were trudging in the direction of the pier. Like so many other Highland families, they no doubt hoped to find a ship that would carry them across the sea. The desperation in their faces and the life they'd lost was caused by the clearances, and it angered Cinaed. He knew their homes had already been destroyed. They had nothing but a long bleak road before them. Pulling a gold sovereign from his pocket, he handed it to the lad as they passed. It was all he could do for them. For now.

A tall man in a battered wide-brimmed hat, leaning against an abandoned cart and eating an apple, watched him. Across the road, two more fellows sat on a low wall. They could have been just passing the time. One was absently whittling a stick, but Cinaed knew their attention never strayed from him.

As he approached, the Highlander by the cart straightened and tossed his apple away. He was dressed in a coat and pants of worn brown wool and a dark green waistcoat. His boots indicated he was no simple farmer, but rather a horseman. And the marked face and flattened nose showed evidence of more than a few rows.

They were approximately the same height and build. He guessed the other man might be a few years older than him, but no more. The Highlander wore a long hunting knife at his belt, and without doubt had at least one sgian dubh tucked into his boots. The riders who came to their rescue on the coach road had been heavily armed with muskets and pistols. If these were indeed the same men, they weren't foolish enough to carry outlawed weapons on the street.

The Highlander touched the brim of his hat. His hand didn't move an inch in the direction of the knife at his belt. He wore the comfortable demeanor of a person who'd been waiting for an old companion.

"Who are you?" Cinaed had no time for pleasantries or pretense.

"Blair Mackintosh."

The quick answer and the name took him by surprise, but there were Mackintosh families spread across the Highlands. "Where from?"

"Dalmigavie, Cinaed."

The years were raindrops disappearing in the grass. He knew he had changed, and the same would be true for others who grew up at Dalmigavie. He didn't recall anyone with the name Blair, but he didn't remember many things from those days. Still, he could easily be kin to this man. The realization was bittersweet, and at the same time clarified a great deal. It made sense now that Searc would have no objection to members of his own clan loitering about the streets surrounding his house. But did this mean that whatever information they had, Searc also knew?

"Did you approach my wife's traveling companion on market day, Blair Mackintosh?"

He used the word "wife" deliberately, hoping he'd be telling these people something they were not aware of, or confirming what they'd heard.

"Aye, that I did. Me and the lads here thought the auld woman and the doctor would want to hear news of their loved ones."

His casual reference to Isabella as "the doctor" was unsettling, but Cinaed's priority right now was to find out more of what they knew.

"Have you heard anything more about John Gordon?"

"That brave lad's had a wee bit more attention than any of us would be wanting." Blair spat in the dirt. "But he's not told them anything, so far as we know. We hear they're moving him soon."

"When?"

"Can't say, as yet. But then again, the weavers upriver have more reliable ears in Fort George than we do. Tonight, when ye see them, ye can ask what the day of the strike is. That'll be the day Gordon is transferred. They're thinking a dozen soldiers sent off to escort a prisoner will be a dozen less sent to town to break up their strike. And that means a handful less folk'll be trampled and killed."

What he said about the day of strikes made sense. The weavers had already asked for protection from Searc. They knew what had happened with every strike in the towns and cities south of here. They were trying to eliminate bloodshed, if possible.

Cinaed focused on what Blair said about the dinner. He even knew who'd been invited tonight. Then again, there were other Mackintosh men who worked inside the house, and all these people had to talk.

"And the girls, my wife's family?"

"We moved them, just to be safe, in case John Gordon couldn't hold fast under questioning."

"Where are they now?"

"Dalmigavie Castle. The lasses are houseguests of the laird."

Lachlan. Cinaed felt the hackles on his neck rise. His uncle's actions were commendable, but why was he going to such lengths? He hated to think he would ever owe him anything.

His men showing up the day of the attack by British soldiers. Taking Isabella's family into the mountains. They must have found out where the girls were from the folk at Stoneyfield House. That was what Isabella had wanted to do that day, but they'd had no time.

Lachlan's letter to him had been an invitation, but the steps he'd taken since made it seem much more serious. Cinaed didn't know what his uncle wanted. The thought occurred to him that perhaps the old gargoyle was feeling a bit burdened with guilt in his advancing years. Maybe he was dying.

"Why is Lachlan doing this?"

"Why?" Blair squinted slightly, confused by the

question. "The laird's doing what's right, I should think. What he sees as his duty. That blue-backed cavalry officer we run off, Hudson, he's been tearing through every village in the countryside, looking for ye and for her . . . and for us. And he's not been too gentle about it, the devil take him. So we're here to watch that ye stay safe and well."

Lachlan hadn't given a straw about him when he was nine years old. Why did he care about him now?

"Your laird sits at Dalmigavie Castle. He's the one who needs protecting."

The Highlander waited until two naval officers passed them on their way toward town, then ushered Cinaed down the quiet lane a ways. "No one can touch the laird there in the mountains. But yer here. And yer the one we been waiting for. Come out, lads."

Blair motioned, and a dozen men appeared from the shadows of the buildings, the alleyways, crumbling cottages, and warehouses. The two who'd been sitting on the wall crossed the road and joined them. More of them were watching the house than he'd seen.

A nod, a tip of the hat, a bow, and a greeting. A few of the faces struck Cinaed as familiar, perhaps from the days of his youth. They were friends and not a threat. One of them had a way of looking at you sideways. Cinaed wondered if this could be the same lad who'd been caught poaching rabbits with him from the laird's private warren. They'd both taken a hiding for that little escapade.

Other memories flowed back, of Dalmigavie, and even of a time before. Images he could make no sense of. Warm summer afternoons. The smell of flowers in a garden. Melodies sung in French. But he fixed his thoughts on the present. "I still don't know why you came after me. Before, I mean."

"We come down from the glen and waited, as Lachlan told us," Blair replied. A few heads nodded in agreement.

Cinaed wasn't getting a straight answer. He gave up and decided to let the man talk.

"When the bells rang that day at Stoneyfield House, we weren't far off, so we came."

"How did you know it was me? No one at the inn knew my name. How could you know I was even there?"

Blair grinned. "Lachlan and a goodly number of other lairds have been waiting—none too patient, neither—for the return of the son of Scotland and the *Highland Crown*. Expecting ye any day. A rider come up from Aberdeen with the message that ye'd sailed for Inverness, so we knew ye were coming. That's when he sent us down."

"Before the storm hit," another Mackintosh man added. "A nasty blow, to be sure."

"Aye," Blair agreed. "We spread out along the shore, looking to spy some sign of ye. One of the lads caught word of a ship running aground, so we set out, combing every village, looking. Just hoping ye'd made it ashore."

Cinaed ran a hand across his brow. How fortunate they'd been that these men had been close enough to that blasted inn to hear the bells.

"My crew," he said. "Searc told me two longboats made it into Nairn. Another boat, with my second mate, is still missing."

Blair gestured to the pair who had been sitting across the road. They nodded and went off.

"Those lads'll find them. Dead or alive, if they come

ashore, we'll bring ye word," he assured him. "Whatever ye need from us, just say the word and it's done."

Ever since he'd been cast out from their midst, Cinaed had always harbored feelings of resentment. But now, surrounded by his kin, he realized his anger had never really been directed toward clan folk. It was Lachlan whom he'd hoped would one day feel his wrath. The fellows around him now were here in Inverness, risking their lives for him under the watchful eye of their British overlords. He owed them his loyalty in return.

All eyes were on Cinaed. They stood in a circle with him at the center.

"Know this. We're yer arm and yer blade when ye need us. And we plan to take back what is rightfully ours."

Cinaed looked from one to the next. Over this past decade, legends had grown up, tales had been exaggerated about his exploits. But the truth was that he'd been blessed with an ability to lead men. It was one thing that made his crews at sea perform their duties with exceptional prowess. Standing here, however, with these Highlanders around him, he was stunned by the sense of unreserved commitment emanating from them.

He took a deep breath, grateful for their support. But he still couldn't understand why they were so willing to provide it. Or why Lachlan was so eager to do anything for him.

The truth suddenly slapped him in the face. The weapons. They were waiting for the arms he'd been smuggling into the Highlands. If they were to fight for their land and their rights, they needed muskets and powder and shot. Cinaed was giving them what they needed to carry on. This was why he was valuable to them.

The Highlanders were waiting, but he didn't know what to say to them. He'd buy another ship. He'd make more crossings and bring more weapons. But none of that was carved in stone at this moment.

For now, he thought, perhaps he could engage them the day he went after John Gordon.

"You're planning to stay here in the Maggot?"

"For as long as ye stay. Lachlan was clear. Be here for when ye need us and protect ye if the need arises."

Isabella. Cinaed needed no protection, but knowing these men lined the streets made him feel better that no British soldiers would be paying any surprise visits to the house. So long as he kept her close to him, and his clan was watching out for him, she was safer here than anywhere, at least until they were ready to sail away from these shores.

"What about Searc? What does he know about my wife and her family?"

Blair shrugged. "He's heard not a word from us. Our ways of doing business ain't quite the same. There's respect both ways, to be sure, but we each keep our own counsel."

Cinaed was relieved. He didn't want to be explaining anything more about Isabella. She was his, and that was all Searc needed to know.

"Will Lachlan send my wife's family to me when it's time?"

Blair frowned. "I wouldn't say that's exactly what the laird has in his head. Them lassies are honored guests and treated as such. Whenever ye want them, ye can come and get them. Not for me to speak for him, of course, but I believe that's Lachlan's thinking."

It was all becoming clearer. Cinaed had to go to Dalmigavie to get Isabella's sister and daughter. That was why Lachlan took them. And he *would* go, for her, when the time was right. But there would be no dealing. No waiting about there.

First, he needed to free Jean's nephew. He'd seen these men in action. He knew they were a match for twice as many British soldiers.

"It's a few days off, but I have something to do and I could use your help with it."

"We'll be here, Cinaed. Just say the word."

With a curt farewell nod, he started to turn back toward the house, but Blair stopped him.

"The Mackintoshes of Dalmigavie celebrate yer return. And we're not the only ones who've been waiting for ye."

He knew. He knew. If all went as planned, he'd be buying a ship tonight and get back to the business of smuggling arms.

CHAPTER 17

Hospitality to the exile, and broken bones
to the tyrant.
— Sir Walter Scott, *Waverley*

Isabella never moved from the window. Though she was at first concerned, fascination quickly set in as she watched Cinaed's interaction with the Highlanders outside.

At one point he was surrounded, and she feared he would hardly be able to defend himself against them. Watching from above, however, she quickly realized no one meant to do Cinaed harm. She thought they were actually forming a protective wall around him. They sent attentive looks in every direction, like watchmen safeguarding a valuable jewel.

Still, she breathed easier when Cinaed was done talking and moved back toward the gate. He paused beneath their window and looked up. Their gazes locked. It might have been her imagination, perhaps not, but she sensed he was pleased with whatever he'd heard outside.

Isabella turned from the window, ready to go down, but she stopped. Her intentions were forgotten when she saw Jean sitting in a chair with her eyes closed. Her lips were moving, as if she were saying a prayer or whispering to herself. Her trembling hand was rubbing a token of some sort, a gift from her nephew. What the token represented, Isabella didn't know. Jean never allowed her or anyone else to see it or touch it. The treasure was kept in a pouch around her neck. During the long days and nights when Isabella was caring for Cinaed, she'd seen Jean doing this exact same thing.

Her heart ached when she thought of how her troubles had disrupted the lives of John Gordon and his aunt. Whatever Sir Walter Scott had offered the young man to convince him to help her, it was not enough to compensate for all he and Jean had given up. And even though she had faith that Cinaed would somehow free John from the clutches of the British, the fact remained the life the young lawyer had built for himself in Edinburgh was gone forever. In the eyes of the authorities, if not the law, he would always be a marked man.

She moved quietly across to Jean and crouched before her. The wrinkles fanning out from the grey eyes were damp. The old woman's hand trembled as she kissed the token and dropped it into the pouch. She put the ribbon around her neck and tucked it into the neckline of her dress.

She waited until Jean opened her eyes before she spoke.

"I owe you my life." Isabella placed a hand on top of hers, softly caressing the weathered skin left by the years and the hard life she'd lived. "You've become the mother that I lost when I was young. I've never known another woman I could call 'friend' until you came into my life. You've been my keeper since the day John dropped me on your doorstep."

The trembling fingers entwined with Isabella's.

"I belong to you now, as you belong to me," she continued as a rush of emotion threatened to choke off her throat. "We'll find John. And we'll bring him back to you."

The old woman nodded as a tear escaped her wizened eyes. Bending her head, she pressed a kiss on Isabella's fingers and touched the ring Cinaed had given her to wear. Drawing their hands to her lips, Isabella returned the loving gesture, kissing her friend's hand.

"Go and fix yer face," Jean said as gruffly as she could manage, patting away a tear from Isabella's cheek. "Ye don't want to be shaming me now."

She smiled and went back to the mirror, tucking an errant lock of hair behind her ear and straightening her shawl. She took a deep breath and thought about all that could go wrong during this dinner.

Jean came and fussed with the dress and arranged the shawl around her shoulders. Finally, she stood back with her hands on her hips. "Not that I've ever seen one afore, nor am I likely to, but damn me if ye don't look like a queen."

Isabella shook her head. "Well, I don't want to be shaming you," she said, smiling. "I should go down."

The older woman went back to the window. "I saw ye watching yer husband talking to them Highlanders in the lane. Kindly find out for me what trouble he's planning now. I'm thinking it'd be comforting to know beforehand, unlike that last time."

Isabella nodded and went out, pausing at the top of the

stairs. She ran a hand down the front of her dress and thought of Mr. Carmichael's warnings about Mondays. This was Searc's day for entertaining the British commander in charge of the port, as well as his staff. But the surgeon said not to trust that schedule. And surely their host wouldn't entertain leaders of the weavers at the same table with so-called gentlemen representing the occupying forces in the Highlands. Besides, Searc had already told Cinaed whom to expect at dinner. And no officers were mentioned.

Still, she took a few breaths to calm her nerves. She wasn't doing this alone, she told herself. Cinaed was waiting for her, and with that bolstering thought, she put one foot in front of the other and descended.

At the bottom of the stairs, Isabella found she was facing a choice of two doors and a corridor. Since the day they'd arrived, she'd never once ventured from the tower chamber. Not remembering that they'd passed through any door as they carried Cinaed up, she directed her steps along the corridor.

She soon realized she'd made a mistake. One passageway led to another. Illuminated only by slivers of light coming through shuttered and barred windows, the corridors seemed to lead in circles. Twice, she was certain she'd passed the same closed door, only to find the passage end at a blank wall. There was no logic to any of this. When she realized one wall of a corridor was the exterior of a building, she decided Searc's house was actually a number of buildings joined together higgledy-piggledy.

Jean had warned her, but now she saw for herself that the house was much larger than it seemed from the outside.

Finally, Isabella came to a door that opened onto a corridor lit by candles in sconces on the wall. Following the smell of food and voices, she found herself looking into the kitchens, which were bustling with cooks and scullery maids and an army of servants.

Isabella had hosted enough dinners to know this was too much preparation for the number of guests she'd been told were coming.

A footman came out, carrying a tray of food, so she trailed him. Within moments, he turned off, but she heard people talking ahead. Before she could follow the voices, someone behind her took hold of her wrist. Cinaed.

"Come with me."

Isabella breathed a sigh of relief. He'd found her. Pulling her behind him, he opened the door into a nearby room and led her in.

"I'm afraid there's been a change in the dinner arrangements." He glanced into the hallway before closing the door. From the far end of the room, twilight slipped past a pair of tall, heavily draped windows and cast a golden glow over him. "I apologize I didn't come in time to escort you down."

Her ability to focus on Cinaed's urgent tone was hindered by the sound of her own heart hammering against the walls of her chest. No ship captain had the right to look as handsome as this man. Even cloaked in the staid attire of a gentleman, he conjured images of pirates and highwaymen. But he was dashing, regardless of what he wore. And the color black suited him perfectly.

He stopped, his gaze moving down her body. "You look beautiful."

She blushed, unable to respond. Her own mind was on him.

His clean-shaven face made the lines and angles of his cheekbones and jaw more pronounced, more handsome, more youthful. Isabella didn't want to guess at his age but imagined he was far younger than she.

Isabella had been considered a spinster when she married Archibald at the age of eight and twenty. Now, six years later, she was mature enough to think clearly and not allow herself to be caught up in foolish dreams or handsome distractions.

But Cinaed Mackintosh was more than a distraction.

She turned away and gaped. They were standing in the most unusual room. Even in this light, she knew she'd never seen anything like it.

"What is this place?"

"My least favorite room anywhere." Cinaed stared at the decorations on the walls. "Searc is getting worse as he ages. He had only about half of these things here when I was a lad."

Outlawed weapons adorned the walls in startling designs. Muskets and swords and pistols laid out in concentric circles, like huge starbursts emanating out from a central buckler or a shield. Rows of crossed swords led upward to wheels of daggers or circular framed portraits. Lines of spears with wicked hooks and axe blades flanked a huge fireplace.

One could start a revolution with the armaments in this chamber.

Isabella had very little familiarity with family coats of arms and no knowledge at all of clan insignia, but on every wall she saw variations of the same crest repeated

over and over. On shields and battle flags, on the handles
of the swords and on brooches pinned to long swaths of
tartan.

"Mackintosh?" She guessed, looking over her shoulder
at Cinaed, waiting for confirmation.

"No other."

Above the fireplace, in a position of honor, hung the
portrait of a young man. Wearing a light grey suit with
a silver star-shaped medallion on his chest, the subject
was wrapped in a red cloak trimmed with white fur,
and a blue sash crossed his chest. He wore the white
powdered wig of the last century. The air of confidence
in his features was timeless.

She didn't need to ask. She knew. Bonnie Prince
Charlie.

Cinaed took a battle-ax off the wall and tested its balance and weight. Watching him now, Isabella could easily imagine him dressed in a kilt, wielding a broad sword
and axe beneath the war banner of his clan, striding into
battle for his king.

She pushed the image away as Cinaed replaced the
weapon on the wall.

"This room holds centuries of the clan's history."

Other than Maisie and Morrigan, Isabella had no
other family. At least none she had any connection with.
When Thomas Murray left Scotland years ago, her father
closed all the doors to his past. Many times, she tried to
bring it up in discussion, hoping there would be aunts
and uncles and cousins, but he offered no clue, no connections that she could seek. Isabella didn't even know
where to look, if she ever decided to search for them.
And in Archibald's family, the Drummonds were his

and Morrigan's relations only. Isabella understood that as his second wife, she held no interest in their eyes. During her marriage, she and Archibald never traveled to Perth, where his family was from, and no one ever came to Edinburgh to visit.

She ran her fingers along the handle of a broadsword mounted on the wall. The weapon was longer than she was tall.

Isabella tried to tell herself it didn't matter that she had no one. She was an independent woman. She had a profession that she could put to use once she arrived in Canada, or wherever they could find a safe haven. An extended family could be both a blessing and a curse. She recalled Cinaed's resentment about how he'd been treated by his kin.

She lifted a smaller sword from the wall. "I'd like to learn how to use one of these."

"A backsword? I can teach you."

A welcome tingle ran along her spine as she realized he stood close behind her. Very close, she corrected, feeling the touch of his lips trailing down the sensitive skin of her neck before settling just below her ear.

"Here? In this room?"

Isabella's voice sounded husky and strange, even to her own ear. She guessed neither of them was thinking any longer about training with swords. She was caught in a breathless wave of sensation as his hands slid across her waist and over the curve of her stomach.

"This already has the makings of the fondest memory I'll ever have of my clan." He tasted the skin of her neck and pulled her closer.

As her buttocks pressed against his groin, she knew

he was as affected as she. Isabella felt herself melting. Her breasts ached for his touch. She'd heard women talk about lusting for a man, but she'd never experienced it. At this moment, however, the desire to have Cinaed inside her suddenly defined the word for her.

"Shall we create a memory?"

She couldn't bring herself to speak, so instead she turned in his arms. Her mouth sought his, and he responded with a kiss that lit a fever within her. Like a butterfly seeking the flame, she threw herself into his warmth even as she risked the scorching heat.

He was the tutor, and she willingly followed his every step. Cinaed's hands squeezed her bottom, drawing her tight against him. Isabella leaned into him, crushing her breasts against his chest. His kiss was a lashing assault of lips and tongue, and she knew exactly what she wanted from him. There was no hesitation on her part. She heard herself moan deep in her throat, and her arms slipped around his neck. Their mouths melded into one.

A man's voice in the hallway startled her, and she pushed away. Detaching herself, Isabella backed away until she collided with a large table covered with swords and daggers.

"Find Captain Mackintosh," the voice called out. "Go and find him *now.*"

Isabella moved around the table as she straightened her dress and tucked in loose tendrils of hair that had escaped their confines. Her lips were numb. Her fingers trembled and searched for a place to come to rest.

"We could be making love there on that bench, and anyone coming into this room would apologize and leave us. We are married, don't forget."

She glanced at the bench, envisioning the two of them together right now. She needed more than a table between herself and Cinaed. She had no willpower against this man's charms.

"What do you say, Isabella?"

How she wished she were brave enough to succumb to a temptation like that at least once in her life.

"We can say we're married to fool other people, but we're not," she asserted, daring herself to look his way.

"Of course, we are. We're in Scotland. We need no clergyman to be married."

He saw every temptation and every hesitation in her face. He was the first man who'd ever really looked at her. The only man who'd ever truly *seen* her.

"A couple is legally married here if the two declare themselves to be married in front of others." His voice was a caress of temptation. "We have more than a dozen witnesses, in this house alone, who will swear to our marriage."

He was no longer teasing. She could see it in his expression, in his eyes. It was thrilling and yet terrifying. Isabella thought of how briefly she'd known him, and of the turbulent and unknown road that lay ahead. She also thought of her first marriage. Archibald had been a familiar face in her father's circle of scholars and friends. She'd known him and worked with him. They'd developed a comfortable and cordial rapport months before her father's death. Afterward, Archibald's proposal had been a reasonable solution to her troubles. In accepting it, she'd thought her future was secure. She'd been wrong.

Marriage was no longer the only answer for her. She needed to find her own path, her own future. The desire she felt for Cinaed, the way she'd come to care for him, had nothing to do with his offer of protection. A husband's role was to cherish and protect. She didn't want to burden him with her life. She wished they could come together, free of their troubles . . . as a man and a woman.

"I suppose I should have gotten down on my knee and proposed properly, since that is the gentlemanly thing to do where you come from."

"Please, let's not talk about this now." Isabella tore her gaze from him and glanced toward the door. She could hear voices approaching again. "You said there was a change in the dinner arrangements."

A knock stopped Cinaed from answering. His expression told her they were not done with the discussion of marriage. He went to the door and opened it.

One of Searc's men stood outside. "They're ready for you, Captain."

"Tell your master we'll be there soon."

He closed the door. The playfulness of a few moments ago was gone from his face.

"Searc's plan for a small dinner tonight has grown." He extended his hand to her. She joined him. "We'll be dining with at least two dozen guests beyond those that we were told about."

Isabella trusted Cinaed with her life, but she still needed to know. "Anyone I should worry about? Do you foresee any unpleasant surprises?"

"No British officers, I can tell you that. And no fat aristocrats getting richer through their support of Crown interests. This much Searc assured me when he explained the change of plans."

Isabella almost asked who was left, but she reminded

herself the main reason for this dinner was to facilitate Cinaed's purchase of a ship. They went out together.

When they reached the drawing room, she held him back for a moment. "Do you know the reason for the last-minute changes?"

"Investors. Searc thinks my endeavor will do a great deal better and grow substantially if its funded by a few of the wealthier reform sympathizers and clan chiefs pooling their money."

Isabella couldn't quiet the apprehensiveness stirring deep in her stomach. She'd thought that Archibald's belief in nonviolent protest to produce change for the better was dangerous to their way of life. And here she was, walking beside a man who helped arm men and women who were ready to fight to the death for those same ideals. She discreetly brushed away a bead of sweat from her temple as one of the footmen ushered them in.

They paused just inside the drawing room, which was grander and far more modern than she would have expected from Searc Mackintosh.

Some guests were smartly dressed in the latest fashions one might see in Edinburgh, others in their best Sunday clothes, but more gentlemen than she would have expected were dressed in kilts of multicolored tartan cloth with wide leather belts across their jackets, fur pouches at their waists, and jeweled daggers at their sides.

She had no time to take in the rest of the chamber, however. At that instant, every guest's gaze swung toward them and a rapt silence swept over the crowd.

Suddenly, those who were sitting scrambled to their feet. Glasses and silver clinked as people freed themselves of any encumbrances. Across the room, men and women straightened their fine clothes and moved to gain a better vantage point. Whispers and murmurs arose on every side. All eyes were upon Cinaed.

Stunned, Isabella had to stop herself from taking a step back. Lord Byron himself wouldn't have been given a more highly charged reception.

As the butler announced them, Searc barreled across the room to greet them.

Immediately, people began to approach, and the introductions began. A queue began to form, and Isabella stepped away from the center. They had come to meet Cinaed, and their enthusiasm was met with his own genuine charm and confidence.

As the guests came forward, she heard the names of clans and families—Fraser, Innes, Chisolm, Munro, Grant, Macpherson, Mackintosh. Isabella could not help but feel the pride of belonging that these Highlanders carried.

Isabella drifted farther away, allowing those attending better access to Cinaed. Searc looked like a man officiating at some high church function, holding some back and presenting others with rigid formality of rank. Toward the end of the line, Mr. Carmichael nodded to her as he approached with men who she surmised, from their clothing, must represent the weavers.

The excitement was palpable. It was as if Cinaed were a foreign potentate, rather than a ship's captain, home from abroad. When the weavers finally reached him, they were more than deferential. Their nervousness was so pronounced they barely looked up.

As he thanked Mr. Carmichael for his help in caring for him, Cinaed looked over his shoulder, searching for

Isabella. Excusing himself, he strode over, linked her arm in his, and led her forward. Immediately, a second hush fell over the crowd.

"I've proved to be a neglectful newlywed husband this evening." He caressed her hand. "I'd like to present my wife, Mrs. Mackintosh."

No one in the drawing room moved or spoke. Every eye was fixed on the ring adorning her finger.

CHAPTER 18

Where shall he find, in foreign land,
So lone a lake, so sweet a strand!—
There is no breeze upon the fern,
No ripple on the lake,
Upon her eyry nods the erne,
The deer has sought the brake;
The small birds will not sing aloud,
The springing trout lies still,
So darkly glooms yon thunder-cloud,
That swathes, as with a purple shroud . . .
—Sir Walter Scott, "Lady of the Lake,"
Canto VI, stanza 15

When the *Highland Crown* hit the reefs in Duff Head, Cinaed was certain his luck had run out. But tonight, his good fortune had seen new heights.

One ship was not the topic of conversation, but three. At least. Plans were for long-term commitments on the part of the investors. Toasts of *Slàinte mhath . . . Slàinte mhòr*, a tribute to the resistance of the old Jacobite cause, rang out over and over. The conversations Cinaed participated in always turned to some vision of a new and independent Scotland, at dinner and afterward.

For years, home had been either Halifax or the *Highland Crown*. When it came to a clan or a homeland, Cinaed had wanted to believe his allegiance was owed only to himself. But tonight was a reminder that no matter how far he'd gone, or how long he'd been away, invisible ties still bound his heart to this land. Talking to these people, he knew he wanted to be involved with creating the changes they believed were coming. They clearly wanted him to be part of it, and he intended to do everything he could.

When Cinaed and Isabella left, only Searc and a small group of guests remained. He entwined his fingers with hers as they worked their way through the house.

"Thank you for being there with me," he told her. "You were absolutely magnificent."

Whether she was at his side or across the room speaking to some of the spouses or to Mr. Carmichael, every time he looked at her, his chest swelled with pride. She was beautiful, intelligent, and insightful in her opinions. Isabella was a rare gem and unlike anyone he'd ever known or dreamed of knowing.

She tucked her hand into the crook of his arm. "You have a bearing, a confidence that is astonishing. Most of those men were far more advanced in years than you, but they sought you out, looked for your opinion, and listened intently. It was quite impressive."

"My ship brings a commodity they all want."

She shook her head. "I'm no expert in how people think. But from what I saw and overheard in the conversations, it's not only your cargo that interests them, but you as a person, you as a man. They're drawn to you."

She may have been exaggerating the guests' response a little, but he was glad Isabella felt this way. It was *her* opinion of him that mattered. He smiled and pressed a kiss on her hand as they started up the stairs into the tower.

She enchanted him, enthralled him with her beauty, with her mind, with the passion that was quick to flare up and light the desire within him.

The stairwell was dark, lit only by a candle at each landing. He felt her tension growing as they ascended. Her hand grew colder, and he could almost feel the blood retreating from her fingers.

He stopped at the door to the tower chamber. Regardless of how much he wanted Isabella, he wasn't about to take advantage of this arrangement he'd forced upon her.

"I'll sleep in the room downstairs where I bathed and changed earlier."

A shadow flitted across her fair features. He hoped it was disappointment.

"That would be best."

"But before I go, I have news of your sister and stepdaughter." Cinaed hadn't wanted to mention it before the reception. At that time, he'd had no idea when he could go after them. Or how he was going to assist Isabella and her family in leaving Scotland. Now he knew.

She didn't wait for him to say any more. But, taking the candle from the wall, she pulled him inside the tower room and closed the door.

"Jean warned me about people coming and going unnoticed. I've become wary that someone might be listening." She leaned her back against the door. "Tell me. Where are they?"

"They're safe with the Mackintosh laird at Dalmigavie Castle."

"The place you came from?"

He nodded. "My uncle arranged for the move."

Isabella put the candle on the table, walked to the window, and looked out into the night. She turned and went to the far side of the room. She couldn't conceal the smile tugging at the corners of her beautiful mouth. She rubbed her hands together and hugged her middle, trying to contain her excitement. He hadn't seen her this eager, this happy since they'd met.

She hurried back to him, looking like a woman who was ready to charge out and go after her family right now.

"You said they're safe."

"They're safe," he repeated.

Cinaed went on to tell her about everything he'd heard from the Highlanders. About how they had found the three of them and come to their rescue on the coach road. And about John Gordon's situation now. He didn't bother to mention that questions about Lachlan Mackintosh's motivation still troubled him. Or the fact that he was puzzled and yet honored by his clan members' seeming dedication to him.

"Can I go there and bring them back?"

Cinaed had guessed at this response on her part. It was understandable she would immediately want to be reunited with them.

"I wouldn't advise it. Not yet. Lachlan has demanded, or at least has hinted, that *I* must travel to Dalmigavie Castle before he lets your family go."

He didn't want to imagine how complicated it would be if Isabella insisted on going into the mountains on her own. Her safety would be at risk every step of the way, and he had no idea about the reception she'd receive once she arrived. Cinaed didn't know what Lachlan wanted. But he guessed Isabella had no role in it.

"I'll take you there myself in a week."

"What happens in a week?" she asked.

Public conversations and private ones had taken place tonight amongst the guests. One that Cinaed made sure he was privy to had been between the weavers and Searc about the impending strike. The Highlanders outside had been correct. One of the weavers mentioned that Fort George would have fewer soldiers next Monday because of a prisoner transfer. They'd decided on the day.

"The weavers have called for all work to stop in Inverness a week from today. They plan to hold a rally."

Sadness darkened Isabella's features, and lines formed on her forehead. Cinaed recalled Hudson taunting her about the death of her husband on a day of strikes in Edinburgh.

"That's the day that I'll go after John Gordon."

Her cheeks grew ashen. Whatever joy the news of her family had given her, it was gone now.

"Are you planning to sneak into Fort George?"

"I don't need to. Gordon and others accused of crimes against the Crown are being moved south. We'll take them on the coach road."

"Do you have help?"

"I have plenty. Between the riders outside and the men Searc will loan me, we'll outnumber the escort soldiers two to one."

She picked up a bottle of ointment from the table and immediately put it back down. She rubbed her arm and began to pace the room. Table to window, window to door, steering wide of where Cinaed stood near the bed.

"You're not well enough," she said, darting a quick look at him. "You still have two bullet holes in your body that have not healed."

He reached out to take her arm and stop her, but she shook off his touch.

"I'll not sew you up again." She put up two hands like a wall. "I refuse."

"You won't need to sew me up. I promise to come back to you unharmed."

"That's an empty promise. It's not your choice." She let out a frustrated breath and glared at Cinaed, her eyes blazing. "There is only so much damage a body can withstand. This time you'll die."

They'd talked about this. She knew he would eventually go after John Gordon. She was present when he'd promised Jean. She hadn't objected then. But now, he studied the passionately irate woman before him and realized what had changed. She cared. She cared for him. Whatever sentiment she'd had for him before, it was all different now.

"Don't worry yourself, Isabella. I'll come back in one piece." He took a step toward her, but she walked away.

"You can send someone else."

"I can't." Aboard ship, he would never put a man in harm's way unless he was willing to do the job himself. Every man's life mattered as much as his own. She was too worked up at the moment, however, for him to explain his position on honor or leadership.

She waved a hand toward the window. "Those Highlanders already know who John Gordon is. They don't need you there."

"Searc's men won't take orders from some riders down from the hills."

"The one group should be enough."

Cinaed shook his head at his bonnie strategist. This time he was quicker. He reached out and caught Isabella's hand, pulling her to him. She didn't have a chance to get away.

She didn't want to, however, and came willingly. Her arms wrapped around him like bands of iron. She buried her face against his chest.

"I don't want to lose you. Don't you see?"

"You won't lose me." He kissed the top of her head.

He was touched deeply by her words, and her worry made his heart ache. Cinaed's fingers delved into her hair. Pins fell to the floor, and her soft tresses tumbled down over her shoulders. He held her so close he could feel the beat of her heart.

He knew what passion was, but he'd never been schooled in love.

The possibility of finding the one person he could not live without, the one whose presence filled him up and brought him joy, whose absence left him incomplete, had to be a miracle. Cinaed was no romantic, but to feel this harmony of heart and mind was to tread on the edges of all in life that was holy.

He ran his hands over her back, gathering her even closer. They'd known each other for only a short time, but *life* was short, with no guarantees of tomorrow. He wanted her in his life, traveling alongside him on whatever road lay ahead, no matter how long they had. What he'd proposed to her in Searc's clan room wasn't to justify the fulfillment of their passion. He'd meant it. They were already husband and wife, if she'd accept him. He wanted to do away with the pretense and move forward.

"Will you have me?" he whispered. "Will you take me as your husband?"

Her hold on him eased, and as she raised her face from his chest, Isabella clutched his coat.

He looked down into her eyes and was troubled to see the tears. "I know I'm not worthy of you. I—"

She placed her fingers against his lips, silencing him. "It's not you. My life is no gift to any husband. What future do I bring to him? What will become of me is a mystery. But aside from that, my decisions are not solely mine to make. I have two other people who rely on me to set them on their paths."

"I'll take them, as well, and I promise to—"

"I can't give you an answer right now." She shook her head. Her voice trembled. She stabbed away a tear.

He was a man who'd walked through life without the love of a family. He'd lived independent of the security of his clan. Isabella cared for him. He could see it as clear as the morning sun rising from the sea. But he also recognized commitment when he saw it.

"I'll ask you again next week, once you're reunited with your family. And I'll ask you again when we sail out of this harbor for Halifax. And I'll ask you again when we arrive there. And I'll ask you time and again until you either accept me or tell me to disappear from your life."

She stabbed away another tear.

"What do you say to that proposal?" he asked, brushing

his thumb across her cheek and smoothing away another glistening pearl.

She retreated from his arms and turned her back to him.

He was disappointed, but he understood her hesitation. He also knew that, as it stood now, he had nothing beyond promises to offer her. Nothing real that would secure her future, or the future of those she was responsible for.

"Can we at least continue with the pretense of husband and wife . . . for the good of everyone involved?"

She half turned toward him and nodded. The candle-light illuminated her profile and the dampness on her cheek. He stood for a long moment, fighting the urge to go to her and pull her into his arms.

Finally, he found the strength to step away. "Good night, Isabella."

He was at the door when she called his name.

"Stay, Cinaed. Stay with me."

They met in the center of the room. She raised her face to him and Cinaed kissed her, tenderly at first, and then with all the passion in his heart. When their lips parted, she took his hand and pulled him toward the bed.

"Isabella, I want you more than I've ever wanted any woman in my life, but—"

"Take me," she said, stopping him. "Make love to me."

However honorable his intentions had been, they were gone. What he'd been about to say to her was forgotten. She pushed his coat off his shoulders, and suddenly he was as exuberant and clumsy as a lad making love for the first time. Excitement and impatience pounded in Cinaed's veins. His hands were blocks of stone as he struggled to remove her dress. A boot accidentally flew across the room. Their heads bumped as she pulled his shirt off his shoulders. He stole kisses from her lips as she tried to be mindful of his wounds. The laces on a blasted undergarment nearly ruined him, but the shift underneath dropped away nicely.

And then it was done. Isabella stood before him as gloriously naked as a goddess.

Her breasts fit his palms perfectly. He squeezed the tips, and a soft moan escaped her. She backed onto the edge of the bed, and he followed, moving in closer and spreading her knees. She reached for him, her hands impatiently unfastening his fall. He groaned as her soft fingers wrapped around him, but he somehow rid himself of his trousers.

She lay back and her strong leg slipped around his waist, urging him on. Cinaed wanted nothing more than to bury himself deep inside her and take what she offered. But his gaze moved along the soft curve of her hips past the perfection of her breasts. Her face was flushed, her lips parted. She was experienced with the marriage bed, and yet her expression was one of a woman making love for the first time. His pleasure would have to wait.

He leaned forward and ran his hand along her cheek and across her lips, sliding a finger into her mouth. He let it trail downward over her chin and throat. When he reached her breasts, he took the time to circle each nipple and watched them rise to his touch.

Her eyes darkened. She watched his every move. Her hips began to stir restlessly.

"Now, Cinaed."

Instead, he smiled and moved ever so slowly downward until he knelt beside the bed.

"We'll get to that soon," he said, and lowered his mouth onto her.

For more than half a decade she'd been married, but the excitement of Cinaed's play beforehand, the ever-increasing passion, and the wild waves of shared release was a gift that Isabella had never known could exist.

Their lovemaking was intense. Cinaed was like some winged god of carnal pleasure who had traveled from Olympus to breathe life into her and her alone. She was a physician, but what he taught her of physical love could not be found in any text. He knew where to touch her, how to love her, when to tease her. He made her body quiver, shudder, and sing.

She'd lived as a married woman, and yet she'd been in a slumber. Now, she was awakened.

Supremely satisfied, Isabella lay sprawled across Cinaed's body, her face near the stitches she'd used to close his chest. Within her line of vision, the bullet hole in his arm looked to be healing well. Her fingers inched toward the wounds that had almost taken his precious life.

He caught her hand and rolled her on the bed until she lay on her back, trapping her with his leg across her belly. "Didn't I exhaust you enough? No thinking of scars or bruises, no worrying about tomorrow or next week. You should rest now and enjoy this moment's peace."

Isabella traced the line of his jaw and realized he was asking for the impossible. She worried about him. She couldn't tell him, but Cinaed held her heart in his hands. She loved him. His proposal had been the most beautiful offer, and if she were a free woman, she would accept it . . . joyfully. But she couldn't. Not the way her life was shaped now.

"Can we at least discuss your rescue plan?"

"Nay. You have your training. I have mine. I respect your expertise. You respect mine."

She rolled her eyes, but she recognized there was no deterring him.

He let his gaze trail down her naked body. "Give me a few more minutes, and I'll have recovered enough to work harder on distracting you."

Distracting, he was also an expert at. And she looked forward to his "recovery," as he'd called it. Isabella reached down and pulled a blanket over her body. Lying naked in a man's arms was not something she was accustomed to.

He tugged the blanket down below her breasts. She pulled it up. He pulled it down again. She let him win.

"Distractions. Very well." She rolled against him. "Tell me about this wife of yours."

"At the moment, I have only one. But she tells me she's not the one, so my plan is to woo her and charm her and make love to her—"

"Stop." She smiled. "Here, you proved my point. You don't know anything about me."

"But I do," he said, wearing a mischievous smirk. "I know your belly is quite ticklish. You moan with every stroke. And you have a mole here under your right breast."

"You're incorrigible." She drove her fingers into his hair and forced him to look above her chin and not below. "I'm asking about *me*. By the way, how old are you?"

"I thought we were talking about you."

"Answer me before I hurt you. And as a physician, I do know how pain is inflicted."

"I'd like you to try, Doctor."

"Cinaed."

"Thirty, at my next . . . or last . . . birthday. And you?"

She let go of his hair and stared at the candle. She'd guessed it. She was so much older.

"But before you answer, I'm telling you now that I don't care about your age. It's what's here and here that I care about." He touched her temple and her heart. "And I'm also quite fond of your breasts. And your hands. And your legs are exceptional. And your bottom makes me want to—"

"Thirty-four. Which means when you're thirty-six, I'll be *forty*."

"So you predict I'll live for at least six more years." He cheered as if she'd awarded him a prize. "Then that means there'll be no trouble when I go for Jean's nephew next week."

"Your logic may need a wee bit of polishing," she scoffed.

"In any event, after I free him and the lads outside take him into the mountains, I'll come back for you. The following morning we'll join him and your lasses at Dalmigavie. And by then, I should have a better idea about when our ship will be ready to sail."

He was, indeed, a master of distraction, and Isabella had to accept it. He didn't care about her age. And he was going through with his plan of attacking an English prisoner escort regardless of what she said. He was pretending it would be as simple as fetching John Gordon from some minister's house or meeting him at the mail coach arriving from Edinburgh.

"Now you tell me about my wife." He touched her chin, drawing her gaze to him. "And I'm not talking about anything as trifling as her age."

"What do you want to know?"

He caressed her face, tucking the loose strands of hair behind her ear. "A physician. Not an easy job for a woman. What made you become one?"

"Where do I begin?" she replied. "I always wanted to know about medicine. I always wanted to heal people."

"You've done a fine job of it with this old sea dog, as our Jean says. But where did it start?"

Isabella thought for a moment. "For as long as I can remember, I followed my father about, watching him with his patients. I was always drawn to his study. The smell of the leather-bound books, pipe tobacco, and whiskey. Other smells, too, intrigued me. Chemicals and fluids that filled large glass jars containing organs and body parts and oddities of nature that I couldn't identify. Even the dusty scrolls and anatomical diagrams on parchment filling work tables by a tall window." She laughed. "He didn't know what to do with me, so he allowed me to be and do as I wished. Because he didn't discourage me, I suppose, my path was set."

"You went to the university as a woman?"

"Indeed. I studied at the university in Wurzburg, where my father held a professor's chair."

"Were there other women there, or were you the first?"

"There were no other women there while I attended,

but many others have taken their degrees before me. Women have been practicing medicine for centuries in many parts of the world. But the direct precedent for my education was a woman named Dorothea Erxleben. She was the first female medical doctor in Germany. Like me, Erxleben was instructed in medicine by her father from an early age."

"So, while other lasses were being taught to do needlework and sketch, you were studying?"

"I would have found that quite gratifying, but I had to learn to paint and arrange flowers and play the pianoforte, as well. I was never proficient in any of those skills, but my efforts with music were particularly horrifying," she admitted. "In fact, I believe because of me there is a music master out there who gave up his art to become a baker."

Cinaed laughed. "I'm very happy your sewing lessons were more successful. I'm a walking sampler of your proficiency."

"Thank you. And I did far better work with my father's tutorials in basic science, Latin, and medicine."

Those years were filled with happiness and hard work, she thought. She never imagined that her life would take her so far from there. Or bring her here to the Highlands of Scotland, to the bed of a man who wanted to marry her.

"And the university accepted you?"

"Not without a fight. But we drew on Erxleben for our argument. In her time, some sixty years before me, the point was made that since women were not allowed by law to hold public office, they also should not hold a medical degree or practice medicine."

"How did they get around that?"

"Three doctors accused her of quackery and demanded she sit for an examination, expecting she would never pass. The rector of the university at Halle decided that practicing medicine was not the same as holding public office. He allowed Erxleben to take her examination. She passed the test brilliantly and was awarded her degree."

"As were you."

She nodded happily. Her father was so proud. "Even now, so many years after Erxleben, my taking of a degree was considered an amazing achievement." She rolled onto her back and gazed up into the darkness above. "Later, I realized the hardest part of the path I'd chosen was not to earn a degree but to be allowed to practice."

"I imagine men could be a problem."

Isabella smiled at him. "And the women. For some reason, we don't trust our own sex. If it weren't for my father and then Archibald, I never would have been able to practice. Though I found that the poor always needed proper care."

"So you provided it."

"Willingly. And I shall always help them. But I couldn't survive on what they could afford to pay, if they had anything at all. My inheritance was modest, and I didn't have only myself to worry about." She thought of her younger sister. "What do you do with a fourteen-year-old who has no dowry? Marrying Archibald was a matter of survival, for Maisie, and for me."

She hadn't planned to mention her husband's name. She had no obligation to explain anything, but the words had simply poured out.

"How much older was he?"

"He was fifty-four. I was eight and twenty."

The difference in their ages was wide and, in many ways, impassable. Suddenly, she realized how wrong it was to talk about him, to mention his age, to think about him even, as she lay in bed with another man. But she couldn't stop herself.

"He was a good man. A talented doctor. Dedicated and gentle. True to his ideals. He truly did me and my sister a favor when he offered . . ."

Isabella hadn't realized she was crying until Cinaed wiped away the tears that had slipped from the corners of her eyes.

"He had to be all of those things and more," he said softly. "Or you wouldn't have married him."

Isabella pinched the top of her nose, but the tears wouldn't stop. Guilt had a tight grip on her throat.

She'd never had the chance to say good-bye. He had dedicated his life to making people's lives better. He'd given his life for his ideals. But she'd never understood. Until now.

And later, after an English bullet had cut him down, his body had been disrespected by Hudson and his barbarous soldiers. Archibald had deserved better.

Cinaed pulled her to his chest as a sob escaped her throat. Then the tears flowed, hot and unstoppable.

Since before she'd left Edinburgh, she'd never had a chance to mourn her husband. But the time had come, and her grief for him now poured out of her.

Finally, Isabella was saying good-bye.

CHAPTER 19

I'll listen, till my fancy hears
The clang of swords, the crash of spears!
These grates, these walls, shall vanish then
For the fair field of fighting men,
And my free spirit burst away,
As if it soar'd from battle fray.
—Sir Walter Scott, "Lady of the Lake,"
Canto VI, stanza 14

Tomorrow, the strikes would shut down Inverness. Tomorrow, he was going after John Gordon.

Word had come yesterday through Blair Mackintosh that the men from the third longboat had joined the rest of his crew in Nairn, but he wasn't thinking about them now.

Six people had gathered to finalize the preparations for the strikes—two of the weavers' organizing committee, Searc, and two of the men from his gang who'd be in the fields assuring the safety of the protestors. And the surgeon, Mr. Carmichael, explaining the measures he'd taken to set up a temporary hospital in an empty book warehouse overlooking the fields. He turned and thanked Cinaed for Isabella's offer to join him tomorrow.

Cinaed stood by the door, trying to control his rising

anger. It wouldn't do. He wouldn't allow it. And he'd put a stop to it right now.

He stalked from the room, passing through a blur of corridors and rooms. What the devil was she thinking? Someone jumped out of his way as he stormed past. All he kept seeing was Isabella, cornered by Hudson and his weasel of a sergeant, in the private dining room at Stoneyfield House. If he hadn't shown up to rescue her, she would have been arrested, tortured, used, and molested. Bloody hell!

Since that day, word had continued to come back to Inverness of Hudson's rampages through the countryside. Davidson had died from Cinaed's bullet, and every Highlander knew the British military rarely shied away from savage reprisals, especially when it suited them. Hudson's Hussars, temporarily stationed at Fort George, had been carving a swath through the area, using violence, coercion, and arrests in their drive to find the "treacherous murderers."

The lieutenant, however, was more single-minded, and he let it be known in every village and farmhouse that Isabella Drummond—an outsider in these Highlands—was an enemy of the people and the cause of their present misery. Three days ago, the bounty on Isabella's head had been doubled—a fortune for any man or woman who would provide information leading to her arrest—and this time the British would take her alive *or* dead.

Cinaed hadn't wanted to worry her with any of this news, so he'd kept it from her. But now he saw he'd been a fool to do so.

Taking the stairs three at a time, he felt his head beginning to pound. He'd like nothing better than to get his hands on that filthy dog Hudson, drag him out of Fort George, and finish him, as he should have done that day on the coach road.

Jean was coming out of the tower chamber just as he reached the door.

"Steady there, Captain, and guard yerself," she warned, going by him. "That wife of yers is raging about like a fishwife on a Friday."

He took a deep breath to calm down, but it had no effect. What the deuce did *she* have to be angry about?

Isabella stood by the window, and she whirled around as he entered. Jean was correct. Her face was flushed, and her eyes were spitting fire. And from the hands fisted at her sides, it was obvious she had a few things on her mind too.

He closed the door behind him, hard enough to let her know how he felt. "So I must hear it from Carmichael?"

"And I need to hear the truth from Blair Mackintosh?" She matched the sharpness of his tone.

Cinaed was stunned for a moment. She'd gone outside. Without him. "When the deuce did you speak to *him*?"

"When I went with Mr. Carmichael to see for myself the arrangements he's made for tomorrow."

Cinaed tried to restrain his temper, but his simmering blood was about to boil over. She'd walked the streets of Inverness. Unprotected. This morning, while he'd been out with Searc and Captain Kenedy.

He hadn't been gone for too long. They'd simply walked to Citadel Quay to inspect the first of the schooners being outfitted. The money Searc had "invested" for him was being put to good use. But they'd passed a dozen British soldiers, if not more. He'd seen new broadsides being put up on the walls of the buildings. He didn't go close enough to read them for fear of attracting Searc's attention, but he guessed they were about Isabella and himself.

The entire time he was out there, his mind was at ease because she was here in the house. Safe. Out of sight.

"Why, Isabella? Why are you doing this?"

"I was about to ask the same question of you."

She'd not just gone outside, but to the fields on the way to Longman. Downstairs, Carmichael had told him no other physician or surgeon in Inverness had agreed to help for fear of the possible violence or retribution later on. Cinaed had been ready to kill the man when he proceeded to thank him. And now he found out she'd already gone there to inspect the site.

"You lied to me," she snapped. "You lied about how many men you were taking to rescue John Gordon. Blair told me that none of Searc's gang could be spared."

"I never mentioned a number."

He may have mentioned a number, but that was beside the point. Cinaed couldn't believe the Highlander would talk so freely, telling Isabella what they were and weren't planning for tomorrow. Chattering away like a drunken magpie.

"You did."

"You're changing the subject," he barked. "But what made you think you could safely go out and talk to those men? I'm certain I was clear about the risk. You *must* assume that everyone who passes you on the street is an enemy who will gladly take the fortune being offered for handing you over to the British. Every blasted one of them—man, woman, or child—cannot be trusted."

"Blair was kind enough to escort me, watch over me, and stand guard while Mr. Carmichael and I looked over the inside of the building." She planted her hands on her hips. "What was I to do? Not speak to him at all? Do you honestly think I wouldn't ask him about how prepared he was to protect my husband tomorrow?"

Cinaed raked a tired hand through his hair. He didn't know if he should continue berating her or make love to her.

"I *am* your husband," he reminded her.

This was only a continuation of the argument they'd been having twice every night of this week. Once before making love and again while they lay in bed exhausted.

"How does that have *anything* to do with this discussion? Who is changing the subject now?"

"I came from Searc's study just now. They're expecting upwards of five thousand people out there. No one knows how many soldiers will come from Fort George. The local magistrates are worried that hotheads from both sides will turn the assembly into a riot and the dragoons will charge in to break up the protest. It could be another Peterloo. As your *husband*, I'm ordering you to stay inside this house tomorrow."

Isabella snorted, letting him know exactly what she thought of his directive.

"We are *not* married." She waved her forefinger like a schoolmaster's birch rod. "And even if we were, I would never allow you to bully me or order me about. I don't care one whit what those wild-eyed clergymen say about the 'sacred vows of matrimony.'"

Cinaed forced himself not to laugh at her imitation of a clergyman's voice. "You think you can wave your finger and make me forget what could happen to you if you were caught up in that violence?"

She threw both hands in the air and started pacing the room. "Then how does this sound? As your wife, fraudulent as that may be, I'm ordering you to send Blair and his men to fetch John Gordon while you stay here in this house with me."

"That's ridiculous."

She arched an eyebrow. "I'm simply turning your own words back on you."

Cinaed had come to understand her so well. Isabella was smart, outspoken, independent. She also didn't do well with authority. He knew he could talk until he hadn't a breath left in his body, but unless he tied her to this bed—not an unattractive thought—she was going to do as she pleased. Since arriving here, day after day, Isabella had grown back the wings that tragedy had clipped in Edinburgh. Day after day, she had become more confident. He'd seen it in the way she dealt with Searc, the way she moved about the house, the way she questioned and challenged him after the nightly dinners downstairs with some guest, whether it was a clan chief or a ship owner or a local politician. She was involving herself in his business.

Cinaed loved her. He wanted her at his side forever. The mention of marriage terrified her, even though to him they were already committed to each other in every way that a husband and wife could be. Still, he was impatient for the day when she would accept his offer.

He realized he was still standing by the door, and she was barricaded behind a table and chair near the window. He strolled to the bed and sat on the edge.

"In two days, we'll be going up through the glens to Dalmigavie Castle. I suspect in less than a fortnight, the schooner I saw today will be ready for us to sail to Halifax. Why are you doing this? Why are you putting yourself in danger?"

He finally had asked a question to which she had no ready reply. Cinaed watched her as she turned her back and stared out the window. He guessed at the answer, but he wasn't going to say it.

She was battling the same conflicted feelings he'd been wrestling with. The emotional groundswell of change in the air, the possibility of making life better for all of Scotland, was powerful. Every night she'd come downstairs with him to dinner, even though she didn't have to. Every conversation she'd listened to intently, even though she held back from offering too much of an opinion, for fear of revealing anything of her past life in Edinburgh.

"My motivation in going to the gathering tomorrow is not as unsullied as it might look." Isabella wrapped her arms around herself as she turned away from the window. "I volunteered to go to be useful to Mr. Carmichael in case of . . . if the need arises, but I also am going for Archibald."

The sadness reached her eyes. On their first night together in this bed, Cinaed had held her as she'd cried. She told him about the years of her husband's political life. They'd each lived two lives. They had two sets of friends. Two political ideologies—one real and the other a façade. Then she spoke of the attack on their house. She wept as she talked about the injured she'd had to leave behind, about the betrayal she'd felt for deserting those who needed her.

He had understood she was finally grieving, not just for her lost husband, but for everyone and everything she'd lost.

"This past week, so many times, I've found myself pausing and imagining what Archibald would have said in a certain situation. Or how proud he would have been to learn that the struggle wasn't dead. And the strikes and speeches tomorrow . . ." She paused and looked out the window again. "It took them months to plan them in Glasgow and Edinburgh, working in secret. Or so they thought. But here in Inverness, the weavers and the other trades, the ministers and the clan chiefs, have courageously and openly gone about organizing, preparing to protest, even though they know other gatherings in other cities have turned deadly."

A beam of light shone on her profile, making her skin glow. She looked to be an angel watching over the town beyond.

"Are you only doing this for your husband?" he asked. "Will you continue to fight *his* battles?"

Her lips parted to answer, but she stopped before any words escaped.

"Did he ever try to persuade you to march on the streets with him?"

"He was a planner. He was not one to move in a more public sphere."

"Then, did he ask you to sit with him at his meetings?"

She shook her head.

"That terrible day, did he ask you to tend to the injured people who were brought to your house?"

"Of course not. I did it myself."

"So how strongly did Drummond demand that you be involved in his fight?"

Once again, she started to respond, perhaps to defend her husband, or to defend herself, but she stopped.

Cinaed had spent enough years on ships to recognize when a sailor came aboard having already mastered his sea legs. This was the same with Isabella. She already had the fight in her.

"He never demanded such a thing," she finally answered. "He was happier when I stayed away from all of it."

Cinaed watched her, waiting to give voice to what was on his mind.

"Who are you doing this for, Isabella?"

He knew she was not taking part in these protests because of him, and not because of her late husband.

"Whose battle are you fighting?" he asked again. "Because I know . . . as surely as we're standing here, two hundred miles from where your journey started."

Her eyes were clear and untroubled as she met his gaze.

"This battle is my own."

CHAPTER 20

Rouse the lion from his lair.
—Sir Walter Scott, *The Talisman*

Like a flowing river of humanity, the marchers swept out of the city into the fields beyond. And Isabella finally knew she was no outsider. She was part of this. Part of the thousands moving together, breathing together, marching together. Her heart beat as one with the crowds. She was with the old tanner, his face lit with the possibility of change. With the schoolmaster, his lads at his heels, wide-eyed and expectant. With the mother, holding her babe in her arms. With the dockworker, his hook on his shoulder and the words of liberty on his lips.

As one, they flowed past the lines of glowering magistrates. Past the lines of mounted dragoons, their faces impassive, their sabers at the ready. Disapproving manufactory owners and landowners staring hard-faced from carriages and from horseback. Their privileged lives blinding them to the pain of those who suffered.

Isabella and her people—*her* people—continued onward without regard for their looks of anger. Their censure meant nothing. The swords and the soldiers and the line of cannon in the distant fields meant nothing. They moved together—one voice, one heart, one goal.

And Isabella marched with them, caught up in the passion of the thousands around her. She marched for the tenants forced from their land and left to wander. She marched for the families torn apart by the violence of their oppressors. She marched for her father, for her husband, for all the generations before them whose noble cause of independence was betrayed. She marched for a lost world where standing up for freedom and justice was now a crime.

And she marched for herself, a woman awakened and willing to fight against the strong-armed tyranny that repressed her people.

A pull on her arm made Isabella blink back the tears. Her immediate surroundings came into focus, and she caught Jean, who'd stumbled. She shielded her from the sea of marchers behind them as the old woman found her footing.

"If ye wish it, I'll walk into battle with ye," she said. "But the sawbones been calling ye that way." Jean motioned to the building they were passing.

Mr. Carmichael. Caught up in the excitement, Isabella had lost track of where she was going.

They'd joined the stream of people on Chapel Street. Soon, however, as they approached Rose Street, their progress slowed. The folk walking from the Maggot and the harbor were merging with those coming from town, and the line stretched back toward the center of the city for as far as she could see.

Isabella counted the tolling bells of church steeples; it

was ten. The crowds jostled them from behind, but she took her instruments bag out of Jean's hand and, holding her friend by the other, cut across.

Mr. Carmichael held the door open for them, and they stepped through it.

"Much larger crowd than was expected. The word has spread. I hear they're coming from as far away as Dingwall and Nairn."

Isabella paused at the open door looking out beyond the ropeworks at the open fields, the destination for the marchers. A large crowd was already filling the space.

"Your husband is the spark, you know. With all he's doing and his return at this moment, he's helped awaken the people of Inverness. Folks are ready to tear down the old and build anew."

Cinaed breathed the smell of pine and horseflesh and looked out from the line of trees where his Highland riders waited, grim-faced and silent, beside him.

He didn't know how long they'd have to wait for the prison escort to pass, but if their information was correct, the wagon bearing John Gordon and the others, protected by a half-dozen mounted dragoons, should be coming soon. He nudged his horse forward and looked up the coach road. No sign of them yet.

Beyond the flat fields, Moray Firth was grey and choppy, and distant storm clouds closed off the skies to the east. Here, though, the sky was clear, and that served them well. Cinaed ran through the plan in his head again. They'd attack the escort after it passed, keeping the bright morning sun behind them and in the soldiers' eyes.

Cinaed had never intended for Isabella to find out he

was taking none of Searc's men. Every available body, every trained fighter, was needed at the gathering in Inverness. He glanced at the riders with him, hoping he'd guessed right and he had enough.

Each man with him was a Mackintosh of Dalmigavie. Over this past week, he'd come to know many of them better. He remembered at least half from his youth. These were tough, committed men, and he had faith in their courage and ability. If the commanders at Fort George decided to send more soldiers, however, the odds would shift. But Cinaed and these men would fight to their very last breath.

His thoughts returned to Isabella, as they had over and over since leaving Inverness. He had no fears for himself. He'd chosen Delnies Wood because it was halfway between Fort George and Nairn. If it came down to a pitched battle to free John Gordon, so be it. At least there would be no reinforcements coming. But Isabella had put herself at the very center of a potentially deadly situation. Cinaed knew how high feelings were running. Highlanders were a hotheaded people to begin with. But for seventy years, the shackles of English rule had been chafing at them. If they saw a way to fight their way free, he worried that Inverness could ignite the powder keg. No matter what precautions Searc and the weavers were taking, if a confrontation arose, no one could predict the outcome.

Blast, he cursed silently. He never should have let her be part of that. She could be hurt. He could lose her. Forever.

Dread soaked him in sweat. He took a deep breath. He couldn't stop her, and he'd be a fool if he tried. Isabella was smart and strong. He knew that. But knowing it did nothing to lessen his worry.

A puff of smoke rose above a low rise far to the west. The signal.

They were coming.

In this larger room of the warehouse, a dozen mats on the clean-swept floors sat ready for patients. At one end, two higher tables had been positioned in case surgery was needed. Isabella walked between the empty beds, remembering the chaos of another time, another day of strikes, and the lives that were lost.

The martial sound of bagpipes playing in the distance, the shouts of "equality, liberty, and fraternity" drifting in through the windows, only served to sharpen the memories.

Thankfully, there were no patients yet. No guns had been fired. No bugle calls. No clash of sabers. No signs of trouble . . . that she was aware of.

Jean sat on a bench, her token in hand, her eyes closed, her lips moving. Isabella shared her old friend's worry. At this very moment, Cinaed could be fighting to free John Gordon. She wanted to sit beside her, hold her hand, and tell her that all would be well. But her fears wouldn't allow her to sit still. She touched the ring on her finger and joined Carmichael at the window.

The crackling energy of a summer storm just to the north hung in the air, and Isabella breathed it in. Many speakers were scheduled for today. She hoped the rain would hold off.

"Those Six Acts passed by Parliament last year make public gatherings of this type illegal," the surgeon said. "But so far, the local magistrates and the mounted soldiers from Fort George are behaving admirably."

She knew about the laws. The deaths at Peterloo and Paisley and Glasgow and Edinburgh were fresh in her mind. But she'd also come to respect the power Searc wielded in Inverness. Looking out the window, she recognized some of his men's faces, intent and serious, mixed with those folks marching to their destinations.

Far ahead, a banner was raised—in itself, an illegal act that could provoke the authorities into responding—but it was quickly pulled down by some of Searc's men. Isabella imagined them thinking deals had to be made, they were in control, but they were not invincible.

A knock on the door in the other room took Mr. Carmichael away. Isabella thought of Cinaed again. He'd promised to come directly here once John Gordon was freed.

Isabella looked over her shoulder at Jean and hoped her friend could handle whatever condition her nephew was in. She'd tended to many who'd undergone the torture the British called "questioning." Their injuries were too often horrifying.

Carmichael was coming back into the room with another man at his heels. Isabella turned around as the voices approached. Her gaze fixed on the man accompanying the surgeon, and he saw her as well.

"Mrs. Mackintosh, may I present one of our distinguished speakers, come from far away." Carmichael turned to the visitor. "Mr. Adams, the head of the Safety Committee of the Association of Operative Weavers in Edinburgh."

Isabella met the small, wiry man's grey eyes and recalled all the times that William Adams had sat at her dinner table and huddled with Archibald afterwards. She remembered how, as one of the leaders of the radical reformers, he knew of all the occasions when she'd cared for those poor souls who'd recently been freed from prison. She thought he understood that she had both discretion and courage.

Isabella had never expected William Adams to be the one who'd put a bounty on her head and call for her death, thinking she had betrayed them or fearing she would.

"Mr. Adams and I have met," she said coldly.

Fourteen sets of eyes were fixed on the red-coated soldiers and the wagon moving steadily along the coach road. Cinaed raised his hand in the air, waiting for the right moment.

At the front of the procession, an officer rode beside a sergeant who was pointing in the direction of Nairn, some four miles distant. A driver and a soldier armed with a musket sat on the heavy transport wagon. A red canvas bonnet enclosed the wagon bed, and an iron band secured the doors in the rear. John Gordon had to be in there. Behind the wagon, six more soldiers rode along, less interested in the possibility of an ambush than a story one of them was telling.

Cinaed had already told Blair and his men what needed to happen after the attack. Gordon needed to be taken to Dalmigavie Castle. Cinaed hoped tomorrow he could bring Isabella and Jean there as well.

Before leaving Inverness, Cinaed told Searc that he was attacking a British prisoner transfer today. He felt it was in everyone's best interest to be aware that retribution might follow. Deals had been made, magistrates and a few key British officers had been paid to head off any attack on the protestors. Cinaed feared his actions now would jeopardize the older man's invulnerability, but Searc had shrugged off his concerns.

The procession reached them and Cinaed signaled to attack.

Storming out from the line of trees, the Highlanders thundered across the narrow space separating them from the road. Their battle cries pierced the air, and the officer at the front drew his pistol from the saddle holster. But before he could discharge his weapon, Cinaed fired, knocking him from his horse. In an instant, the riders had the escort surrounded, pistols pointed. The soldiers raised their hands, choosing to surrender with grace rather than fight. Only the guard on the wagon stood and raised his musket, but he immediately laid it down.

The soldiers never knew what hit them. The battle was over as quickly as it started.

While Blair relieved the sergeant of his weapons, Cinaed dismounted beside the officer, who was squirming in pain on the road. The ball had struck the man in the wrist.

"You'll live," Cinaed told him, picking up the pistol. "Who has the key to the wagon?"

"Bugger off, Scotch scum," he said through gritted teeth.

The officer howled when Blair stepped on his hand.

"Not the most gentlemanly of responses," Cinaed remarked. "Care to try again?"

The man motioned to the sergeant, who pulled the keys from his belt.

As Cinaed reached the back of the wagon, he found the mounted soldiers and the driver sitting in the road with two of Blair's men watching them. The horses were being strung together for the journey into the mountains.

Prepared for any unexpected company, he unlocked the door. He needn't have been concerned. The guard riding with the prisoners was kneeling with his musket on the wagon bed and his hands in the air.

Two other men were in the wagon, and neither were in very good condition. Cinaed climbed in, quickly released them from their shackles, and handed them out into the Highlanders' waiting arms.

"Which of you is John Gordon?" he asked when they were both on the ground.

One of the prisoners—the one in worse shape—nodded. His curly brown hair was mottled with blood from gashes in his scalp, his torn shirt was bloodied, and one side of his face was swollen badly. Only one eye was open. His arm had been broken, and a splint had been half-heartedly applied.

"Who are you?" he asked.

Cinaed crouched in front of him, speaking only to him. "Isabella sent me."

"Mrs. Mackintosh." Adams bowed. "I believe you must be mistaken. I have an excellent memory, and your lovely face is not one easily forgotten."

Isabella was never fond of games, and this kind of charming deceit repelled her the most. She could imagine what he was thinking. He was a Lowlander traveling among strangers. Everyone here seemed to have accepted her as one of their own. The surgeon, the men Searc positioned across the street to watch the building, even the old woman sitting nearby—all of them would take her part, regardless of any accusation he made, for to them she was Cinaed Mackintosh's wife. But that was only true for this morning. What would happen at the end of the day, or tomorrow? How long would it take for this man to spread the word that she was in Inverness? How long before the wolves came after her?

One of the town magistrates at the door drew Mr. Carmichael out of the room. She looked at Jean. The pouch had been tucked away, and she was watching the newcomer like a hawk.

In that moment, Isabella realized it was anger and not fear that she was feeling. And before Carmichael returned, she would speak her mind.

"I know you, Mr. Adams. Just as I know your wife, since she's been a patient of mine for the past five years. I have treated all four of your children whenever they've fallen ill. You've been to my home, and I've been to yours. So let's be honest with each other."

He bowed, but deeper this time. "Dr. Drummond, my apologies. My intention was to save you from any awkward situation that the truth might place you in."

"*Save* me?" she asked in a tone sharp enough to draw Jean's attention. But she thought nothing of it. Her friend knew everything there was to know about her past. "Explain to me exactly how you define 'saving'?"

"I . . . I understand this is an awkward situation."

"For you. Not for me. But what an interesting choice of words, coming from you. Do you consider my life these past months just awkward? Is running for my life *awkward*?" She stepped close to him and snapped her words into his face. "I *helped* your friends and colleagues. When you brought them to my house, I stitched them and set broken bones. I healed them and saved more than one life, if you recall. When one of your friends was too badly injured to be carried anywhere, how many times did I refuse to go?"

Adams's face had colored the deepest scarlet. He stared at the tips of his shoes.

"How many times?" she demanded.

"Never."

"Even if I'd done none of that, I was still the wife of your friend." Her voice cracked, but she cleared it, holding her anger in place. "How could you treat me with such cold callousness? As if I were someone completely unknown to you? How could you justify putting a bounty on my head?"

"You disappeared after the day of the strikes. We didn't know what happened to you."

"So you ordered to have me killed?"

"We never called to have you killed. We simply wanted you returned to us. You knew . . . you know everything about us. We wanted you found, that's all."

"That's a lie."

The man raised his hands in defense. "I swear to you. It's the truth. The committee decided to offer a reward after the government declared you an enemy of the Crown and advertised a bounty for your arrest. We thought that by making a counter offer, we might have a chance to have you returned to us before the authorities laid their hands on you."

"Dead. You wanted me *dead*," she repeated. "At every inn coming north, I heard those words."

"The rumors were out of our control. We couldn't paste up broadsides or pass out handbills. We needed to rely on word of mouth. But what we said took on a different meaning. That was never what we intended."

"And what good would your intentions have been for me or my family if we'd been identified? We could have suffered violence anywhere along the road." She scoffed. "There is an expression, Mr. Adams, about good intentions and the road to hell."

"Dr. Drummond, please believe me." His voice was low and meek, and his shame was written across his features. "Please believe me when I say our intentions were noble, but we failed."

"Exactly. You failed," she repeated, turning away from him, "but at what cost to me and my family?"

The backs of her eyes burned, her chin was quivering, but she was not about to let him see her break down. Isabella recalled the desperation of their days in hiding. Sir Walter Scott—hardly a friend to this cause—was able to find them, and he sent John Gordon after them. These people—William Adams and the others—could have done the same thing.

She rubbed her forehead and remembered the dead. The radical reformers had suffered great losses. She'd heard what was happening. Their committees had been decimated. Many were running for their lives. She looked over her shoulder at his bent back. His hair was grey at the temples where it had been black this past spring. The lines around his eyes were deeper. He'd suffered, but he hadn't needed to fear for his life due to the actions of his so-called friends.

"We, too, were in hiding—my family and I—for weeks," he said.

He went on and mentioned other names she knew.

Men who were friends of Archibald. Men she held responsible for adding to the dangers facing her. He told her what each person had needed to do to escape the gallows.

This past April, Isabella's mind could not dwell on anything but her responsibility for Maisie and Morrigan. The struggles of those committee members seemed insignificant compared with her family's plight. She took a deep breath and listened to the sounds of the people marching by outside. She'd come quite far since then.

"They gutted our cause. They broke our hearts and crushed our spirit," he said softly. "Until now."

She turned around to face Adams. She understood. She could almost forgive.

"What do you intend to do about the bounty on my head?" she asked.

"Word is being spread as widely and quickly as possible that it was a mistake. The offer has been rescinded, though I know the danger to you does not go away instantly."

"It's gone? It's over?"

"I was already in Aberdeen en route to Inverness when I received word from this weavers' committee," he explained. "I'd suspected I would find you here."

Isabella shook her head in confusion.

"Mr. Searc Mackintosh. In return for his efforts to protect those gathered today from any attack, he demanded the bounty be removed. He has vouched for your name and for your integrity."

The thunderclouds parted. God was watching.

Standing at the edge of the crowd, Cinaed saw the golden glow of heaven break through and shine down on these people. The summer sun was descending in the west, beyond the tall steeples of High Church and the Tolbooth. Here in the fields of Inverness, legions of angels had come to side with their cause. Despite the raised voices of the orators on the platform, despite the clamorous cheers that greeted each pause, despite the wail of the bagpipes, a sense of harmony infused this assembly.

Cinaed waded into the sea of Highlanders. Thousands had turned out. Tradesman and farmers, sailors and wharfies, ministers and magistrates. And families, everywhere. With each step he took, a path opened in front of him, like a parting of the sea. Folk on every side stood back, turning their faces toward him and making way. As he looked out over the heads of those around him, he felt a sense of belonging coursing through his veins. Here he was, amongst thousands, one with them.

He could feel nothing but the deepest love and respect for them. It was reflected in every face that looked upon him. They were fearless. With a gang of armed men, he had freed two so-called enemies of the Crown, but these people—born with the same Highland blood that flowed through his body—had come here with nothing but empty hands and raised voices. They'd come to this protest, crying out for reform, for freedom, for justice, armed only with a free, clear conscience . . . and their courage.

He once thought he'd lost them, but now he knew he'd never lost anything. They were always here.

He moved closer to the front of the crowd, to where two hay wagons had been maneuvered into place to create a hustings for the speakers and guests. The heads of the weavers' organizing committee were on the platform, several local Whig politicians, the minister from the High Church, two ladies promoting suffrage for women, and some others.

Small groups of cavalrymen sat astride their horses on the outskirts of the gathering, and a few hundred yards off to the east, across the fields towards Longman, the British were making a stronger presence known. A temporary encampment was visible, and he could see red-coated dragoons along with the blue coats of Hudson's Hussars. They'd even thought to bring a number of field guns. But Cinaed had no eyes for these things as he scanned the energized crowds for Isabella.

He saw her, standing far to the left, at the very front, and her shining eyes turned to him. Like two falcons sailing across the skies, they moved toward each other. When they met, he saw the question in her face.

"It's done," he murmured.

As their fingers entwined, they turned together toward the speaker who was exhorting the crowd.

"If a people cannot reform an unjust government, then that system has failed. And if that system has failed, a nation is destined for ruin and for change of the fiercest kind. So I say to you now, change is our destiny. The Highlands' destiny. Scotland's destiny!"

As he finished, the crowd picked up the cry, "*Destiny! Destiny!*"

And Cinaed and Isabella raised their voices with them.

CHAPTER 21

The rose is fairest when 't is budding new,
And hope is brightest when it dawns from fears;
The rose is sweetest washed with morning dew,
And love is loveliest when embalmed in tears.
—Sir Walter Scott, "Lady of the Lake,"
Canto IV, stanza 1

As the candle beside the bed flickered, Isabella looked one last time at Cinaed's powerful arms stretching over to her side of the bed, even in sleep trying to hold her. A dark tendril of his hair lay across his cheek, and she fought the urge to push it back and kiss his face before leaving the room. Dawn was upon them, and he'd just fallen sleep.

She slipped through the door and moved quietly down the steps, her mind continuing to dwell on the love they'd shared by the candle's light. After what they each had gone through yesterday, there had been great hungering need in both of them. But their lovemaking had known no hurry, and their touches were tender and lingering, as if they had years lying ahead of them.

She had sighed out his name; he had made her tremble. He'd shuddered in ecstasy at the things she'd done to his body. They had not talked of the past. They both pretended a million tomorrows would follow to-night's rapture.

As she hurried through the labyrinth of corridors, Isa-bella thought about their plan to leave for Dalmigavie Castle around midday. With the long summer evenings, they would have plenty of time to get there, Cinaed told her. He was looking forward to getting this sojourn over with, and his business with his uncle would not take long, but Isabella was looking forward to reuniting with her sister and stepdaughter. She also hoped John Gordon's injuries were not too severe, for she already knew that when the time came to leave Scotland, he and Jean would need to come with them. They certainly had no future left to them here.

An ache was already growing inside her when she thought about the man lying in her bed. Last night might have been their final time together. Isabella had known it all along. Too many obstacles lay in their path. Their future was about to be washed with a new color, but nei-ther of them had any real idea what hue their life would take on.

One of Searc's men stood at the study door. Seeing her approach, he stood respectfully and greeted her.

"Is he in there?" she asked.

"Aye. Never left since last night."

"Will you let him know I've come to see him?"

Isabella waited as the man tapped on the door and dis-appeared inside. She told Cinaed last night about her meeting with William Adams and explained everything she'd learned from him.

Regardless of her first impression of Searc, since staying here, she'd come to respect his influence and admire his shrewdness. But more than that, she was indebted to him for wanting to save her life, even though she and Cinaed had withheld the truth of her identity. Somehow, he'd learned who she was anyway.

Last night, Cinaed told her he'd speak to him this morning, offer their apologies, and explain. But Isabella felt the responsibility was hers and no one else's. She wanted to talk to Searc herself.

"Himself'll see you now, mistress. Don't mind his temper. Can't say when was the last time he ate or slept."

Isabella entered the study, once again awestruck by the range and multitude of treasures Searc had collected. A candlestick on the desk was the only source of light. The curtains had been drawn tight. This was the first time she'd come here without Cinaed, and she was surprised when the burly little man came to his feet and bowed politely.

"You shouldn't come down here without an escort."

He thought she was concerned about her reputation, but Isabella was far beyond such worries.

"I came down to say thank you," she answered, deciding it would be better to say what was on her mind.

"For what?"

"For your kindness. For your efforts on my behalf. For standing surety for me and for my character, even though I lied about who I am. For convincing the weavers to rescind their offer for my head."

"You are most welcome."

Searc went around the chair, and she noticed his face was drawn, his shoulders sagging. He *was* tired, she decided. He paced to his desk and back, but she thought his usually energetic steps were dragging.

"But I didn't do it for you. I did it for Cinaed."

She'd guessed as much. Whatever his motivation, she was grateful for all he'd done.

"I've lived my life accumulating wealth," he said gruffly. "I learned early on the power of controlling commodities. I also learned that information is perhaps the most valuable commodity. No information of any value gets past me . . . in this house or in this town."

She should have known he'd find out about her, but she wondered how he would have treated her if he'd found out that first night that she was a wanted woman worth a great deal of money. She, too, would have been a commodity.

"A physician. A female physician. And one willing to get her hands dirty."

She nodded. His shrewd eyes studied Isabella as if she were some exotic insect.

"I won't ask you how you became one. That information has no value for me. And I don't care to know how you and Cinaed came to know each other. It's none of my business."

Isabella was grateful for that. Even though she'd come down to thank him, her marital status—real or feigned—was truly none of his business.

He paused for a moment from his pacing and pointed roughly in the direction of the tower chamber. "But I owed you a great deal for saving Cinaed's life. Carmichael told me it was not his skill but yours that saved the lad. What you did before you brought him here made the difference."

Mr. Carmichael's comments must have sown the seeds of suspicion about her. But she was absolutely certain the surgeon's words, whatever they were, had been spoken to give her credit.

Searc looked her in the eye. "I've never had a lad of my own, that I know of. Never will. But Cinaed has always been the closest thing to a son to me. In some ways, he's more precious than if he *were* my own. And he might know it or not, but for all his life, I've kept my eye on him. Here or in Halifax, it never mattered. He thinks he was alone, but there have always been folk out there watching him. *I* was watching. He imagines he built his life alone, but I've always looked after his interests. He had to prove himself to them others, but not to me. I knew he'd come out on top. I always told them so."

Isabella had no idea who *everyone* and *them* might be, but Searc appeared to be talking as much to himself as to her. Even though the room was cold, he was perspiring. His meaty hand dashed away a bead of sweat running down the side of his face. He was breathing heavily. The physician in her raised her head.

"And, truth be told, I've come to like you, in my own way. I'm not so old a fool that I can't see he loves you, and that you feel the same. But that's not the way it'll be when you go to Dalmigavie Castle. It'll be an uphill battle, and a bloody one. Lachlan has other plans for him."

Isabella stepped toward him as Searc held on to the back of a chair to steady himself. She was focusing on him now and not his words.

"Please allow me." She took him by the arm and encouraged him to sit. "Tell me what's wrong."

"Nothing. Tired, is all. I want you to go to your husband. Rouse him. Tell him I need to speak to him."

She checked his pulse. It was rapid, but not exceptionally so. The skin on his face was mottled and covered with perspiration. The first thing that came to her mind was that he was suffering from a heart disease. But any other time she'd seen him, he'd never shown any symptoms. He always appeared to be in perfect health. She decided this episode could easily be the result of exhaustion. "Do you have pain in your chest or in your abdomen?"

"It's not my blasted body that's the problem. It's my supposed friends who are betraying me."

Perhaps he was talking about Cinaed. Or her. She had no idea. "When was the last time you ate or drank or slept?"

"Yesterday, I think. But I . . ." He stopped, cocking his head toward the door and scowling fiercely.

"Are you . . . ?" Isabella gasped when he caught hold of her wrist and pulled her close.

"Hush, lass. I didn't think the scoundrels would dare come into my house, at least not this soon. But they're here." He motioned to the cases on the farthest wall. "Go. Hide. No matter what you hear, no matter what happens, you don't show your face."

The knock on the door had an urgency to it. He let go of her wrist, and she slipped away to where he'd ordered.

Behind a tall easel upon which a huge map had been mounted to a board, two display cases came together in a dark corner of the study. A narrow space had been left between them, and Isabella managed to fit herself into it. The shadows cast by the single candle and the screen helped hide her, but if anyone came close enough, she'd be exposed. Searc's man opened the door and came in.

"Apologies, master. But soldiers are in the street. Two officers—"

He never had a chance to finish as he was shoved aside, and two men entered.

"Stay outside with this miscreant and shoot anyone who tries to come in here."

The order was directed toward whoever waited in the hall. But Isabella recognized the voice.

Lieutenant Hudson.

The sound of horses and rattling swords in the lane beneath their window pushed into Cinaed's sleeping brain like a long, sharp needle. The shift from deep sleep to instant alertness was quick. He slid across the floor, knife in hand.

Ten soldiers stood outside and inside the gate below, four of them wearing the blue coats and tall black busbies of the Hussars. They were waiting, alert to any movement around the house or in the lane. He counted horses. Others had to be inside the house.

"Isabella," Cinaed called in a low voice, looking over his shoulder. She wasn't in the room.

His heartbeat became a battle drum. He pulled on his clothes and boots. His mind raced as he thought of where he had to go in the house to get weapons, how to attack. He wouldn't let these devils take her with them. He'd fight them to the death.

Knife in hand, he pulled open the door and Blair appeared, pushing Cinaed back in and blocking his way. He didn't know any of the Highlanders were back.

"Make way, I have to go after my wife."

"Wait." He spoke in a low voice. "Hudson's here. And

an officer they tell me is a regular visitor. Colonel Wade. Commander of the port, he is. This might just be business with Searc and nothing to be worrying us."

He never knew of any British officers who made casual visits at dawn. Certainly not with that many soldiers in the street.

"How many men do you have with you?"

"Four. The rest went up to Dalmigavie."

Four would do. Cinaed tried to think how many men Searc kept here overnight. It didn't matter. They'd handle them. They weren't taking her.

"Where is Isabella now?"

"Last someone saw her, she was going into Searc's study."

"And Hudson?"

"Searc's study."

Cinaed pushed for the door, but Blair stopped him again. "Wait. We won't let them walk out with her. But let them make the first move. Be patient. We don't want to make it any more dangerous for her, I should think."

"Colonel Wade, you know I don't take kindly to anyone barging into my house." Searc's voice was hard and gruff. "But since you're here, why don't you introduce your spirited junior officer?"

The colonel had no chance to speak. Hudson cut in, introducing himself, his jangling voice filling the room, loud and arrogant. "Lieutenant Ellis Hudson, of the 10th Royal Hussars."

Isabella's blood ran cold at the nearness of the man.

She pressed her face against one of the cases to see what was happening. Only a small sliver of the room was

visible. She thought worriedly of Cinaed, hoping someone had awakened him. Perhaps Jean had gone up. Hudson wouldn't come here unless he had an army with him.

"What can I do for you, Colonel?" Searc appeared to
be intentionally ignoring the newcomer.

"You will address me and *not* Colonel Wade," Hudson barked, moving into Isabella's field of vision.

She shrank back involuntarily, but only for a moment.

"I've been sent here from Edinburgh on a mission of
the utmost importance to the Crown, and I answer only
to my commander there."

"I didn't know that's the way the British army worked,"
Searc put in. "New military protocol, Colonel?"

Hudson continued to talk, ignoring the barb. "And
nothing you say or offer me . . ." He paused and sent a
degrading glance at Colonel Wade. "Nothing will dis-
suade me from accomplishing what I've been assigned to
do." He looked around the study. "And that includes any
effort on your part to bribe me with gifts, favors, or whatever else you use in this barbaric corner of the kingdom
to induce others to do your bidding."

Even before he finished talking of bribes, the map on
the board near Isabella's hiding place drew his interest.
Her heart stopped as he moved toward it.

"Why are you here, Lieutenant?" Searc asked sharply.

Hudson paused and looked back at him. "Yesterday,
there was an attack on a prisoner escort on the way to
Nairn. You will hand over those responsible."

The lieutenant's broad back was to her. Isabella
wished she had a knife. A broken stick would do.

"I have no knowledge of any attack. How would I
know who was responsible?"

"Your reputation and your web of spies are well known to us," he said, turning his back on Searc and coming closer to the map . . . and Isabella. "You're lying."

"Careful what you say, laddie. Slander is still taken quite seriously by the courts here."

Hudson scoffed. "You paid local officials as well as—I suspect—military officers to attend your seditious gathering and stand on the perimeter like so many puppets, allowing violence against the Crown to be incited from the platform. And while these treasonous acts were taking place, you knew exactly what was happening on the coach road."

"You give me far too much credit," Searc growled. "And you haven't a shred of evidence to back your outlandish claims."

"Give the order to search the house," Hudson barked at Colonel Wade. "There has to be plenty of evidence in this ruin that will incriminate him of this crime or some other. There isn't a Scot in the Highlands who doesn't have something to hide."

An item on a shelf in the case beside the map drew Hudson's attention. He was only a few feet from where she hid.

"We spoke of this before we came in here, Lieutenant." Wade cleared his throat uncomfortably. "We have no desire to create a situation which could result in bloodshed or destruction of property. And if you still intend to take Mr. Mackintosh from his home, his household will—"

"Save your breath, Colonel. Our duty is to the Crown, not some scoundrel in this vile place." He wheeled his tall frame and glared. "Are you a loyal officer, or are you not? I tell you this man is guilty of nefarious crimes. Whom do you fear?"

Searc's men, Isabella thought. She recalled all the weapons hidden in this house, in this very room. They were probably better armed than the soldiers. They wouldn't go down without a fight.

"I advised against it, but we are here at your insistence."

Appearing satisfied, Hudson turned back to the case and approached. Isabella had nowhere to go.

"Very well. Take me to Fort George," Searc snapped, stopping the lieutenant in his tracks. "I'll go willingly, without any trouble. My men won't stand against you. I'm certain we can resolve whatever misunderstandings we have and avoid any complications that will surely arise here."

Surprise and then smug satisfaction registered on Hudson's face as he slowly turned and faced the others. "Indeed. Take him into custody, Colonel. Now."

CHAPTER 22

*Revenge, the sweetest morsel to the mouth that
ever was cooked in hell.*
—Sir Walter Scott, *The Heart of Mid-Lothian*

Cinaed had to keep Isabella out of the room. He couldn't allow her to think she had any responsibility in this. She believed Searc sacrificed himself for her that morning by volunteering to go with the British soldiers to keep her from being discovered. He tried to make her understand that Hudson had come to the house to arrest Searc, using force if he had to. No other reason explained arriving so early. The streets were empty of people, and he brought a sufficient number of men to do it.

"Trespass on property of the Crown. Illegal assembly. Incitement to commit violence. Sedition. Conspiracy to commit treason."

Cinaed paced the room as Philip Kenedy read the charges from the printed handbill. The notices were being plastered all over the waterfront. All the other men who'd gathered with him in the study—Blair, Carmichael, the leadership of the weavers, and several of Searc's men—also knew.

He cursed himself for allowing Hudson to take Searc. But his own men believed that their master could talk himself free of any situation. He was a friend to the commander of the port of Inverness. He knew the Deputy Governor of Fort George very well, but the man was at Fort William, according to the weavers.

In the absence of the general, Hudson was abusing his power. Because the assembly had been held on "ship lands," controlled by the Royal Navy, the lieutenant was taking it on himself to make the arrest under military law. Same-day trial. Same-day judgment. Treason and "compassing to levy war against His Majesty" was his justification.

"Hang by the neck until dead unless . . ." Kenedy stopped and threw the handbill on the table.

Cinaed knew the rest of it, what was being offered. For the capture and delivery of Isabella Drummond, a reward of two thousand pounds, and Searc Mackintosh's punishment would be commuted to transportation for life. Hudson was counting on a link between Searc and Isabella. As for Cinaed, he had no name and only his description was printed on the notice.

Since this morning, the news of the arrest had spread through Inverness like a spring flood tide. Kenedy had come immediately, while many of Searc's other connections had sent messages, offering assistance. He was the dealmaker, unethical and mercenary, but he made the town click like a well-oiled clock. From his house in the Maggot, Searc played both sides of the political chessboard between Highlanders and English authorities. And he was the heart of Inverness. Everyone—merchants, ship-owners, tradesman, and even the poor—relied on him for their survival.

Cinaed knew no one would have any difficulty identifying the woman on the notices. Too many of Searc's friends had been introduced to Isabella at the reception and at the dinners that followed. No one wanted to lose Searc in this way; he was too valuable to the working of the city and the area . . . and the cause. But if he was already lost to them, and many believed that to be the truth, then two thousand pounds sterling in exchange for a Lowlands woman would be ample motivation for anyone.

Cinaed looked around the room and had no doubt these men knew the truth.

"Hudson cares nothing about Searc," he said. "It's Isabella he wants."

"I'll take her up into the mountains. To Dalmigavie," Blair offered. "I swear to protect her with my life."

Cinaed shook his head. "My wife's escape will not end this. Hudson won't hesitate to execute Searc when he feels he serves no further purpose." He turned to others around him. "Hudson has been embarrassed by his failures here, by his loss of men and his loss of John Gordon. He needs to get his hands on Isabella. Right now, he's a mad dog who's chewed through his muzzle. So, before someone above him gets a grip on his leash, he'll continue to overstep his authority. Today, he took Searc. Tomorrow, it'll be you." He motioned to Kenedy. "The next day, he'll start to arrest you and you and you. And he'll manufacture charges if he needs to."

Men nodded one at a time.

"He won't stop until he has this town by the throat. He'll arrest and execute everyone who came out to those fields. Speakers, protesters, and bystanders—one by one until every one of us is hanging by the neck in the parade grounds at Fort George."

These men were older than Cinaed. Some of them had to know the stories handed down of what happened in Inverness after Bonnie Prince Charlie and the Jacobite forces were defeated in the fields of Culloden a few miles away.

"Were you never told the story of William Rose? Just a few hundred yards from here, twelve wounded men were carried out of his house and shot in a hollow."

He paused, waited for acknowledgment from the others.

"Or the story of an elderly gentleman named MacLeod who was pursued by two dragoons to a hill near the cattle market. He went down on his knees and begged for his life, but the dogs shot him through the head."

More nods.

"Or the poor fellow shot dead by a soldier at the door of a widow on Bridge Street?"

Someone else continued Cinaed's story. "Aye, and then the fiends went and hacked off the arms of the bairns next door."

Cinaed had grown up hearing tales of the atrocities done by the Duke of Cumberland's troops after the battle. All in the name of the Crown. Those histories had remained banked fires within him and no doubt fueled the life he'd pursued.

"How many men in the town had their throats cut for no reason?" Kenedy asked.

"The treatment of prisoners kept in the bell tower of the High Church was monstrous," Mr. Carmichael interjected quietly. "Few nightmares can compare."

"My auld granddad told me they gave those men a handful of meal a day but no water to swallow it," one of Searc's men said.

"Many lay sick with wounds that festered until they died in the utmost agony." Carmichael tore the notice in his hand in half. "The minister Hay sent his bishop a catalogue of atrocities."

"My great-grandfather, Murdoch McRaw," another said bitterly, "was hanged by the road from an apple tree out on Haugh Brae. Them demons left his naked body out fer two days and a night . . . and whipped it fer their devilish amusement."

Cinaed nodded. They all remembered. They were Highlanders. Inverness was their home. They never forgot.

"Are we to allow Hudson to do the same to us now?" he asked.

The answers came as one. "Nay!"

Cinaed looked at the faces around the room. They were few, but they all had sound hearts and courage enough. Attacking Fort George to free Searc would be impossible and foolish to try. They'd be cut down before they got over the walls. The Deputy Governor of Fort George and his staff had fattened their purses and built their reputations on keeping the Highlands quiet, thanks to Searc. They wanted no trouble and would get Hudson back in harness.

Cinaed needed a way to bring those commanding officers back to Inverness in a hurry, but if he could draw Hudson out and destroy him before their return, all the better.

He turned to Kenedy. "What English ships are in port?"

The deserted malt house across the lane from Searc's house fit Isabella's needs perfectly. The growing rooms were large and dry, and with some help cleaning the place up, it would serve a much greater purpose than sitting shuttered and empty.

She understood what Cinaed planned to do tonight and tomorrow. She worried, but she couldn't chastise him. And she wouldn't try to change his mind. A battle lay ahead, and she understood the value of strategy and preparation.

At the same time, she wasn't about to keep herself locked away in the tower chamber, pacing the floors and feeling useless. No matter what Cinaed said, she still felt completely at fault for what was happening to Searc Mackintosh. She knew about the offer Hudson had circulated to encourage people to hand her in. But Isabella wasn't afraid. She'd been in this situation before. She wasn't going to be intimidated again.

Right now, they each had a task to accomplish. Hers was to get a temporary clinic ready, in case of reprisals for the attack on the prisoner escort and for what Cinaed had planned.

"We're up to twenty-five lasses," Jean announced as she ushered in two more women who'd come to help.

"And their children?"

"Told 'em to bring the bairns along. Cook is sending over food enough for all."

"And you told them they'll receive an honest day's wages so long as they stay."

"Aye."

Isabella had seen enough hungry faces on Maggot Green to know Jean's offer would be popular. Cleaning the large growing-rooms was the priority, and she'd arranged to have bedding and blankets brought over from Searc's house and from Carmichael's temporary clinic in the book warehouse later.

In the event of trouble, the clinic by the fields would have been an ideal place, but she knew Cinaed would be concerned about her safety if she decided to work that far away from the house. Also, by starting to renovate the malt house, she decided it might be a good place as a temporary shelter in the future. She'd seen a number of them in Edinburgh, and the need existed here as well. Too many women and children in the Maggot were wandering the riverbanks.

She rolled up her sleeves and was about to join her small army of workers when she saw Cinaed come in.

All work stopped. All conversation ceased. Everyone was openly staring at him. Isabella had seen the same reaction the night they'd walked into Searc's reception. Even during the speeches, she'd watched the heads turn as he came through the crowd to her. Cinaed was impressive. More than impressive, she corrected herself. He was beautiful.

He filled the doorway, his shoulders blocking the light. He searched the low-ceilinged room until his gaze connected with hers, and then a smile tugged at the corners of his lips as he took his time walking through. He spoke to the women, nodded at whatever they said to him, patted a child on the head. With every step he took closer to her, Isabella felt her heart beat faster.

Their time together felt like stolen minutes. Each time she saw him, kissed him, made love to him, Isabella feared it was their last. And every time they came together again, she thought of it as a gift.

He reached out and the tips of his fingers touched hers. "What would these women say if I lifted my wife off the ground and kissed her?"

"I'm not afraid of what they'd say, but what they'd do. You're not like any man they have, if they have one at all. And if I'm your woman . . . well, jealousy is a terrible thing."

"Then we need to be careful not to stir up such feelings in them." He took her by the hand and pulled her out of the nearest door.

Drawing her past the ruin of the kiln, she followed him into a darkened hallway beyond, where he encircled her with his arms and crushed her breasts against him.

"You *are* my woman. My love, my wife, and all I hold dear."

He kissed her, and she felt the hunger in the assault of lips. There was no hesitation on Isabella's part. She moaned deep in her throat, and her mouth opened under the pressure of his.

He looked up and down the dark corridor and pulled her into a storeroom. He began to open her dress, and she helped him, wanting to feel his hands on her breasts.

"I ache for you," he growled. "I want to bury myself deep inside of you."

They had no time to go back to their tower room. He was leaving soon, and she couldn't desert the people she'd assembled here.

Isabella lifted up her skirts with a smile.

"Now? Here?"

"Now, Cinaed," she replied softly, sliding her hand inside his trousers. "We must make the most of every minute we have."

Across the black waters of the canal's wide basin, *HMS Pitt*, a third-rate ship of the line, sat at the new Merkinch Wharf. According to Captain Kenedy's friends in the harbor master's office, the vessel was delivering, along with kegs of gunpowder, a special shipment of experimental weaponry—exploding shells for the long guns at Fort George. Unloading would begin in the morning.

Cinaed could not have asked for better.

He and Blair crouched in the tall grass, wearing only their trousers, waiting for the clouds to cover the moon. Time was running out. The few short hours of darkness in the summer night were being made even shorter by the light of the white half-moon shining over Inverness.

Cinaed felt Blair's soot-blackened hand on his arm. He pointed to the armed sentries patrolling the wooden drawbridge at Telford Street. The men were talking with three sailors in a small skiff in the basin. The muzzles of the muskets, on the bridge and in the boat, gleamed in the moonlight. A moment later, the skiff pulled away and moved the length of the ship and continued down the row of smaller vessels. They'd be back in just a few minutes.

Nothing would awaken the British military authorities

faster than losing prized weaponry. Inverness, a conquered town to them for more than fifty years, was a forgotten place, beaten and subdued. Cinaed believed this was why Hudson, after the protest assembly and the day of strikes, felt emboldened to do as he pleased.

Everything was about to change.

A red-coated marine patrolling this side of the waterway came along, his musket and equipment signaling his approach from fifty yards off. The two men, still and silent as death, watched him come closer. When he was no more than ten feet away, he stopped. Standing by the edge of the water, he unbuttoned the fall of his breeches and pissed down the bank.

They waited impatiently until the sentry moved off, buttoning himself up as he went.

As a cloud slipped across the face of the moon, Cinaed and Blair moved to the water's edge and waded in. It took only a few minutes to cross the canal, and they used the tow lines hanging down the side to climb to an open port hole on the lower gundeck.

They crept stealthily amidships between the rows of guns and hammocks and descended to the cargo holds. As Blair stood watch, Cinaed set the fuses and lit them. Moments later, they were back in the water, swimming for the far shore.

When the ship went up, a series of fireballs rose in quick succession high in the sky, as one hold after another detonated. Without doubt, the explosion would be visible as far as Fort George.

Come out of your hole, Hudson, Cinaed thought as they gathered their clothes. Come out and play.

CHAPTER 23

That day of wrath, that dreadful day,
When heaven and earth shall pass away,
What power shall be the sinner's stay?
How shall he meet that dreadful day?
—Sir Walter Scott, "Hymn for the Dead,"
Canto VI

Two miles west of the city, Cinaed sat astride his mount on a rocky rise, looking out over the tiny cluster of fishing cottages at Clachnaharry. The mud flats of Beauly Firth lay below him, along with the narrow cart path that his foe would need to travel to reach the half-built monument outside of the village. Whitecaps crowned the chop on the grey firth, and the wooded hills behind offered a lush, green place to hide his men. Toward the port, a few small plumes of smoke were all that remained of the ship they'd destroyed last night.

Stretched out along the ridge on either side of him, fifty Highland fighters waited. With his men, gathered from the area's clans—Fraser and Innes, Macpherson and Chisolm, Grant and Mackintosh—he would finish this mad dog today, as he should have done the day they met.

"The lads are all in position," Blair said, reining in his horse beside him.

Cinaed nodded and looked across the canal toward the city. Immediately after the ship exploded, he'd sent one of Searc's men out to Fort George with a message for Lieutenant Hudson. The woman on the handbills, he'd been told, had been found and would be turned over to him at the half-built monument at Clachnaharry at noon today. The message had come back that Hudson and his men would be there to take her into custody.

He glanced at the fighters. Situated where they were, they would cut the Hussars down with the same lack of mercy Hudson had been showing throughout the country-side for the past fortnight.

Ever since the ship had burned and sank at its berth in Inverness last night, Fort George had reportedly been in an uproar. Word from the weavers had come that dispatches had already gone out to Fort William, where the Deputy Governor of Fort George was meeting with the Governor of the Highlands. The expectation was that the two generals would be coming north directly, which meant Hudson's time off the leash of his superiors was coming to an end.

Taking Isabella into custody would mean the successful completion of the lieutenant's mission to the Highlands. Cinaed knew Hudson would never be able to resist the bait.

And he'd be waiting.

"By the devil, Cinaed. Look." Blair was pointing toward Inverness.

An hour ago, the skies over the city had been grey. Now, however, beyond the canal and the River Ness, smoke was rising, thick and black as the fires of hell.

* * *

The Maggot was ablaze, and it seemed to Isabella the end of the world was upon them.

Wounded men and women, hacking and coughing, were staggering in faster than she could find space for them to sit, never mind lie down. Thankfully, Mr. Carmichael had joined her earlier in the day, and the surgeon was working relentlessly to treat those in the worst pain.

She'd been expecting saber cuts and broken bones, but burns were by far the most prevalent injury. Gathering together a few of the local women who'd stayed to help, she sent them off to fetch pitchers of water. The best way to help those with burns was to cool what was left of the charred skin and flesh. She saw Carmichael carrying in two buckets of water himself.

"How close is it to us?" she asked him.

"Roofs of buildings bordering the Green are on fire."

"How did it start?"

A group of coughing children came in, and the surgeon motioned to them to come closer.

"It's Hudson's Hussars," he replied. "They're burning the town."

Her heart clawed its way into her throat. Isabella looked at the crowd of people needing help all around her. She didn't know what they would do if the fire reached this building.

"Where is Cinaed?"

"I'm afraid Hudson saw through his plan," the surgeon said in a low voice. "The blackguard came here instead of going out to Clachnaharry."

A young boy standing in the middle of the crowded floor began to cry out hysterically for his mother. Isabella went to the child and lifted him in her arms. Taking another little one by the arm, she hurried them to a corner where a group of bairns huddled around Jean.

Her friend opened her arms, and both boys crawled onto her lap.

A man cried out in pain on the far side of the room. Two young ones coughed dreadfully as they tried to tend to their unconscious mother. Calls for help surrounded her. Isabella moved from one person to the next. A sip of wine. Positioning a bucket of water for three people to share and immerse their burned hands and arms in. Soaking cloths in pitchers of wine, hoping it would be sufficient until more water arrived.

The smell of smoke was getting stronger. She feared the fire had reached them. Isabella rushed to the door and stepped out into the lane. The sky had disappeared, replaced by a billowing charcoal blanket. The roar of flames competed with the shouts and screams of people in pain. The report of a gun pierced the air. Where the lane ended at the river, she saw people filling buckets and moving back toward the blaze.

A horse stamped and neighed behind her, and Isabella spun around. In front of her, mounted atop the wheeling animal, a blue-jacketed officer sat, seemingly oblivious to the chaos.

Hudson had come for her.

Isabella glanced at the door to the malt house where her patients lay.

Unwilling to lead him to them, she ran in the opposite direction, toward Searc's gate.

Before Cinaed and his men even reached the bridge across the River Ness, he could see the smoke and flames were

rising above the crowded buildings and alleys around
Maggot Green.

As they spurred their horses through the wild-eyed
crowds streaming out of the Maggot, Cinaed worried
about Isabella. He'd been able to see the fires had not yet
reached the lane between Searc's house and the malt
house where he'd left her, but he feared it might just be a
matter of time.

They reached the smoke-filled green and found panic
and pandemonium everywhere. A light rain began to
fall, adding to the chaos. The streets were choked with
abandoned carts loaded with household goods. Some
still had terrified goats and cows tethered to them. People
were running in every direction. Unattended children
wandered in the smoke and rubble. Near the distillery,
the entire block was aflame.

It was clear the fires had been started in different
parts of the Maggot. Several lines of courageous residents
were trying to pass buckets of water hand to hand, but
their efforts were being thwarted. Blue-jacketed soldiers
on horseback were charging back and forth across the
green, swinging their sabers and scattering the lines. At
the river, a line of Hussars was forming to clear out those
trying to reach the Ness with their buckets.

This was a nightmare come to life. These were his
people, and he would not stand aside.

Signaling to his Highlanders, Cinaed drew his sword
and they charged.

CHAPTER 24

And come he slow, or come he fast,
It is but Death who comes at last.
—Sir Walter Scott, "Marmion," Canto II

Take her alive or order the house burned with her in it? Have his men run her down or capture her himself?

Counting on Hudson's arrogance, she decided he was certain to follow her across the lane and take her on his own. At least, that was what she prayed as she raced through the open doorway of Searc's home. The most important thing at that moment was to lead him away from the innocent people lying helpless on the malt-house floor.

In the great hall, the housekeeper stood, uncertain in her panic as to what she should do. "All the men have gone to help with the fire, mistress. And only the cook and I and—"

"Take the tunnel to the river." She dragged her toward the corridor on the far side of the hall. "The soldiers might set this house on fire too. Gather whoever is left in the house and go. Go now!"

"Come with us, mistress."

"Not now. I'll join you."

Thankfully, the older woman didn't argue and yelled to a serving girl rushing from the kitchens. They both disappeared.

Isabella reached into the pocket of her apron for the scalpel she'd tucked there earlier. She could hardly hope to throw it with any success at the monster, but she was still prepared to fight him to the end.

She faced the door across the great hall. The labyrinth of corridors lay behind her. She knew her way through them now. She could disappear, and he would never find her. She could leave the building. But she wasn't going to run away. She was the one who'd brought Hudson to Inverness, and one way or the other she would send him away from here.

The door from the lane flew open with a smash. He swaggered in and stopped across the great hall when he saw her, his face at once smug and triumphant. Thank God, she thought, he'd chosen to come after her alone.

"Good day, Dr. Drummond. Or is it Mrs. Murray today? Wait, I believe you must be Mrs. Mackintosh, the lovely wife of this new son of Scotland everyone speaks so highly of."

Of course, word would have reached Fort George. *Son of Scotland*. She'd heard the term used over and over. She knew they were referring to Cinaed. She took a couple of steps back. The door behind Hudson stayed open, but no one else appeared.

"How did you find me?"

"It was easy," he said, strolling casually toward her. "A fine-looking woman with a Lowlander's accent who happens to have medical knowledge."

She retreated, backing into a wide corridor leading into the house. "If you knew where I was, why burn this neighborhood? Why not just take me and drag me back to Edinburgh with you? Why make these people suffer?"

"A little late for such talk, don't you think?" he asked, continuing to follow her. "But I'm not here to take you back. I no longer need you. I no longer need the names of your troublemaking friends."

Isabella shot a quick glance over her shoulder. She kept backing away, slow enough to keep him coming. He was enjoying this. She was a mouse, trapped between his cat claws. In a moment, he'd become bored with the game. The time for toying with her would be over. And then he'd pounce.

"You don't need me?" she asked, stalling.

"Not at all. You've given me something greater. Another husband. Another enemy of the Crown. You have a keen interest in traitors."

She bit back her words.

"Thanks to you, I now know the man who is fast becoming the heart of all our future troubles here."

Isabella didn't need to ask. Cinaed.

"Unlike you, he is a true enemy of the Crown, wanted for years. Sinking government ships. Bringing illegal arms into the Highlands." He shook his head like he expected better. "It wasn't too difficult to realize what was on the *Highland Crown*. I hear the explosions lit up the sky before it sank."

"Much like that ship not a mile from here," she taunted.

"As you say. But you've given me another charge to attach to his name."

"I've given you nothing," she spat.

"He is a bold one, and shrewd. I'll give him that. Bleeding, smelling like a dead fish, and still he bursts into that dining room to rescue you. But if for nothing else, I'll enjoy seeing him hang for killing Sergeant Davidson."

The length of his stride was longer than hers. He was closing the distance between them.

"I do enjoy a spirited competition, when it benefits me," he said. "And our little game has benefited me greatly since the day you two escaped Stoneyfield House. Now, I have a face for every treasonous act that has occurred since we arrived here."

She backed around a corner into another hallway, and he followed.

"The rescue of John Gordon." He smiled. "The destruction of *HMS Pitt* in retaliation for Searc's pending execution. More celebration for me. And of course, hearing our spies constantly speaking of this *liberator* who's returned to his people. With his Lowland bride on his arm. It all came together for me last night. My superiors in Edinburgh . . . in London . . . will be falling over themselves in their gratitude and their desire to decorate me."

"Still, why take Searc Mackintosh?"

"Ah, women never understand the art of war. It's difficult for you to appreciate the brilliance of a finely wrought military maneuver." He dragged his nails along the wall as he advanced. "All corruption leads back to this house. Pull Searc Mackintosh from his lair, and the so-called son of Scotland would surely show his face."

Panic clutched Isabella's chest. It wasn't only her own

life that she worried about, but Cinaed's. Hudson knew everything about him. Because of her, they had a name. And then wherever he was, be it Inverness, Dalmigavie Castle, Halifax, or the far side of the Antipodes, they'd go after him.

"I believe your husband's weakest move came this morning. Such a simpleton, after all. To think I'd ever go to a place so convenient for an ambush, even to have *you* turned over to me."

She backed away quicker, and he lengthened his strides.

"You can kill me," she told him. "But you will never have him."

"Well, my dear. Killing you is only an eventuality. You'll serve me much better as bait. I've seen how he reacts when you're in trouble. And in my hands, you're about to learn what real trouble is."

Isabella turned and yanked open a door. Dashing through it, she found what she wanted.

Hudson entered, and his eyes lit up. He stared at the portrait above the fireplace as if he'd found the Holy Grail.

The rain was falling harder, an unexpected gift from the heavens. The fires were coming under control, though it appeared the distillery would be lost.

Buckets continued to be passed from hand to hand, men and women working hard to douse the flames and keep the fires from spreading farther.

Cinaed stepped out of the line and drew his saber when he spotted two Hussars at the end of a lane. Seeing him, they quickly wheeled their horses and put the spurs to their flanks. It hadn't taken long to rout Hudson's men, and those who hadn't already fled were fast disappearing.

"That coward Hudson never showed his ugly face." Blair walked up the lane behind him. "No one's caught even a whiff of the poxy cur."

"I'll find the devil, wherever he is hiding. And I'll make him pay with his blood for all of this."

An old man staggered from an alley and leaned exhausted against a wall. Cinaed nudged his steed closer and saw his hands were burned.

"I'll take yer place in the line," Blair offered, "if ye want to take him to get them hands looked at."

They'd arrived at the Maggot in the midst of a disaster. But his mind had never strayed from Isabella. He knew how close she was to the danger.

Helping the old man into the malt house a few minutes later, he handed him into Jean's care and looked around for Isabella.

The floor of the entire room was crowded with people. As he walked through, the smell of burned flesh and wool stung his nostrils. The wide eyes of children looked up from soot-covered faces. He took buckets of water from a lad and carried them across the room. A man needed to be helped in from the lane. Picking up a lost child, he searched until he found a neighbor who knew her. Cinaed remained there, helping where he could.

These were his people. The keen edge of guilt cut into him, for he knew that he was as responsible as Hudson for the pain reflected in their lives. He'd expected a reprisal, but he thought he could control it. He'd been out-flanked, and it hurt him. Next time, he'd be smarter.

Isabella. He hadn't seen her. He looked over the crowd and found Carmichael, instead. When was it he'd seen the surgeon last? He couldn't remember. The man's shoulders sagged from the suffering around him.

"Where is she?" he asked the surgeon when he reached him.

Carmichael straightened and looked around. "I . . . I don't know."

"When did you last see her?"

The surgeon shook his head. Cinaed forced himself to stay calm and moved to one of the women he'd seen earlier. And then on to the next, asking the same question. Finally, a young woman holding a small soot-covered child told him she thought she'd seen his wife go out into the lane, but that was ages ago.

Ages ago?

He didn't know how he found his way out of the building, for his eyes were blind to everything as he searched for a glimpse of her. He couldn't hear anything beyond the roaring in his head. His brain was telling him over and over that no one had seen Hudson. Now Isabella was missing.

Searc's housekeeper, coming from the direction of the river, ran up the lane to him. "She came into the house . . . Aye, long ago. She told me to run. She was worried the house would go up in flames."

Cinaed ran down the lane to the gate. Finding the door standing open, he felt another cold wave of doom wash over him, threatening to push him under. He forgot how to breathe.

No one was inside. No servants. None of Searc's men. He called her name from the bottom of the tower stairwell. Nothing. In the great hall, he shouted up the wide stairs toward the drawing room.

A weak answer came, but from the bowels of the house.

Too afraid to hope, but praying she was unharmed, he called again, moving through the corridors in search of her.

Cinaed found her down the hall from Searc's clan room, sitting on the floor, her back against the wall. As he approached, he saw she was covered in blood.

"By the devil!" he exclaimed, rushing toward her.

"Not mine." She stood and threw herself into his arms as he reached her. "It's his blood. Hudson's. I had to do it. I had no choice. I had to kill him."

Cinaed held her, caressed her, spoke softly in her ear. She was shaking uncontrollably. Her face was wet, though he didn't think she even realized she was crying. He understood. She'd spent her life saving lives, and today she'd been forced to take one.

He kissed her furrowed brow and leaned her against the wall. She was reluctant to release him.

"I need to make sure," he said softly.

The clan-room door was open. Cinaed entered and found Hudson on the floor. The backsword had pierced his heart. His eyes stared blankly at the portrait on the wall, the throes of death etched across his face.

CHAPTER 25

Time will rust the sharpest sword,
Time will consume the strongest cord;
That which molders hemp and steel,
Mortal arm and nerve must feel.
—Sir Walter Scott, "Harold the Dauntless"

Deep in the Highlands, in a remote glen of the River Findhorn, Dalmigavie Castle sat on a craggy hill overlooking the valley. Around its ancient stone walls, far-off mountain peaks soared, kissing the sky.

Cinaed knew and loved these hills. He was nearly home, but he wasn't home either. He was happy to meet the folk he'd grown up amongst, but he feared the bond of kinship had already been severed with too keen a blade. As they climbed ever higher into the mountains, he enjoyed seeing the excitement build in Isabella and Jean. The old woman's face lit up with every turn of the narrow road, thinking they had perhaps arrived. They were eager to be reunited with their families, and he tried to hide his own ambivalence.

They'd needed to wait a week before leaving Inverness for the journey to Dalmigavie. After the sinking of the ship and the fire at Maggot Green, the city streets had been crawling with patrols of armed soldiers, but in a few days, calm returned. After a brief investigation, the explosion on *HMS Pitt* was called a "tragic accident." The bodies of Lieutenant Hudson and a number of his men were discovered in several of the burned buildings. Searc had been released as soon as the Deputy Governor of Fort George returned from Fort William, with the general's apology for the rogue officer who'd demonstrated irrational behavior and acted without authority. Searc appeared to be in good health. Regarding Isabella Drummond, the search was finished in Inverness. The lieutenant's orders were being referred back to London for review.

Cinaed knew all of this because of Searc and his unabated flow of information. He'd managed to become even more controlling and influential after the incident at the hands of Hudson. No one, be it Highlander or Englishman, wished to have their relationship with the burly man damaged.

With the turmoil of Hudson's inquisition behind them, Searc decided to accompany them on this visit to Dalmigavie.

The Mackintosh clan throughout the Highlands was fond of celebrations, and Blair had already warned him a great feast and ceilidh was being organized for him. Cinaed had no desire to arrive under false pretenses, however. He didn't want to be the center of such festivities when he had no intention of staying.

They were perhaps only an hour or so from the castle when he stopped the carriage and their escort of riders. He took Isabella for a walk in the nearby meadow overlooking the river.

The smell of pine on the breeze, the deep azure sky, the sun on the majestic mountain peaks, the sparkling river tumbling toward the next bend and the unknown beyond all teased his memories. A piece of him belonged here, though he found it hard to admit.

"Lachlan has agreed to meet with me at an old lodge at this end of the glen," he told Isabella. "You and Jean will continue to the castle with Searc and the rest of the men."

She didn't argue. She knew about his past and understood his concerns. "Will you send a message and let me know where you go from here? We'll be ready, whenever you decide we should come. That is, if you want us to join you."

"There are no ifs." He pulled her into his arms. Cinaed held her, inhaled the scent of her hair, thankful that she was in his life. She completed him.

"I love you," he told her. "And whether I remain in that lodge or go elsewhere, I'll wait for you until you're ready. Searc can arrange it all. He'll bring you to me."

"And I love you, Cinaed Mackintosh. But know this, whatever you decide is your path, whatever your people's plans turn out to be, I'll not allow my past to hinder your—"

He silenced her with a kiss. Cinaed didn't know what she'd been told or by whom, but several times this past week she'd hinted about the need for going separate ways, about not being a burden to him. He wouldn't have it. He wouldn't allow it.

Too soon, he had to let her go. Cinaed watched until Jean and Isabella were on their way before mounting his horse and riding toward the hunting lodge.

Though he'd been here only a few times as a lad, he had no difficulty finding it. As he approached, however, he realized how different his perception of the place was now from what he remembered. What had once been an impressive building had turned into a moss-covered stone edifice. The roof of a nearby stable had fallen in on itself. A single horse was grazing in the meadow.

Cinaed had asked for Lachlan to come alone, and he was satisfied to find his request had been honored.

His uncle was not the man that Cinaed remembered, either. The years had been tough on the laird who'd once been a tall and strapping man. He was now grey, bone thin, and his face was deeply marked with the lines of age.

Seeing the ravages of time in Lachlan, he felt a sadness emerge in him. In spite of anything he'd done, this man was his closest kin.

"Cinaed."

"Lachlan."

No formalities. No affection. Cinaed's sadness evaporated. They were simply two men meeting in a sparsely furnished, dust-covered lodge with no servants or attendants to break the heavy silence. A saddlebag lay open on a table and beside it, a bottle of whiskey and two silver cups.

He motioned, and Cinaed sat across from him.

"You have no wish to be greeted properly by your clan."

"I have no clan. Or rather, they've shown they don't wish to have me." He sat back, surprised by the stinging bitterness in his tone.

"Time will rust the sharpest sword, but not yours, I see."

"I need no poetry," Cinaed replied. "I asked you to come here because I want to hear the truth, without the fanfare of a 'homecoming.'"

The wind whistled down the chimney, and the smell of ancient fires filled the room. The ghosts of their ancestors were making their presence known, and he felt their eyes on them. On him.

"When I received your message, I nearly laughed. So fitting that you should want to meet here at this lodge." Lachlan looked around him with affection in his eyes. "It makes me believe that somewhere deep inside, the past is a part of you."

Cinaed watched the older man stare into the corners of the lodge. He imagined him seeing it in a different time, perhaps in a time when he was young. Perhaps even before his time, when clan chiefs were the protectors of their people, when fathers and mothers grew old together and children never left the land.

Lachlan reached for the bottle, poured two drinks and pushed one across the table.

"After the battle at Culloden," he began, turning his gaze to Cinaed, "many of the defeated Highlanders fled into these hills, bloodied and heartbroken. This building sheltered many in those dark days. But a fortnight later, this lodge became a place of great honor for the Mackintosh clan. Your grandfather decided to stay here."

Lachlan drank his whiskey, waiting to be asked the next question. Cinaed knew nothing about any grandfather. He'd never given any thought to it. He'd barely been given any information about his father. But he knew plenty about those who'd suffered at Culloden.

Lachlan poured another drink. Cinaed's sat untouched on the table.

To witness moments of grandeur and then to taste defeat. This lodge and Lachlan had both weathered storms.

Cinaed couldn't stop unexpected emotions from creeping in. Pity? Empathy? He couldn't say. This man wanted to share information with him, but right now was not the time to be distracted by family history.

"Why did you send me that letter? Why did you want to see me?"

Lachlan shook his head and smiled. "Impatient as always. You haven't changed a whit from when you first arrived at Dalmigavie as a bairn."

When he first arrived? The man was a master of misdirection, but Cinaed let him have his way, for now.

"When did I first arrive at Dalmigavie?"

He feared his earliest memories of childhood were more imagined than real. He'd always felt he was an outsider, always looking on, rather than being one with other children. Later, he became a castaway. He was correct to feel he didn't belong. But why?

Lachlan sat back in his chair. "Do you remember anything of your past? Of a time before you came to us?"

Cinaed didn't know what he was supposed to remember. Sometimes, when he was drifting off to sleep, another time and place would slip into the edges of his dreams. A soft whisper in French. Songs hummed over a basket of flowers. The skirts of a woman who loved to whirl around and lift him into her arms to dance. It wasn't his mother. He couldn't place these memories.

Every time he thought of them, he wiped them away and recalled the hard face of his mother, Anne Mackintosh.

"When did I first arrive at Dalmigavie?" he asked again, his tone sharper than before.

"You were almost four years of age when your mother sent you to us."

Four. No wonder he didn't belong. He *was* an outsider. The words finally sank in. *Sent.* He was sent here.

The thick walls of the past were crumbling around him, stone by stone, allowing long-forgotten memories to filter through like sunlight through colored glass.

Mon fils, mon bébé. Je suis ta maman. The gentle murmur of the words was in his head. He couldn't shake them or make them go away. Cinaed had always known French. He spoke the language like someone born to it.

The face of a fair young woman with curls that hung around her face came to his mind.

Je suis ta maman. I am your mother.

"*Who* is my mother? Who sent me here?"

"I'll not speak of her. She'll be the one to tell you who she is. How and why she gave you up is not for me to be telling either. But I'll tell you this, my sister Anne was no more blood kin to you than that horse you rode in on."

He wanted to deny it, but he couldn't. Anne Mackintosh's coolness, her lack of affection made sense to him now. He was raised by others. By the clan. She never called him "son." The only time he recalled her being kind to him was on her deathbed, when she'd handed him the ring.

His real mother was alive. Alive. In his mind, he ran down a dark tunnel, trying to find the light, trying to recall memories. He wanted to remember her face.

"But you won't have long to wait. She's making arrangements to come to the Highlands, though I know it'll be difficult to manage, considering who she is. But she's determined to meet you."

Cinaed ran his hand over his face, fighting to pull

back the curtain still stretched across his memory. But the darkness wouldn't lift.

"What of my father? Was he a Mackintosh?"

Lachlan shook his head and leaned forward, planting his elbows on the table. "I've had to wait years until I could reveal the truth to you. But I believe the time has come."

His curiosity was aroused. But none of this mattered. He had his own life. He had Isabella. His past had no hold on him. Whatever "truth" this man was about to throw at him, it was only a thistle seed in the wind.

"You are . . ."

Cinaed knew who he was. As a child he'd wanted to know more, but a father's name meant nothing to him now.

"Your true name is Cinaed James Stuart." He paused, letting the sound fade from the air. "You are the only male alive descended directly from our Bonnie Prince."

Cinaed stared, not comprehending. His father was a sailor. He'd been lost at sea before Cinaed was born.

This was foolishness. The ravings of a man too long here in the mountains. Cinaed knew the history, the same as all Highlanders knew it. Bonnie Prince Charlie died in exile, and his only acknowledged heir was his daughter, Charlotte. She, too, was already dead.

"I don't believe you."

The old man shrugged. "Your father, Jamie, was a bastard, a year older than Charlotte, born and raised in secret."

Lachlan wore the smile of a man who'd just bestowed on him the most precious gift on earth. But Cinaed felt no richer for it. He had a thousand questions—not the least of which was why his so-called father's existence was a secret, with only Lachlan Mackintosh privy to it. But his greatest wish was to walk out of this lodge and leave this nonsense behind.

Cinaed had seen enough Highlanders, displaced from their homes and their land. He knew how far people would go, how desperately they would cling to a misbegotten belief, to keep their hope alive.

"I don't believe it," he repeated.

Lachlan sat back and shook his head. His sad smile told Cinaed he was not surprised by his reaction.

"Where is the ring you were given?"

"My wife is wearing it. My mother, your sister, gave it to me."

"That ring signifies the truth of your parentage. It was a gift from your father to your true mother. Did you never wonder why it's a crowned thistle?"

"This is madness."

"You don't need to believe me. You'll meet her. And you *will* believe her, for she has undeniable proof. You'll believe her just the same as all of us believed her when she sent us a four-year-old lad to raise, to prepare him for his destiny."

He still didn't believe Lachlan. Or *her*, whoever she was. And he wasn't going to waste his time here with this insanity.

Cinaed rose abruptly to his feet and walked a few steps away, but then stopped and turned around.

"You sent me away. Why?"

"Your grandfather was the rightful king of Scotland, but he couldn't gather enough support in '45. He couldn't bring the people together. Your father was born on a foreign land and not even half the man Prince Charlie was. But it didn't matter; it was too soon. The Highlands were still bleeding. But you—"

"What does that have to do with a lad of nine years? How does any of that justify tearing a child from the only home he's ever known and casting him out to sea?"

Lachlan came to his feet. "We had to keep you safe. You were our last chance. You think we cast you out, but you were always watched, always protected."

Cinaed thought of all the help Searc had given him over the years.

"Until now," the old man continued, his eyes flashing. "Cinaed James Stuart, you are the true son of Scotland, and the Mackintosh clan and a score of others are ready to march with you."

They'd been apart for only a few short weeks, but Isabella saw immediately that Maisie and Morrigan were no longer the naïve young women she'd been worrying about.

Both of them were happy to see her. They were in good health and appeared extremely well adjusted to life in these mountains, regardless of having spent all their years in the cities.

Her half-sister, Maisie, in particular, had matured considerably in the days since they'd said good-bye on the coach road outside Inverness. She'd always been quiet and amiable, but she now showed no hesitation about speaking her mind when she was told of their schedule and travel plans to Halifax.

"Isabella, listen to me," she said. "I'm twenty years old. I love you as a sister, but none of the problems that drove us from Edinburgh affect me. There is no reward on my head. No one chasing after me. I'm not going to be coerced into moving to the other end of the world. I need to find my own way, and I've decided it will be here in Scotland."

As the three of them walked in the courtyard of the castle, Morrigan was listening closely to the younger sister. Seeing the pursed lips and restless hands, Isabella knew Morrigan's impatience, at least, hadn't changed. She clearly had a few things on her mind, and she was doing her best to wait her turn to share them.

Isabella felt the many eyes on them, especially on her, since she'd so newly arrived. There'd been some polite greetings and curious looks, but no warm welcome. She didn't know how Searc had explained her, or if he'd said anything about her at all. The laird was meeting with Cinaed at the hunting lodge, and not a single person approached to greet the carriage when they arrived, except the two young women on either side of her.

"Are you ready for my opinion of the move to Halifax?" Morrigan asked bluntly.

"Let me guess, you're no longer fond of our original plans either?"

"They were always your plans, Isabella, and not mine. Not ours," she corrected, sending a look at Maisie. Morrigan, a year older, had never in six years shied away from expressing an opinion for both of them. To Isabella, it was a blessing that her reserved younger sister had a person to stand up for her.

People walked past them, sending Isabella a few nods. Some were coming close enough to eavesdrop. But this was not the time or place to continue this conversation. Neither of the young women wanted to hear her reasoning. They were without friends and penniless.

They had no place to live, no means of feeding themselves or clothing themselves. Still, they each had a strong mind and a good education. They also had courage.

Isabella took a deep breath, trying to calm her worries. Because she'd always played the role of mother, now that she'd returned, they were eager to express their opinions and remind her of their independence.

She noticed Blair following at a respectful distance. Even within the safety of these castle walls, Cinaed was making sure someone was watching over her.

"Very well. Each of you should formulate your own plan for the future. When you're ready, I'll be open to hearing what you've decided." She looked from one to the other. "And whatever it is, I'll be there to support you."

Isabella left them looking at each other, surprised expressions on their faces. She wanted to see John Gordon.

She found Jean sitting with her nephew in a tiny room off a gallery above the castle's great hall. A week had passed since the young man had been brought up here. His arm was set, and his bruises were mending. Still, sitting beside him, she could tell he was wrestling in his mind with the torture he'd endured. His aunt spoke to him, told him that Isabella had come to see him, but she didn't think he heard or noticed her. She'd seen this before in Edinburgh, when prisoners came to them after being subjected to the brutality of the authorities.

"He'll recover, won't he?" Jean asked her.

Isabella crouched beside her friend and took the old woman's quivering hand in her own. "With you beside him, he will."

"Do ye promise me?"

How many times she'd been asked that same question. A desperate mother or wife wanting some guarantee that a wound would heal. How many times she'd given an answer based on hope rather than on medical knowledge.

"I promise." She kissed Jean's hand and stood.

Her life, the future Isabella had imagined she'd be building in Halifax with all of these people, was quickly fading. The two young women she'd traveled north with would make their own plans. John Gordon was better off staying in one place until the scars in his mind had a chance to heal. Dalmigavie Castle was a fortress in the mountains, safe. It could provide a sanctuary for John . . . and perhaps for her as well. She hoped he'd be allowed to stay here, along with her sister and stepdaughter. No matter what Maisie and Morrigan thought right now, they would need time to form a rational plan for their future.

Standing by the railing and looking down into the great hall, she thought of Cinaed. Her love for him warmed her. For so long, she'd thought she hadn't the freedom to decide her own future. Things seemed to be changing. Her fight was not over, but she now had the power to decide her own road. But would the man she wanted wait a year, six months, or a month for her to join him in Halifax . . . or wherever he'd set sail for?

She started toward the room she'd be sharing with her family, but Cinaed suddenly stepped in front of her.

She hadn't expected him to come here. As she reached for his hand, Isabella knew he was the light of her life, the air in her lungs, the blood in her veins. She could not do without him. Regardless of everything facing them, the thought of being apart from him was too painful to imagine.

"Come with me."

There'd been nothing to indicate his arrival—no cheering, no sounds of excitement.

"Does anyone know you're here?" she asked when he pulled her into an empty room.

"No one knows but you." He closed the door behind them and took her in his arms.

She held him. She pressed her face against his chest and held him tight. Their love for each other was the only certainty she had now in this tumultuous life.

"The lasses. How are they?"

"They're fine. Both girls have been well taken care of by your clan." Isabella looked up into his face and cradled his cheek. "You're upset. What did Lachlan tell you?"

He shook his head. "First, I want to hear about your family. Are they anxious to go? And Gordon? How is he faring?" He paused. "Are you ready to leave?"

A fist squeezed Isabella's heart as she relayed the conversation she'd had with Maisie and Morrigan. "They need time. And it's the same with Jean's nephew. It would be best if he wasn't moved right now. But I don't want to abuse the Mackintosh clan's hospitality."

He caressed her face, looked into her eyes. "Do *you* want to stay here?"

She *wanted* to go with Cinaed, but she couldn't. Not yet. Her voice struggled, but she cleared it. "I need to stay, if your uncle allows it. I can't leave them, any of them. They need me."

Perhaps it was her imagination, but Isabella saw some of the tension lift from his shoulders. He nodded and rested his forehead against hers. His hands cupped her face. Their lips were only a breath apart. She'd felt the storm raging through him before. Now that seemed to have passed, but the respite was momentary, and clouds appeared in his eyes.

"What did Lachlan tell you?" she asked again.

"Stories and fairy tales about my parentage. None of which I believe."

She wanted to know all of it, and she waited.

"He claims . . . he says . . . he imagines . . ." Cinaed stepped away from her. Going to the window, he looked outside.

Isabella hated to see him so tormented, but she didn't know how to soothe the pain.

"He believes in a lie." He turned around to face her again. "He's asked me to stay here at Dalmigavie until my mother arrives."

"Your mother?" she asked, surprised. "I thought she was dead."

He shrugged. "I guess that was another lie. I was told today that she is well and making arrangements to come to the Highlands."

"Who is she?"

He shook his head. "She's either a brazen liar or a queen. And my father was the son of . . . of Bonnie Prince Charlie."

Isabella found herself unable to utter a sound. Questions on top of questions whirled in her brain. But amid the storm of confusion, she thought about the way Cinaed had been received by those in power when the two of them had entered Searc's drawing room. She recalled the way those far less fortunate were drawn to him. So many times, she'd heard the words *son of Scotland*. She'd even heard them on Hudson's lips.

He walked back toward her. "I left Lachlan, ready to go where you go, be there at your side, wherever our lives lead us."

Emotions choked her. Tears sprang to her eyes.

"I love you, Isabella." Taking her hand, he dropped down on one knee.

"Cinaed—"

"My life has changed. My future no longer lies across the sea. I belong here in Scotland, it appears. Here in the Highlands and, for a while at least, here at Dalmigavie. But I shall refuse all of it. I want none of that if I can't have you."

She went down on her knees. His handsome face shone with an inner light.

"Will you be my wife, Isabella, forever? Will you stay with me? Will you love me as I love you?"

"I do love you, Cinaed Mackintosh, more than any person has ever loved another since the beginning of time. And I'll stay by you and walk beside you wherever you go. I'm yours, now and forever, if you'll have me."

His kiss was her answer.

The clouds of uncertainty were gone, and the sun had once again risen high in the sky. A road lay before them. They both knew it was a road fraught with twists and turns, with unseen dangers, but they'd be facing those perils hand in hand, together.

AUTHOR'S NOTE

One story comes to an end, only to begin the next.

As you've already guessed, *Highland Crown* is the opening chapter of Cinaed and Isabella's life together. They are hardly finished with their search to solve the mystery of his birth and find the role each of them will play in the future of a nation.

In the next two novels, *Highland Jewel* and *Highland Sword*, we'll also follow the adventures of Maisie and Morrigan as they become entangled in the social and political struggles of a nation searching for its identity.

And as we continue this romantic adventure series, questions arise that must be answered. Who is Cinaed's mother? Stay tuned. We promise to reveal it in *Highland Jewel*.

In *Highland Crown* we've attempted to depict a place and a time in a way that mingles the real and the imagined. Much of the action in this novel is loosely based on real events.

After the end of the Napoleonic wars, social unrest spread through England and Scotland due to economic disparity and unfair laws. The British government responded with heavy-handed measures and increasingly repressive laws that made public gatherings criminal and speaking out in protest sedition. The Cato Street conspiracy was an entrapment effort on the part of British authorities, and the notoriety of the case was used to justify laws that robbed citizens of their rights. Peterloo, which we refer to in the novel, was also an actual event. In Manchester, sixty thousand people were peacefully protesting when government forces attacked, killing and injuring hundreds of innocent citizens. The newspaper called it the "Peterloo Massacre" despite the government's efforts to suppress information about the event.

In the novels that follow, we'll continue to weave fiction and history and try to entertain you. So stay with us.

As authors, we love feedback. We write our stories for you. We'd love to hear what you liked, what you loved, and even what you didn't like. We are constantly learning, so please help us write stories that you will cherish and recommend to your friends.

Please visit us on our website at www.MayMcGoldrick .com for our latest news.

Finally, if you enjoyed *Highland Crown*, please leave us a review . . . and recommend it to your friends. We greatly appreciate your support!

Wishing you peace and health!

Nikoo and Jim, writing as May McGoldrick

Don't miss the next book in
the Royal Highlander series

HIGHLAND
JEWEL